Pra

'James Lee Burke is one … a. His prose is an uncom… -quence' *Los Angeles T…*

'A threnody of grief for the American dream . . . What keeps the pages turning is the pace and unpretentious clarity of the writing, along with the tension generated by the unpredictable collision of motives and interests. But it is the bitterness and anger underpinning the novel that makes *Red Ponies* fascinating . . . a nightmarish vision, which finds insistent parallels in today's (and tomorrow's) headlines . . . serious and interesting' Mike Philips, *Guardian*

'Dave Robicheaux is a detective to be reckoned with, more interesting than Spenser, more complex and satisfying than Travis McGee . . . James Lee Burke is a writer to be remembered' *USA Today*

'The best crime writer alive today' Elmore Leonard

'Burke's most self-evident strengths are two; the luminosity of his writerly voice, and the rich, vivid, fascinating terrain of Southern Louisiana, which that voice renders with both love and despair . . . James Lee Burke is something special' *Washington Post*

'James Lee Burke has a sophisticated and brilliantly expressed vision of humanity and one can see, smell and taste the America of which he writes' *Washington Post*

'Burke can embroider a gangster yarn with prose of tremendous lyrical power' *Independent*

'A thrilling piece of fiction, at once exciting and elegiac . . . In *Purple Cane Road* he writes with a depth of feeling that is rare in the mystery genre' *Observer*

James Lee Burke is the author of twenty-six novels, including sixteen featuring Detective Dave Robicheaux, and a volume of short stories. *The Lost Get-Back Boogie* was nominated for a Pulitzer Prize; *Black Cherry Blues* won the Edgar Award in 1989; and *Cimarron Rose*, Burke's first novel featuring Billy Bob Holland, won the 1997 Edgar Award. In 1998 *Sunset Limited* won the CWA Macallan Gold Dagger for Fiction. He lives with his wife, Pearl, in Missoula, Montana, and New Iberia, Louisiana. Visit his website at www.jamesleeburke.com.

By James Lee Burke

DAVE ROBICHEAUX NOVELS

The Neon Rain
Heaven's Prisoners
Black Cherry Blues
A Morning for Flamingos
A Stained White Radiance
In the Electric Mist with Confederate Dead
Dixie City Jam
Burning Angel
Cadillac Jukebox
Sunset Limited
Purple Cane Road
Jolie Blon's Bounce
Last Car to Elysian Fields
Crusader's Cross
Pegasus Descending
The Tin Roof Blowdown

OTHER FICTION

Half of Paradise
To the Bright and Shining Sun
Lay Down My Sword and Shield
Two for Texas
The Lost Get-Back Boogie
The Convict and Other Stories
Cimarron Rose
Heartwood
Bitterroot
White Doves at Morning
In the Moon of Red Ponies
Jesus Out to Sea

JAMES LEE BURKE

THE NEON RAIN

PHOENIX

A PHOENIX PAPERBACK

First published in Great Britain in 1989
by Mysterious Press UK
This paperback edition published in 2005
by Phoenix,
an imprint of Orion Books Ltd,
Orion House, 5 Upper St Martin's Lane,
London WC2H 9EA

An Hachette Livre UK company

A CIP catalogue record for this book is available from the British Library.

Printed and bound in Great Britain by
Clays Ltd, St Ives plc

The Orion Publishing Group's policy is to use papers that are natural, renewable and recyclable products and made from wood grown in sustainable forests. The logging and manufacturing processes are expected to conform to the environmental regulations of the country of origin.

www.orionbooks.co.uk

To the family of Walter J. Burke of New Iberia, Louisiana, with great affection for their gentle spirit and kind ways

1

The evening sky was streaked with purple, the color of torn plums, and a light rain had started to fall when I came to the end of the blacktop road that cut through twenty miles of thick, almost impenetrable scrub oak and pine and stopped at the front gate of Angola penitentiary. The anti-capital-punishment crowd – priests, nuns in lay clothes, kids from LSU with burning candles cupped in their hands – were praying outside the fence. But another group was there too – a strange combination of frat boys and rednecks – drinking beer from Styrofoam coolers filled with cracked ice; they were singing 'Glow, Little Glow Worm,' and holding signs that read THIS BUD IS FOR YOU, MASSINA AND JOHNNY, START YOUR OWN SIZZLER FRANCHISE TODAY.

'I'm Lieutenant Dave Robicheaux, New Orleans police department,' I said to one of the guards on the gate. I opened my badge for him.

'Oh, yeah, Lieutenant. I got your name on my clipboard. I'll ride with you up to the Block,' he said, and got in my car. His khaki sleeves were rolled over his sunburned arms, and he had the flat green eyes and heavy facial bones of north Louisiana hill people. He smelled faintly of dried sweat, Red Man, and talcum powder. 'I don't know which bunch bothers me worse. Those religious people act like we're frying somebody for a traffic citation, and those boys with the signs must not be getting much pussy over at the university. You staying for the whole thing?'

'Nope.'

'Did you nail this guy or something?'

'He was just a low-level button man I used to run in once in a while. I never got him on anything. In fact, I think he screwed up more jobs than he pulled off. Maybe he got into the mob through Affirmative Action.'

The guard didn't laugh. He looked out the window at the huge, flat expanse of the prison farm, his eyes narrowing whenever we passed a trusty convict walking along the dirt road. The main living area of the prison, a series of two-story, maximum-security dormitories contained within a wire fence and connected by breezeways and exercise yards and collectively called the Block, was as brilliantly lit as cobalt in the rain, and in the distance I could see the surgically perfect fields of sugar cane and sweet potatoes, the crumbling ruins of the nineteenth-century camps silhouetted against the sun's red afterglow, the willows bent in the breeze along the Mississippi levee, under which many a murdered convict lay buried.

'They still keep the chair in the Red Hat House?' I said.

'You got it. That's where they knock the fire out their ass. You know how the place come by that name?'

'Yes,' I said, but he wasn't listening.

'Back before they started putting the mean ones in lockdown in the Block, they worked them down by the river and made them wear striped jumpers and these red-painted straw hats. Then at night they stripped them down, body-searched them, then run them in the Red Hat House and threw their clothes in after them. There wasn't no screens on the windows, and them mosquitoes would make a Christian out of a man when a baseball bat couldn't.'

I parked the car and we entered the Block, passed through the first lockdown area, where both the snitches and the dangerous ones stayed, walked down the long, brilliantly lit breezeway between the recreation yards into the next dormitory, passed through another set of hydraulic locks and a dead space where two hacks sat at a table playing cards and where a sign overhead read NO GUNS BEYOND THIS POINT, into the rec and dining halls where the black trustys were running electric waxers on the gleaming floors, and finally walked up the spiral iron steps to a small maximum-security corner where Johnny Massina was spending the last three hours of his life.

The guard from the gate left me, and another one pulled the single lever that slid back the cell door. Johnny wore a white shirt, a pair of black slacks, and black Air Force shoes with white socks. His wiry gray and black hair was dripping with sweat, and his face was the color and texture of old paper. He looked up at me from where he was seated on his bunk, and his eyes were hot and bright and moisture was beaded across his upper lip. He held a

Camel cigarette between his yellowed fingers, and the floor around his feet was covered with cigarette butts.

'Streak, I'm glad you come. I didn't know if you were going to make it,' he said.

'How you doing, Johnny?'

His hands clutched his thighs and he looked at the floor, then back at me. I saw him swallow.

'How scared you ever been?' he said.

'In Vietnam I had some moments.'

'That's right. You were over there, weren't you?'

'Way back in '64, before it got real hot.'

'I bet you were a good soldier.'

'I was just a live one, that's all.'

I felt instantly stupid, at my remark. He saw the regret in my face.

'Don't worry about it,' he said. 'I got a whole bunch of shit to tell you. Look, you remember when you took me to a couple of those AA meets, that step you guys take when you want to confess something, what'd you call it?'

'Step Five, admitting to yourself, God, and somebody else the exact nature of your faults.'

'That's it. Well, I done it. To a colored preacher, yesterday morning. I told him every bad thing I ever done.'

'That's good, Johnny.'

'No, you listen. I told him the truth and I come clean with some really heavy shit, sexual things I always been ashamed of and I never understood. You know what I mean? I didn't keep nothing back. I also told him about the two guys I whacked in my life. I dumped one guy over the rail of a passenger liner on the way to Havana, and in 1958 I took out

Bugsy Siegel's cousin with a shotgun. You know what it means to ice a relative of Bugsy Siegel? After I confessed it to the preacher, I told the guard and the assistant warden about it. You know these dumb cocksuckers couldn't care less?

'Wait a minute, let me finish. I told all this stuff because somebody's got to believe I didn't snuff that broad. I wouldn't throw no young girl out a hotel window, Streak. I got no kick coming about being fried. I figure it all comes out even in the end, but I want these bastards to know I only pushed the button on guys that played by the same rules I did. Can you relate to that?'

'I think so. I'm glad you did a fifth step, too, Johnny.'

He smiled for the first time. His face glistened in the light. 'Hey, tell me something. Is it true Jimmie the Gent is your brother?'

'You hear a lot of bullshit in the street.'

'You both got that black Cajun hair with a white patch in it, like you got skunk blood in you.' He laughed. His mind was now moving away from the ride he would take in three hours, manacled in a waist chain, to the Red Hat House. 'Once he contracted us for some poker machines for his places. After we put them in we told him he gets all his machines from us – cigarettes, Pac-Man, and rubbers. So he says no rubbers, he's got class clubs and he don't put rubber machines in them. So we tell him he don't have a choice, he either buys the whole line or he don't get linen service, the Teamsters put a picket up on his sidewalk, and the parish health office finds out his dishwashers got leprosy. So what's he do? He invites Didoni

Giacano – Didi Gee himself – and his whole family for lasagna at his restaurant, and they arrive on Sunday afternoon like a bunch of *cafoni* that just got off the boat from Palermo, because Didi thinks Jimmie has got respectable connections and is going to get him into the Knights of Columbus or something. Didi Gee probably weighs three hundred pounds and he's covered with hair like an animal and he scares the crap out of everybody in downtown New Orleans, but his mama is this little dried-up Sicilian lady that looks like a mummy wrapped in black rags and she still hits Didi on the hands with a spoon when he reaches across the table and don't ask.

'So in the middle of dinner Jimmie starts telling Mama Giacano what a great guy Didi Gee is, how everybody down at the Chamber of Commerce and Better Business Bureau think he's a big plus for the city, and how Didi don't let anybody push his friends around. For example, he says, some scumbags tried to put some machines in Jimmie's restaurants that Jimmie, a Catholic man, don't want. Mama Giacano might look like she's made out of dried-up pasta, but her hot little black eyes tell everybody she knows what he's talking about. Then Jimmie says Didi tore them machines out, smashed them up with hammers, and run a truck up and down on them behind the restaurant.

'Didi Gee's got a mouthful of beer and raw oysters and almost chokes to death. He's spitting glop all over his plate, his kids are beating him on the back, and he coughs up an oyster that could plug a sewer main. Mama Giacano waits till his face ain't purple anymore, then tells him she didn't raise her son to eat like a herd of pigs and says he should go wash out his mouth in the bathroom because everybody else at the table is getting sick looking at him, and when he don't get up right away she busts him across the knuckles with her spoon. Then Jimmie says he wants to take the whole family out on his sailboat and maybe Didi Gee ought to join the Yacht Club, too, because all these millionaires think he's a swell guy, and besides, Mama Giacano would really love the Italian-American celebrations they have on the Fourth of July and Columbus Day. And even if Didi don't join, which everybody knows he won't because he hates the water and pukes his guts out just crossing the Mississippi ferry, Jimmie is going to drive out and get Mama Giacano whenever she wants and sail her all around Lake Pontchartrain.'

He laughed again and ran his hand through his wet hair. He licked his lips and shook his head, and I saw the fear come back in his eyes.

'I bet he already told you that story, didn't he?' he said.

'They didn't give me too long, Johnny. Is there something else you wanted to tell me?'

'Yeah, there is. You always treated me decent and I thought maybe I could repay you a little bit.' He wiped the sweat out of his eyes with the flat of his fingers. 'I think maybe I got some heavy dues to pay on the other side, too. It don't hurt to try to square what you can now, does it?'

'You don't owe me.'

'A guy with my track record owes the whole fucking earth. Anyway, here's the deal. Yesterday this punk by the name of L. J. Potts from Magazine

Street is pushing a broom out in the corridor, clacking it against my bars and making all kinds of noise so I can't sleep. So I say I ain't working on the Good Housekeeping award and would this punk take his broom somewhere else before I get my hands on it and shove it up his hole. So the punk, who's got a brother named Wesley Potts, tries to impress me. He asks if I know a New Orleans homicide roach named Robicheaux, and he's smirking, see, because he thinks you're one of the cops that nailed me. I tell him maybe, and he keeps smirking and says, well, here's some good news because his brother Wesley has it that this particular homicide roach has stuck his nose in the wrong place and if he don't stop it he's going to get whacked.'

'He sounds like a gasbag, Johnny.'

'Yeah, he probably is, except the difference with him and his brother is I think they're connected up with the greasers.'

'The Colombians?'

'Fucking A. They're spreading around the country faster than AIDS. They'll take out anybody too – whole families, the children, the old people, it don't matter to them. You remember that bar on Basin that got torched? The greaser that did it stood in the doorway in broad daylight with a fucking flamethrower on his back and because he was in a good mood he gave everybody one minute to get out of the place before he melted it into a big pile of bubbling plastic. You watch out for those cocksuckers, Streak.'

He lit a fresh Camel from the butt in his hand. He was sweating heavily now, and he wiped his face on his sleeve and smelled himself simultaneously. Then his face got gray and still and he stared straight ahead with his palms gripped on his thighs.

'You better leave now. I think I'm going to get sick again,' he said.

'I think you're a stand-up guy, Johnny.'

'Not on this one.'

We shook hands. His hand was slick and light in mine.

They electrocuted Johnny Massina at midnight. Back in my houseboat on Lake Pontchartrain, with the rain beating on the roof and dancing on the water outside, I remembered the line I had heard sung once by a black inmate in Angola:

I ax my bossman, Bossman, tell me what's right.
He whupped my left, said, Boy, now you know
what's right.
I wonder why they burn a man twelve o'clock
hour at night.
The current much stronger; the peoples turn
out all the light.

My partner was Cletus Purcel. Our desks faced each other in a small room in an old converted fire station on Basin Street. Before the building was a fire station it had been a cotton warehouse, and before the Civil War slaves had been kept in the basement and led up the stairs into a dirt ring that served both as an auction arena and a cockfighting pit.

Cletus's face looked like it was made from boiled

pigskin, except there were stitch scars across the bridge of his nose and through one eyebrow, where he'd been bashed by a pipe when he was a kid in the Irish Channel. He was a big man, with sandy hair and intelligent green eyes, and he fought to keep his weight down, unsuccessfully, by pumping iron four nights a week in his garage.

'Do you know a character named Wesley Potts?' I asked.

'Christ, yes. I went to school with him and his brothers. What a family. It was like having bread mold as your next-door neighbor.'

'Johnny Massina said this guy's talking about pulling my plug.'

'Sounds like bullshit to me. Potts is a gutless lowlife. He runs a dirty movie house on Bourbon. I'll introduce you to him this afternoon. You'll really enjoy this guy.'

'I've got his file right here. Two narcotics, six obscenity busts, no convictions. Evidently one serious beef with the IRS.'

'He fronts points for the greasers.'

'That's what Massina said.'

'All right, we'll go talk to him after lunch. You notice I say "after lunch," because this guy is your real genuine bucket of shit. By the way, the parish coroner in Cataouatche returned your call and said they didn't do an autopsy on that colored girl.'

'What do you mean, they didn't do one?' I said.

He said they didn't do one because the sheriff's office didn't request it. It went down as a drowning. What's all this about, anyway, Dave? Don't you have enough open cases without finding work down in Cataouatche Parish? Those people down there don't follow the same rules we do, anyway. You know that.'

Two weeks before, I had been fishing in a pirogue on Bayou Lafourche, flycasting popping-bugs along the edge of the lily pads that grew out from the banks. The shore was thickly lined with cypress trees, and it was cool and quiet in the green-gold morning light that fell through the canopy of limbs overhead. The lily pads were abloom with purple flowers, and I could smell the trees, the moss, the wet green lichen on the bark, the spray of crimson and yellow four-o'clocks that were still open in the shade. An alligator that must have been five feet long lay up close to some cypress roots, his barnacled head and eyes just showing above the water line like a brown rock. I saw another black swelling in the water near another cypress, and I thought it was the first alligator's mate. Then an outboard boat passed, and the wake rolled the swelling up in the cypress roots, and I saw a bare leg, a band, a checked shirt puffed with air.

I set down my fly rod, rowed closer, and touched the body with my paddle. The body turned in the water, and I saw the face of a young black woman, the eyes wide, the mouth open with a watery prayer. She wore a man's shirt tied under her breasts, cut-off blue jeans, and for just a second I saw a dime tied on a string around her ankle, a good-luck charm that some Acadian and black people wore to keep away the *gris-gris*, an evil spell. Her young face looked like a flower unexpectedly cut from its stem.

I looped my anchor rope around her ankle, threw the anchor back into the trees on the bank, and tied my red handkerchief on an overhanging branch.

Two hours later I watched the deputies from the parish sheriff's office lift the body onto a stretcher and carry it to an ambulance that was parked in the canebrake.

'Just a minute,' I said before they put her in. I lifted up the sheet to look again at something I'd seen when they had pulled her out of the water. There were tracks on the inside of her left arm, but only one needle hole that I could see inside the right.

'Maybe she gives blood to the Red Cross,' one of the deputies said, grinning.

'You're a pretty entertaining guy,' I said.

'It was just a joke, Lieutenant.'

'Tell the sheriff I'm going to call him about the autopsy,' I said.

'Yes, sir.'

But the sheriff was never in when I called, and he didn't return calls, either. So finally I telephoned the parish coroner's office, and now I discovered that the sheriff didn't believe an autopsy for a dead black girl was that important. Well, we'll see about that, I thought.

In the meantime, I was still curious as to why the Colombians, if Johnny Massina was right, were interested in Dave Robicheaux. I went through my case file and didn't see any connection. I had a whole file drawer of misery to look at, too: a prostitute icepicked by a psychotic john; a seventeen-year-old runaway whose father wouldn't bond him out of jail and who was hanged the next morning by his black cellmate; a murder witness beaten to death with a ball-peen hammer by the man she was scheduled to testify against; a Vietnamese boat refugee thrown off the roof of the welfare project; three small children shot in their beds by their unemployed father; a junkie strangled with baling wire during a satanic ritual; two homosexual men burned alive when a rejected lover drenched the stairwell of a gay nightclub with gasoline. My drawer was like a microcosm of an aberrant world populated by snipers, razor-wielding blacks, mindless nickel-and-dime boost artists who eventually panic and kill a convenience-store clerk for sixty dollars, and suicides who fill the apartment with gas and blow the whole building into a black and orange fireball.

What a bunch to dedicate your life to.

But there was no umbilical cord that led to the south-of the-border account.

Cletus was watching me.

'I swear, Dave, I think your feelings are going to be hurt unless you find out the greasers got the hots for you,' he said.

'We don't have a lot of perks in this business.'

'Well, I'll tell you what. Let's go to lunch early, you buy, and I'll introduce you to Potts. The guy's a delight. Your day is going to be filled with sunshine.'

It was hazy and bright when we drove into the Quarter. There was no breeze, and the palm fronds and banana trees in the courtyards were green and motionless in the heat. As always, the Quarter smelled to me like the small Creole town on Bayou Teche where I was born: the watermelons, cantaloupes, and strawberries stacked in crates under the scrolled colonnades; the sour wine and beer with sawdust in the bars; the poor-boy sandwiches dripping with shrimp and oysters; the cool, dank smell of old brick in the alleyways.

A few genuine bohemians, writers, and painters still lived in the Quarter, and some professional people paid exorbitant rents for refurbished apartments near Jackson Square, but the majority of Vieux Carré residents were transvestites, junkies, winos, prostitutes, hustlers of every stripe, and burnt-out acidheads and street people left over from the 1960s. Most of these people made their livings off middle-class conventioneers and Midwestern families who strolled down Bourbon Street, cameras hanging from their necks, as though they were on a visit to the zoo.

I couldn't find a place to park by Pearl's Oyster Bar, and I kept driving around the block.

'Dave, when does a guy know he's got a drinking problem?' Cletus asked.

'When it starts to hurt him.'

'It seems I've been getting half-stoned near every night of recent. I can't seem to go home unless I stop at the joint on the corner first.'

'How are you and Lois getting along?'

'I don't know. It's the second marriage for both of us. Maybe I've got too many problems, or maybe both of us have. They say if you don't make it the second time around, you ain't going to make it at all. You think that's true?'

'I don't know, Clete.'

'My first wife left me because she said she couldn't stay married to a man that brought a sewer home with him every day. That was when I was working vice. She said I smelled like whores and reefer all the time. Actually, vice did have its moments. Now Lois tells me she doesn't want me to bring my gun home at night. She's into Zen, meditates every day, sends our money to some Buddhist priest out in Colorado, and tells me she doesn't want her kids growing up around guns. Guns are bad, see, but this character out in Colorado that takes my bucks is good. Two weeks ago I came in wired, so she started crying and blowing her nose into a whole box of Kleenex. So I had a couple more hits of Jack Daniel's and told her how you and I had spent the afternoon combing pieces of a fourteen-year-old kid out of the garbage dump with a garden rake. Fifteen more minutes of tears and nose-honking. So I cruise for some booze and almost get nailed on a DUI. Not very good, huh?'

'Everybody has family trouble sometimes.'

He was frowning out the window, his thoughts collecting in his eyes. He lit a cigarette, drew in deeply, and flicked the match out into the sunlight.

'Man, I'm going to be a chainsaw by two o'clock,' he said. 'I'm going to have a couple of beers with lunch. Sedate the brain, the stomach, mellow the nerves. Does that bother you?'

'It's your day. You can do whatever you want to with it.'

'She's going to split. I know the signs.'

'Maybe y'all will work it out.'

'Come on, Dave, you didn't get off the boat yesterday. It doesn't work that way. You know how things were just before your wife took off.'

'That's right, I do. I know how things were. Nobody else does. You get my drift?' I grinned at him.

'All right, I'm sorry. But when it's going down the toilet, it's going down the toilet. You don't turn it around by leaving your piece in a locker. Pull into that truck zone. It's too damn hot out here.'

I parked in the loading zone by Pearl's and cut the engine. Cletus was sweating in the sunlight.

'Tell me honestly,' he said, 'would you have done something like that just to please your wife?'

I didn't even want to think about the things I had done to please my wife, my pale, dark-haired, beautiful wife from Martinique who left me for a Houston oilman.

'Hey, lunch is on you after all,' I said.

'What?'

'I didn't bring any money.'

'Use your MasterCard.'

'They wouldn't renew it. Something about exceeding my credit limit by four hundred dollars.'

'Great, I've got a buck thirty-five. What a class act. All right, we eat on the tab. If he doesn't like it, we tell him we're calling Immigration about the Haitians he's got working in his kitchen.'

'I didn't know he had any.'

'Me either. It'll be fun to see what he says.'

The pornographic theater was right on Bourbon Street. Bourbon had changed since I used to come here as a college student over twenty years ago. The old Dixieland bands like Papa Celestin's and Sharky Bonnano's had been replaced by imitation country bands made up of kids in designer jeans, vinyl vests, and puffed white silk shirts with lace brocade, like mambo dancers or transvestites would wear. The burlesque houses had always been seedy places where the girls hustled drinks between sets and hooked loose johns before closing, but the city code had required them to wear G-strings and pastics, and there hadn't been any dope around, except a little reefer among the desperate, burnt-out musicians who played in a small, dark pit at the bottom of the runway. But now the girls danced completely nude on the stage, their eyes glowing with black speed, their nostrils sometimes still twitching and wet from snorting coke through a rolled-up dollar bill.

The windows of Plato's Adult Theater had been walled up with cinder blocks so no one could see in, and the interior of the small, gold and purple lobby was decorated with erotic art that might have been painted by blind people. We went through the lobby into the office without knocking. A thin man with a pointed, shiny face looked up, startled, from his desk. He wore a powder-blue polyester suit and patent-leather shoes with silver buckles, and his receding, oiled hair glistened in the light from the desk lamp. Cans of movie reels were stacked in a wooden rack against one wall. The surprise and fear went out of the man's face, and he scratched his cheek with one hand and picked up a filter-tipped cigar from the ashtray.

'What do you want, Purcel?' he said indifferently.

'Dave, meet Wesley Potts, our resident bucket of shit,' Cletus said.

'I don't have time for your insults, Purcel. You got a warrant or something?'

'That's what they say on television, Pottsie,' Cletus said. 'You see any TV cameras, Dave?'

'I don't see any TV cameras,' I said.

‘On television some guy is always saying “You got a warrant?” or “You got to read me my rights,”’ Cletus said. ‘But in big-people land we don’t do it that way. You ought to know that, Pottsie.’

‘I thought you didn’t work vice anymore,’ Potts said.

‘That’s right. I’m in homicide now. My partner here’s last name is Robicheaux. Does that make your swizzle stick start to tingle?’

The man behind the desk blew cigar smoke out in front of him and looked into it with his eyes flat, but I saw his fingers crimp together on the desk blotter.

‘Your little brother up at Angola says you’re blabbing it around that Dave here is going to get snuffed,’ Cletus said.

‘If that’s what my brother says, you ought to be talking to him. I don’t know anything about it.’

‘The people up at Angola don’t like cops hitting on their convicts. Bad for their image and all that,’ Cletus said. ‘But you and us, well, that’s a whole different caper, Wes.’

Potts’s eyes were small and hot and staring straight ahead.

‘Lighten up,’ Cletus said. ‘You’re a businessman, you pay taxes, you’re reasonable. You just got diarrhea of the mouth and you been spreading rumors around, and we want to know why you been doing that. It’s no big deal. Just straighten us out about this strange stuff we heard, and you can get back to entertaining the perverts. Look at the material you got here. This is classy stuff.’ Cletus began to bang through the film cans on the wooden rack. He picked up one in both hands, and looked at the penciled title with a critical eye. 'This one is state-of-the-art porn, Dave. In one scene a guy kills a naked broad with a nail gun. She screams and begs, but the guy chases her around the house and staples pieces of her all over the woodwork.' Cletus opened the can, held on to one end of the film, and dropped the reel bouncing on the floor. He held the film strip up to the light. 'The funny thing, Wes, is sometimes a john goes apeshit and tears a hooker up, and I get the feeling that maybe the guy just finished eating popcorn out there in your theater. What do you think?'

'I never look at that stuff. I couldn't tell you what's in it. I just manage the place. It's a movie house, with a license, with fire exits, with sanitary bathrooms just like any other movie house. You don't like the place, go talk to the people that give out the permit.'

Cletus began opening the other film cans, dropping the reels to the floor, and walking on them as he worked his way down the rack. Thick tangles of film were looped around his ankles and shoes.

'You cut it out, you bastard,' Potts said.

'How'd you get into the IRS beef?' Cletus said.

'Fuck off.'

'You're fronting points for the spicks, aren't you?' Cletus said. 'You probably don't have fifteen people out there right now, but you show profits like you have the patent on the wheel. Why is that?'

'I sell lots of popcorn.'

'All that coke and brown scag money finds a ledger to get written down on,' Cletus said. 'Except the Treasury boys are about to ream your butthole.'

'I don't see any Treasury men. All I see is a plain-clothes prick that never grew up from high school,' Potts said. 'Where the fuck you get off with this stuff? You smash up my films, you come down on me because of something my little brother said which I don't even know he said, and you give me some bullshit about Mexican scag, when if I remember right you never busted anybody more serious than a junkie with a couple of balloons in his crotch. Maybe you took a little juice while you were in vice, huh? You're a fucking joke, Purcel.'

'Listen to this man carry on,' Cletus said. 'We're going to have to have privacy. Does this door go into the theater? Thanks, that's what I thought.'

He opened a side door that gave onto a small theater that looked like a remodeled garage. In the flickering darkness a dozen or so men stared fixedly at the screen.

'What's happening, geeks?' Cletus said loudly, and began flicking the light switch on and off. 'I'm the New Orleans heat. I just wanted to make sure everything was working all right. Enjoy your show.'

They rose quickly from their seats and moved as a group up the aisles farthest from Cletus and went through the curtained exit.

'Big deal. The same guys'll be sitting out there tonight,' Potts said.

'Could you leave me and Wesley alone a few minutes?' I said.

'I thought you might say that,' Cletus said, and crunched again through the tangle of ruined film on the floor and closed the door behind him.

I sat on the corner of Potts's desk and folded my hands on my thigh.

'How do you think this is going to end?' I said.

'What d'you mean?'

'Just what I said. Do you think you can tell people somebody is going to blow me away and I'm just going to walk out of here?'

He sucked in his lips and looked at the wall.

'Tell me what you think is going to happen,' I said.

'I don't know. I never saw you before. Why would I go around talking about you?'

'Who wants to drop the hammer on me, Wes?'

'I don't know any such thing.'

'Do you think I'm a dumb guy?'

'I don't know what you are.'

'Oh, yes you do. I'm the guy you never thought you'd see, just a vague figure in your mind you could laugh about getting snuffed. I've sort of showed up like a bad dream, haven't I?'

'I got nothing against you,' he said. 'I run a legal business. I don't cause you guys no trouble.'

'But I'm sitting here on your desk now. It's like waking up with a vulture on your bedpost, isn't it?'

'What are you going to do? Trash the place, knock me around? Big fucking deal.'

I took out my five-inch, single-blade Puma pocket knife and opened it. The blade could fillet bass like a barber's razor. It trembled with light.

'Jesus Christ, man, what are you doing?' he said.

I picked up his cigar from the ashtray, sliced off the burning end on the desktop, and put the still-warm stub in Potts's shirt pocket.

'You can smoke the rest of that later,' I said.

'What the fuck! Are you crazy, man?' he said. His face had gone white. He swallowed and stared at me, his eyes full of fear and confusion.

'You know who Didi Gee is, don't you?'

'Sure, everybody does. Why you ask about –'

'What's he do?'

'What d'you mean?'

'What's he do? Tell me now.'

'Everything. Whores, numbers, unions, y'all know that.'

'We're going to have lunch with him and I'm going to tell him what you told me.'

'What?'

'He has lunch in Jimmie the Gent's restaurant every Tuesday at two o'clock. You and I are going to sit at the next table and have a chat with the fat boy himself. Believe me, he'll find you an entertaining guy.'

'I ain't going.'

'Yes you are. You're under arrest.'

'What for? I didn't do anything,' he said desperately.

'You said something about cash. That sounded like an attempted bribe to me.'

His eyes flicked back and forth frantically. Pinpoints of sweat broke out on his forehead.

'I said "trash." I said "trash the place."'

'I'm hard of hearing. Anyway. I'll think about it on the way over to the restaurant. Do you believe that story about Didi Gee's aquarium, the one full of piranha? I heard he held a Teamster's hand in it for a full minute. Maybe that's just another one of those bullshit Mafia stories, though. Put your hands out in front of you, I'm going to cuff you. You can carry your coat across your wrist if it embarrasses you.'

'I don't rattle. You're running a game on me.'

'You dealt the hand, Wes. Play it out. But right now you put your wrists in front of you or I'm going to break open your fucking worthless face.'

He was breathing loudly now, his hands clenched in fists on the desk blotter.

'Listen, Lieutenant, I heard the other guys say something. Lot of times they're just blowing gas. It don't necessarily mean anything. I didn't hear it from Mr. Segura. It didn't come from Mr. Segura. You understand that? It's just street talk, a bunch of guys' bullshit.'

'You're talking about the Colombian?'

'He's from Nicaragua.'

'Go on.'

He wiped his lips with his fingers, then pulled at the flap of skin under his chin.

'It's got something to do with a nigger girl. I think she used to be a street whore. Didn't you pull a nigger out of the bayou in Cataouatche Parish?'

'You just keep telling me what you know, Wes.'

'Jesus Christ, Lieutenant, what d'you think I am? I'm just a theater manager. Maybe once a month Mr. Segura has a bunch of guys out to his place on the lake. A buffet, a lot of booze, some broads in the pool. He shakes everybody's hand, maybe has a collins with us or plays cards a few minutes under the beach umbrella, then disappears inside.'

'What's the girl have to do with Julio Segura?'

'You're not understanding me, Lieutenant. He don't tell me things like that. He don't talk to me about anything, in fact. Look, this a heavy-metal cat. I think he's wired into big people. Why mess with him? The feds deal with guys like this.'

I continued to stare silently at him. His hands

flicked on the desk blotter as though wires were attached to them.

'They say you're making noise about a nigger girl you found in another parish,' he said. 'That ain't your territory, so they wonder why the interest. For some reason they think you're after them. Don't ask me why. I don't even like to be around that kind of talk. I walk away from it. That's the God's truth.'

'You really bother me, Wes. I have great concern about your sincerity. I also have the feeling you think you're omniscient.'

'Wha – '

'Tell me if I'm wrong. You think you can intuit exactly what I'll accept. You're going to jerk me around and tell me bedtime stories, then snort a line or two after I'm gone to calm your nerves, and your day will be back intact again. That indicates a serious problem with vanity and pride. What do you think?'

'Look –' he began, his mouth smiling, his eyes cast down self-deprecatingly.

'No, no, it's time for Wes to listen and me to talk. You see, when you shoot off your mouth about the murder of a police officer, you invite some dangerous complications into your life. Number one, foreknowledge can make an accomplice out of you, Wes. Then, on a more basic level, there are several men I work with who would simply cool you out. Are we communicating here?'

'Yes,' he said weakly.

'There's no confusion?'

'No.'

'All right, Wes. We'll talk again later. You understand that, don't you?'

'Yes.'

I stood up from his desk and walked toward the door. I could hear him expel his breath.

Then: 'Lieutenant?'

I turned and looked at him. His face was small and pale.

'Will this get back to Mr. Segura?' he said. 'A couple of the Latin guys that work for him . . . cruel guys . . . they were cops or national guardsmen or something in Nicaragua . . . I don't like to think about the stuff they do.'

'No guarantees. You sniff something bad in the wind, come to us and we'll get you out of town.'

The sun was blazing outside. Across the street, three black kids were tap dancing for the tourists in the shade of the scrolled iron colonnade. The huge taps they wore sounded like drumsticks clicking on the metal. Cletus stood out of the sunlight's glare, watching, with his seersucker coat over one arm. 'What'd you get from old Pottsie?'

'It was the black girl I found in Bayou Lafourche. It's got the smell of dope and the Barataria pirates. Did you ever run up against Julio Segura when you were on vice?'

'You better believe it. He's your genuine, certified greaseball. The guy's got Vitalis oozing out of every pore.'

'I thought he was a Colombian.'

'He's hooked in with them, but he's from Managua. I heard he owned a hundred whorehouses down there. They say the Sandinistas shot holes all over his plane just as it cleared the field. The guy's a survivor. We tried to get him two or three times. I think he's got a lot of high-up juice going for him.'

We walked in the warm shade back toward Royal Street, where we had left the car parked in front of the oyster bar. I went into a small, dark grocery store cooled by a wooden-bladed overhead fan, and bought a *Times-Picayune*. The interior of the store smelled of bananas, coffee, blocks of cheese, and big wooden bins filled with grapes and plums. I opened the *Picayune* to the sports page as we walked along.

'Y'all want to go to the races tonight?' I said.

'Forget the races. Let's front the spick. We tell the captain about it first, then we go out to his house and flip his necktie in his face.'

'Nope. Too soon.'

'Bullshit. The only way to handle these guys is jump up and down on their nuts. In this case we want the guy to know it's personal. We deliver the Candygram right in his living room.'

'I appreciate it, Clete, but I'll let you know when it's time to toggle out there. Don't worry. You won't miss out on the party.'

'You're too laid back. I'm telling you, this guy is subhuman. He makes an animal like Didi Gee look like the archbishop by comparison.'

'Damn,' I said.

'What's wrong?'

'Next time, we take your car to lunch.'

'What for?'

'That's my car on the back of that tow truck.'

The light was soft on the lake as I dressed on the houseboat that evening. Up the shore I could see the palm and cypress trees blowing in the wind off the Gulf. The air smelled like rain again. I felt very alone and quiet inside, and I wondered if my feeling of confident solitude, my peculiar moment of serenity inside, was not a deceptive prelude to another turbulent time in my life. Maybe it was just a brief courtship with narcissism. My body was still hard and lean, my skin brown, the old scar from the dung-tipped *pungi* stick like a broken gray snake embossed on my stomach. My hair and brush mustache were still as black as ink, except for the white patch above one ear, and I convinced myself every morning that living alone was no more a mark of age and failure than it was of youth and success. The dark purple clouds piled on the Gulf's southern horizon trembled with heat lightning.

I sat alone in a box at the races that night and looked with the same quiet and tranquil fascination at the lighted track, the dampened and raked sod, the glistening clipped grass in the center field. It was the kind of vague, almost numb euphoria that I used to feel when I slid off the edge of a two-day binge into delirium tremens. I had become omniscient; my white tropical suit glowed from the arc light overhead; I cashed three place bets and two wins in a row. The peach-complexioned waitresses in the clubhouse brought me shelled shrimp on ice, and lobster and steak, and brushed their hips unnecessarily against my arm when they took away my soiled napkin and blood-streaked plate.

Someone once told me that the gambler's greatest desire, knowledge of the future, would drive us insane. On that warm summer evening as I drove back home, with the moon denting the lake and the fireflies lighting in the palm and oak trees, I felt a thin tremolo inside me, like the faint tinkling of crystal or the almost silent vibration of sympathetic guitar strings, just a hint of Cassandra's tragic gift, and I tried to ascribe it to my old alcoholic fears that writhed in the unconscious as blind snakes would. But a winner at the track usually cares little for caution or moonlit nuances.

2

Early the next morning I drove southwest of New Orleans, into the bayou country. It was the south Louisiana I had grown up in, around New Iberia. Oak, cypress, and willow trees lined the two-lane road; the mist still clung like torn cotton to the half-submerged dead tree trunks back in the marsh; the canebrakes were thick and green, shining in light, and the lily pads clustered along the bayou's banks were bursting with flowers, audibly popping, their leaves covered with drops of quicksilver. The bream and bass were still feeding in the shadows close to the cypress roots; egrets were nesting in the sand where the sun had risen above the tree line, and occasionally a heron would lift from its feeding place on the edge of the cattails and glide on gilded wings down the long ribbon of brown water through a corridor of trees.

Now these same bayous, canals, and marshlands where I had grown up were used by the Barataria pirates. But their namesakes, Jean Lafitte's collection of brigands and slavers, were romantic figures by comparison. The current group was made up of marijuana, cocaine, and heroin smugglers who would murder a whole family out on the Gulf simply for the one-time use of their boat, after which they'd open up the cocks and sink it. Occasionally the Coast Guard would find one half-filled with water and beached on a sandbar, the gunwales painted with blood.

But why should this shock or revile? The same people sometimes killed infants by injection, embalmed the bodies, and filled the stomachs with balloons of heroin so women transporters could walk through customs as though they were carrying their sleeping children.

The Cataouatche Parish sheriff was not at the courthouse. He was at his horse farm outside of town, galoshes on his feet, feeding two Arabians in a side lot. His house had a fresh coat of white paint and a wide screen porch, and was surrounded by azalea bushes and flaming hibiscus. The long white fence along the back horse pasture was entwined with climbing roses. The Sheriff was around fifty, a man in control of his property and his political life. His blue uniform fitted tightly on his compact, hard body, and his round, freshly shaved face and direct eyes gave you the impression of a self-confident rural law officer who dealt easily with outside complexities.

Unfortunately for him, I proved to be the exception.

'She drowned,' he said. 'My deputies said a bucket of water came out of her when they flipped her off the gurney.'

'She had tracks on her arms.'

'So? Addicts drown too. You need an autopsy to tell you that?'

'Do you know if she was right-handed or left-handed?'

'What the hell are you talking about?' he said.

'She'd been shooting regularly into the left arm, but she had only one needle hole on the right. What's that tell you?'

'Not a goddamn thing.'

'When a junkie flattens the vein in one arm, he starts on the other. I don't think she'd been shooting up that long. I think somebody gave her a hotshot.'

'The parish coroner signed the death certificate. It says "drowned". You take it up with him if you want to pursue it. I'm late for work.' He walked out of the horse lot, pulled off his muddy galoshes on the grass, and slipped on his polished, half-topped boots. His round face was turned away from me as he bent over, but I could hear the repressed anger in his breathing.

'Those are fine Arabians,' I said. 'I understand they can bring thirty thousand or so when they're trained.'

'That wouldn't touch them, Lieutenant. Like I say, I don't mean to be rude, but I'm late. You want me to introduce you to the coroner?'

'I don't think so. Tell me, as a matter of speculation, how do you figure a healthy young woman, wearing all her clothes, would come to drown in a narrow bayou?'

'What's going to make you happy, Lieutenant? You want somebody to write down for you that she died of a hotshot? You want to take that back to New Orleans with you? All right, you have my permission. It's no skin off our ass. But how about her family? She was raised up in the quarters on a sugar plantation about five miles south of here. Her mother is feeble-minded and her daddy is half-blind. You want to drive out there and tell them their daughter was a junkie?'

'Everything in this case stinks of homicide, Sheriff.'

'I've only got two more things to say to you, podna, and it's important you understand this. I trust what my deputies told me, and if you got a complaint, you take it to the coroner's office. And number two, this conversation is over.'

Then he looked away at his horses in a distant field, as though I were not there, slipped on his pilot's sunglasses, got into his Cadillac, and drove down his pea-gravel lane to the blacktop. I felt like a post standing in the ground.

The dead girl's name had been Lovelace Deshotels. Her parents lived in one of the weathered, paintless shacks along a dirt road on the back of a corporate sugar plantation. All the shacks were identical, their small front porches so evenly aligned that you could fire an arrow through the receding rectangle of posts, roofs, and bannisters for the entire length of the quarters without striking wood. The thick green fields of cane stretched away for miles, broken only by an occasional oak tree and the distant outline of the sugar mill, whose smokestacks in the winter would cover these same shacks with a sickening sweet odor that made the eyes water.

The shack was like thousands of others that I had seen all my life throughout Louisiana and Mississippi. There was no glass in the windows, only hinged board flaps that were propped open on sticks. The walls had been insulated with pages from the Sears catalog, then covered with wall-paper that was now separated and streaked brown with rainwater. The outhouse, which was set next to a small hog lot, had a rusted R.C. Cola sign for a roof.

But there were other things there that leaped at your eye when you walked through the door: a color television set, an imitation Bavarian clock above the woodburning stove, plastic flowers set in jelly glasses, a bright yellow Formica breakfast table next to an ancient brick fireplace filled with trash.

The parents would tell me little. The mother stared vacantly at a game show on television, her huge body stuffed in a pair of lime-green stretch pants and a man's army shirt cut off at the armpits. The father was gray and old and walked with a cane as though his back were disjointed. He smelled of the cob pipe in his shirt pocket. His eyes were scaled over and frosted with cataracts.

'She gone off to New Orleans. I tolt her a colored girl from the country dint have no business there, her,' he said, sitting on the couch, his hand curved along the top of his cane. 'She only a country girl. What she gonna do with them kind of people they got in New Orleans? I tell her that, me.'

'Who did she work for, Mr. Deshotels?'

'What I know about New Orleans? I ain't got no truck there, me.' He smiled at me, and I saw his toothless blue gums.

'Do you believe she drowned?'

He paused and the smile went out of his face. His eyes seemed to focus on me for the first time.

'You think they care what some old nigger say?' he said.

'I do.'

He didn't answer. He put his dead pipe in his mouth, made a wet sound with his tongue, and stared blankly at the television screen.

'I'll be going now,' I said, standing up. 'I'm sorry about what happened to your daughter. I really am.'

His face turned back toward me.

'We had eleven, us,' he said. 'She the baby. I call her *tite cush-cush* 'cause she always love *cush-cush* when she a little girl. He'p me walk out front, you.'

I put my hand under his arm and we stepped out into the bright sunlight on the porch. The wind was ruffling the green fields of surgarcane on the opposite side of the road. The old man's arm was webbed with veins. He limped along with me to my automobile before he spoke.

'They kilt her, them, dint they?' he asked.

'I think they did.'

'She just a little colored jellyroll for white mens, then they throw her away,' he said. His eyes became wet. 'I tolt her "Jerryroll, jellyroll, rollin' in the cane, lookin' for a woman ain't got no man." She say "Look the television and the clock and the table I give Mama." She say that, her. Little girl that don't know how to read can buy a five-hundred-dollar television set for her mama. What you gonna do when they nineteen? Ain't no listenin', not when she got white men's money, drive a big car down here from New Orleans, tellin' me she gonna move us up North, her. Little girl that still eat *cush-cush* gonna outsmart the white mens, her, move her old nigger daddy up to New York. What she done they got to kill her for?'

I didn't have an answer for him.

I was on an empty stretch of road bordered on one side by a flat, shimmering lake and on the other by a flooded woods, when I saw a blue and white patrol car in my rearview mirror. The driver already had on his bubblegum light, and when he drew close to my bumper he gave me a short blast with his siren. I started to pull to the shoulder, but there were shards of beer-bottle glass like amber teeth shining in the weeds and gravel. I tried to drive on to a clear spot before I stopped, and the patrol car leaped abreast of me, the engine roaring, and the deputy in the passenger's seat pointed to the side of the road with an angry finger. I heard my tires crunch over the beer glass.

Both deputies got out of the car, and I knew it was going to be serious. They were big men, probably Cajuns like myself, but their powerful and sinewy bodies, their tight-fitting, powder-blue uniforms, polished gunbelts and holsters, glinting bullets and revolver butts made you think of backwoods Mississippi and north Louisiana, as though they'd had to go away to learn redneck cruelty.

Neither of them had a citation book in his hand or pocket.

'The siren means pull over. It don't mean slow down, Lieutenant,' the driver said. He smiled back at me and took off his sunglasses. He was older than the other deputy. 'Step out of the car, please.'

I opened the door and stepped out on the road. They looked at me without speaking.

'All right, I'll bite. What have you got me for?' I said.

'Sixty in a fifty-five,' the other deputy said. He chewed gum, and his eyes were humorless and intent.

'I didn't think I ever got over fifty,' I said.

''Fraid it creeped up on you,' the older man said. 'On a pretty morning like this you get to looking around, maybe looking at the water and the trees, maybe thinking about a piece of ass, and before you know it you got lead in your pecker and foot, both.'

'I don't guess we're going to have an instance of professional courtesy here, are we?' I said.

'The judge don't allow us to let too many slide,' the older man said.

'So write me a ticket and I'll talk to the judge about it.'

'Lot of people from outside the parish don't show up in court,' the older deputy said. 'Makes him madder than a hornet with shit on its nose. So we got to take them down to the court.'

'You guys didn't get completely dressed this morning,' I said.

'How's that?' the other deputy said.

'You forgot to put on your name tags. Now, why would you do that?'

'Don't worry about any goddamn name tags. You're coming back to the courthouse with us,' the younger deputy said. He had stopped chewing his gum, and his jawbone was rigid against his cheek.

'You got a flat tire, anyway, Lieutenant,' the older man said. 'I figure that's kind of our fault, so while you ride in with us I'll radio the tow to come and change it for you.'

'Facts-of-life time,' I said. 'You don't roust a City of New Orleans detective.'

'Our territory, our rules, Lieutenant.'

'Fuck you,' I said.

They were both silent. The sun was shimmering brilliantly on the flat expanse of water behind them. The light was so bright I had to force myself not to blink. I could hear both of them breathing, see their eyes flick at each other uncertainly, almost smell the thin sweat on their skin.

The younger man's shoe shifted in the gravel and his thumb fluttered toward the strap on the holster that held his chrome-plated .357 Magnum revolver. I tore my .38 out of the clip holster on my belt, squatted, and aimed with two hands into their faces.

'Big mistake, podjo! Hands on your head and down on your knees!' I shouted.

'Look –' the older deputy began.

'Don't think, do it! I win, you lose!' My breath was coming hard in my throat.

They looked at each other, laced their hands on their heads, and knelt in front of their car. I went behind them, pulled their heavy revolvers from their holsters, and pitched them sideways into the lake.

'Take out your cuffs and lock up to the bumper,' I said.

'You're in over your head,' the older deputy said. The back of his suntanned neck was beaded with sweat.

'That's not the way I read it,' I said. 'You guys thought you'd be cowboys and you got your faces shoved into the sheepdip. What was it going to be, a day or so in the tank, or maybe some serious patty-cake in the backseat on the way to the jail?'

They didn't reply. Their faces were hot and angry and pained by the rocks that cut their knees.

'Put the cuffs through the bumper and lock your wrists,' I said. 'You didn't answer me, which makes me wonder if I was going to make the jail. Are you guys into it that big?'

'Kiss my ass,' the younger deputy said.

'Tell me, are y'all that dumb? You think you can pop a New Orleans cop and walk out of it?'

'We'll see who walks out of what,' the older deputy said. He had to twist sideways on his knees and squint up into the sun to talk to me.

'The Sheriff is letting you clean up his shit for him, isn't he?' I said. 'It looks like lousy work to me. You ought to get him to spread the juice around a little more. You guys probably rip off a little change now and then, maybe get some free action in the local hot-pillow joint, but he drives a Cadillac and raises Arabians.'

'For a homicide cop you're a stupid bastard,' the older deputy said. 'What make you think you're so important you got to be popped? You're just a hair in somebody's nose.'

'I'm afraid you boys have limited careers ahead of you.'

'Start figuring how you're going to get out of here,' the younger deputy said.

'You mean my flat tire? That is a problem,' I said thoughtfully. 'What if I just drive your car down the road a little ways with you guys still cuffed to it?'

For the first time their faces showed the beginnings of genuine fear.

'Relax. We have our standards in New Orleans.

We don't pick on the mentally handicapped,' I said.

In the distance I saw a maroon car approaching. The two deputies heard it and looked at each other expectantly.

'Sorry, no cavalry today,' I said, then squatted down at eye level with them. 'Now look, you pair of clowns, I don't know how far you want to take this, but if you really want to get it on, you remember this: I've got more juice than you do, more people, more brains, more everything that counts. So give it some thought. In the meantime I'm going to send somebody back for my car, and it had better be here. Also, tell that character you work for that our conversation was ongoing. He'll get my drift.'

I flagged down the maroon car with my badge and got in the passenger's seat before the driver, a blond woman in her late twenties with windblown hair and wide eyes, could speak or concentrate on the two manacled deputies. Her tape player was blaring out Tchaikovsky's First Concerto, and the backseat was an incredible litter of papers, notebooks, and government forms.

'I'm a New Orleans police officer. I need you to take me to the next town,' I shouted above the music.

Her eyes were blue and as round as a doll's with surprise and fear. She began to accelerate slowly, her eyes sliding past the handcuffed cops but then riveting on them again in the rearview mirror.

'Are those men locked to the car?' she said.

'Yes. They were bad boys,' I yelled back. 'Can I turn this down?'

'I'm sorry, but I have to do this. You can go ahead and shoot if you want to.'

And with that she slammed on the brakes, dropped the transmission into reverse, and floorboarded the car backwards in a screech of rubber and a cloud of black smoke. My head hit the windshield, then I saw my old Chevrolet coming up fast. 'Watch it!' I shouted.

But it was too late. Her bumper caught my front fender and raked both doors. Then she careened to a stop, flipped off the stereo, leaned across me, and yelled at the deputies, 'This man says he's a police officer. Is that true?'

'Call the Cataouatche Sheriff's office, lady,' the older deputy said. He was squatting on one knee, and his face was strained with discomfort.

'Who is this man in my car?'

'He a piece of shit that's going to get ground into the concrete,' the younger deputy said.

The woman yanked the car into low, pushed the accelerator to the floor, and roared past my car again. I felt her back bumper carom off my front fender. She drove like a wild person, papers blowing in the backseat, the lake and flooded woods streaking past us.

'I'm sorry about your car. I have insurance. I think I still do, anyway,' she said.

'That's all right. I've always wanted to see the country from inside a hurricane. Are you still afraid, or do you always drive like this?'

'Like what?' Her hair was blowing in the wind and her round blue eyes were intent over the wheel.

'Do you still think I'm an escaped criminal?' I said.

'I don't know what you are, but I recognized one of those deputies. He's a sadist who rubbed his penis all over one of my clients.'

'Your clients?'

'I work for the state handicapped services.'

'You can put him away.'

'She's scared to death. He told her he'd do it to her again, and then put her in jail as a prostitute.'

'God, lady, look out. Listen, there's a restaurant on stilts just across the parish line. You pull in there, then we're going to make a phone call and I'm going to buy you lunch.'

'Why?'

'Because you're wired and you don't believe who I am. By the way, what you did back there took courage.'

'No, it didn't. I just don't give rides to weird people. There's a lot of weirdness around these days. If you're a police detective, why are you driving a wreck of an automobile?'

'A few minutes ago it wasn't entirely a wreck.'

'That's what I mean by weirdness. Maybe I saved your life, and you criticize my driving.'

Don't argue with God's design on a sun-spangled morning in a corridor of oak trees, Robicheaux, I thought. Also, don't argue with somebody who's doing eighty-five miles an hour and showering rocks like birdshot against the tree trunks.

The restaurant was a ramshackle board place with screen windows, built up on posts over the lake. Metal Dixie 45 and Jax beer signs were nailed all over the outer walls. Crawfish were out of season, so I ordered fried catfish and small bowls of shrimp gumbo. While we waited for the food, I bought her a drink at the bar and used the phone to call my extension at First District headquarters in New Orleans. I put the receiver to her ear so she could hear Clete answer, then I took the receiver back.

'I'm having lunch with a lady who would like you to describe what I look like,' I told him, and gave the phone back to her. I saw her start to smile as she listened, then her eyes crinkled and she laughed out loud.

'That's outrageous,' she said.

'What'd he say?'

'That your hair is streaked like a skunk's and that sometimes you try to walk the check.'

'Clete's always had satirical ambitions.'

'Is this how you all really do things? Chaining up other cops to cars, terrifying people on the highway, playing jokes over the phone?'

'Not exactly. They have a different set of rules in Cataouatche Parish. I sort of strayed off my turf.'

'What about those deputies back there? Won't they come after you?'

'I think they'll be more worried about explaining themselves to the man they work for. After we eat, can you take me back to the city?'

'I have to make a home call at a client's house, then I can.' She sipped from her Manhattan, then ate the cherry off the toothpick. She saw me watching her, and she looked out the window at the lake, where the wind was blowing the moss in the cypress trees.

'Do you like horse racing?' I said.

'I've never been.'

'I have a clubhouse pass. Would you like to go tomorrow night, provided I have my car back?'

She paused, and her electric blue eyes wandered over my face.

'I play cello with a string quartet. We have practice tomorrow night,' she said.

'Oh.'

'But we'll probably finish by eight-thirty, if that's not too late. I live by Audubon Park,' she said.

See, don't argue with design and things will work out all right after all, I told myself.

But things did not go well back at the District the next day. They never did when I had to deal with the people in vice, or with Sergeant Motley in particular. He was black, an ex-career enlisted man, but he had little sympathy for his own people. One time a black wino in a holding cell was giving Motley a bad time, calling him 'the white man's knee-grow, with a white man's badge and a white man's gun,' and Motley covered him from head to foot with the contents of a can of mace before the turnkey slapped it out of his hand.

But there was another memory about Motley that was darker. Before he made sergeant and moved over to vice, he had worked as a bailiff at the court and was in charge of escorting prisoners from the drunk tank to morning arraignment. He had seven of them on a wrist-chain in the elevator when a basement fire blew the electric circuits and stalled the elevator between floors. Motley got out through the escape door in the elevator's roof, but the seven prisoners were asphyxiated by the smoke.

'What do you want to know about her?' he said. He was overweight and had a thick mustache, and his ashtray was full of cigar butts.

'You busted her three times in a month – twice for soliciting, once for holding. You must have had an interest in her,' I said.

'She was a ten-dollar chicken, a real loser.'

'You're not telling me a lot, Motley.'

'What's to tell? She was freebasing and jacking guys off in a massage parlor in Decatur. She was the kind a john cuts up or a pimp sets on fire. Like I say, a victim. A country girl that was going to make the big score.'

'Who went her bail?'

'Probably her pimp. I don't remember.'

'Who was he?'

'I don't remember. There's a new lowlife running that joint every two months.'

'You know anybody who'd have reason to give her a hotshot?'

'Ask me her shoe size. When'd she become your case, anyway? I heard you fished her out of the bayou in Cataouatche Parish.'

'It's a personal interest. Look, Motley, we cooperate with you guys. How about being a little reciprocal?'

'What is it you think I know? I told you she was just another brainless whore. They all come out of the same cookie cutter. I lost contact with her, anyway.'

'What do you mean?'

'We busted the massage parlor a couple of times and she wasn't working there anymore. One of the other broads said Julio Segura moved her out to his place. That don't mean anything, though. He does that all the time, when he gets tired of them, gives them a few balloons of Mexican brown, and has that dwarf chauffeur of his drive them to the bus stop or back to the crib.'

'You're unbelievable.'

'You think a guy like him is interested in snuffing whores? Write it off, Robicheaux. You're wasting your time.'

Fifteen minutes later, Captain Guidry walked into the office I shared with Clete. He was fifty and lived with his mother and belonged to the Knights of Columbus. But recently he had been dating a widow in the city water department, and we knew it was serious when the captain began to undergo a hair transplant. His gleaming bald scalp was now inlaid with tiny round divots of transplanted hair, so that his head looked like a rock with weeds starting to grow on it. But he was a good administrator, a straight arrow, and he often took the heat for us when he didn't have to.

'Triple-A called and said they towed in your car,' he said.

'That's good,' I said.

'No. They also said somebody must have broken all the windows out with a hammer or a baseball bat. What went on over there with the sheriff's department, Dave?'

I told him while he stared at me blankly. I also told him about Julio Segura. Cletus kept his face buried in our file drawer.

'You didn't make this up? You actually cuffed two sheriff's deputies to their own car?' the captain said.

'I wasn't holding a very good hand, Captain.'

'Well, you probably had them figured right,

because they haven't pursued it, except for remodeling your windows. You want to turn the screws on them a little? I can call the state attorney general's office and probably shake them up a bit.'

'Clete and I want to go out to Segura's place.'

'Vice considers that their territory,' Captain Guidry said.

'They're talking about killing a cop. It's our territory now,' I said.

'All right, but no cowboy stuff,' he said. 'Right now we don't have legal cause to be out there.'

'Okay.'

'You just talk, let him know we're hearing things we don't like.'

'Okay, Captain.'

He rubbed his fingernail over one of the crusted implants in his head.

'Dave?'

'Yes, sir?'

'Forget what I said. He's threatening a New Orleans police officer and we're not going to tolerate it. Put his head in the toilet. Tell him it came from me, too.'

Oleander, azalea, and myrtle trees were planted thickly behind the scrolled iron fence that surrounded Segura's enormous blue-green lawn. Gardeners were clipping the hedges, watering the geranium and rose beds, cutting away the dead brown leaves from the stands of banana trees. Back toward the lake I could see the white stucco two-story house, its red tile roof gleaming in the sun, the royal palms waving by the swimming pool. Someone sprang loudly off a diving board.

A muscular Latin man in slacks and a golf shirt came out the front gate and leaned down to Clete's window. There were faded tattoos under the black hair on his forearms. He also wore large rings on both hands.

'Can I help you, sir?' he said.

'We're police officers. We want to talk to Segura,' Clete said.

'Do you have an appointment with him?'

'Just tell him we're here, partner,' Clete said.

'He's got guests right now.'

'You got a hearing problem?' Clete said.

'I got a clipboard with some names on it. If your name's on it, you come in. If it ain't, you stay out.'

'Listen, you fucking greaseball . . .' Without finishing his sentence, Clete got out of the car and hit the man murderously in the stomach with his fist. The man doubled over, his mouth dropped open as though he had been struck with a sledgehammer, and his eyes looked like he was drowning.

'Got indigestion troubles? Try Tums,' Clete said.

'What's the matter with you?' I said to him.

'Nothing now,' he said, and pushed back the iron gate so we could drive through. The Latin man held on the fence with one hand and labored to get his breath back. We drove up the driveway toward the stucco house. I continued to look at Clete.

'You never worked vice. You don't know what kind of scum these bastards are,' he said. 'When a greaseball like that gets in your face, you step all over him. It defines the equations for him.'

'Did you get drunk last night?'

'Yeah, but I don't need an excuse to bash one of these fuckers.'

'No more of it, Clete.'

'We're in, aren't we? We're the surprise in Julio's afternoon box of Cracker Jacks. Look at that bunch by the pool. I bet we could run them and connect them with every dope deal in Orleans and Jefferson parishes.'

About a dozen people were in or around the clover-shaped pool. They floated on rubber rafts in the turquoise water, played cards on a mosaic stone table and benches that were anchored in the shallow end, or sat in lawn chairs by the slender gray trucks of the palms while a family of dwarf servants brought them tall tropical drinks filled with fruit and ice.

Clete walked directly across the clipped grass to an umbrella-shaded table where a middle-aged man in cream-colored slacks and a yellow shirt covered with blue parrots sat with two other men who were as dark as Indians and built like fire hydrants. The man in the print shirt was one of the most peculiar-looking human beings I had ever seen. His face was triangular-shaped, with a small mouth and very small ears, and his eyes were absolutely black. Three deep creases ran across his forehead, and inside the creases you could see tiny balls of skin. On his wrist was a gold watch with a black digital dial, and he smoked a Bisonte with a cigarette holder. The two dark men started to get up protectively as we approached the table, but the man in the yellow and blue shirt gestured for them to remain seated. His eyes kept narrowing as though Clete's face were floating toward him out of a memory.

'What's happening, Julio?' Clete said. 'There's a guy out front puking his lunch all over the grass. It really looks nasty for the neighborhood. You ought to hire a higher-class gate man.'

'Purcel, right?' Segura said, the recognition clicking into his eyes.

'That's good,' Clete said. 'Now connect the dots and figure out who this guy with me is.'

One of the dark men said something to Segura in Spanish.

'Shut up, greaseball,' Clete said.

'What do you think you're doing, Purcel?' Segura asked.

'That all depends on you, Julio. We hear you're putting out a very serious shuck about my partner,' Clete said.

'Is this him?' Segura asked.

I didn't answer. I stared straight into his eyes. He puffed on his cigarette holder and looked back at me without blinking, as though he were looking at an object rather than a man.

'I heard you been knocking the furniture around,' he said finally. 'But I don't know you. I never heard of you, either.'

'I think you're a liar,' I said.

'That's your right. What else you want to tell me today?'

'Your people killed a nineteen-year-old girl named Lovelace Deshotels.'

'Let me tell you something, what's-your-name,' he said. 'I'm an American citizen. I'm a citizen because a United States senator introduced a bill to bring me here. I got a son in West Point. I don't kill people. I don't mind Purcel and his people bothering me sometimes. You got *la mordida* here just like in Nicaragua. But you don't come out here and tell me I kill somebody.' He nodded to one of the dark men, who got up and walked to the house. 'I tell you something else, too. You know why Purcel is out here? It's because he's got a guilty conscience and he blames other people for it. He took a girl out of a massage parlor in the French Quarter and seduced her in the back of his car. That's the kind of people you got telling me what morality is.'

'How'd you like your teeth kicked down your throat?' Clete asked.

'I got my attorneys coming out right now. You want to make threats, you want to hit people, you'll make them rich. They love you.'

'You're a pretty slick guy, Julio,' I said.

'Yeah? Maybe you're a cute guy, like your partner,' he answered.

'Slick as Vaseline, not a bump or a handle on you,' I said. 'But let me tell you a story of my own. My daddy was a trapper on Marsh Island. He used to tell me, "If it's not moving, don't poke it. But when it starts snapping at your kneecaps, wait till it opens up real wide, then spit in its mouth." What do you think of that story?'

'You're a mature man. Why you want to be a fool? I didn't do nothing to you. For some reason you're finding this trouble for yourself.'

'What's the worst thing you've ever seen happen to somebody, Julio?' I asked.

'What're you talking about?' he said. His brow was furrowed, and the tiny balls of skin in the creases looked like strings of purple BBs.

'I hear you have some cruel guys working for you.

Probably some of Somoza's old national guardsmen, experts in garroting journalists and murdering Catholic priests.'

'You don't makc no sense.'

'Sure I do,' I said. 'You probably got to visit the basement in some of Somoza's police-stations. You saw them hung up by their arms, with a cloth bag soaked in insecticide tied over their heads. They screamed and went blind and suffocated to death, and even a piece of shit like yourself had a few nightmares about it. You also knew about that volcano where the army used to drop the Sandinistas from a helicopter into the burning crater. It's pretty awful stuff to think about, Julio.'

'They really sent us a pair today. A Vice cop with *puta* in his head and another one that talks like a Marxist,' he said. Some of the people around the pool laughed.

'You're not following my drift,' I said. 'You see, to you a bad fate is what you've seen your own kind do to other people. But once you got away from the horror show down there in Managua, you figured you were safe. So did Somoza. He got out of Dodge with all his millions, then one day his chauffeur was driving him across Asunción in his limo, with a motorcycle escort in front and back, and somebody parked a three-point-five bazooka rocket in his lap. It blew him into instant lasagna. Are you following me, Julio?'

'You going to come after me, big man?' he asked.

'You still don't get it. Look, it's almost biblical. Eventually somebody eats your lunch, and it always comes from a place you didn't expect it. Maybe a redneck cop puts a thumbbuster forty-five behind your ear and lets off a hollow-point that unfastens your whole face. Or maybe they strap you down in the Red Hat House at Angola and turn your brains into fried grits.'

'You ought to get a job writing comic books,' he said.

'Then maybe you're sitting by your pool, secure, with your prostitutes and these trained monkeys around you, and something happens out of sequence,' I said, and picked up his tropical drink full of ice and fruit and poured it into his lap.

He roared back from the table, raking ice off his cream-colored slacks, his face full of outrage and disbelief. The squat, dark man seated across from him started from his chair. Clete slammed him back down.

'Start it and we finish it, Paco,' he said.

The dark man remained seated and gripped the wrought-iron arms of his chair, staring at Clete with a face that was as flat and latently brutal as a frying pan.

'There's a good fellow,' Clete said.

'You get out of here!' Segura said.

'This is just for openers. The homicide people are a creative bunch,' I said.

'You're spit on the sidewalk,' he said.

'We've got a whole grab bag of door prizes for you, Julio. But in the end I'm going to send you back to the tomato patch,' I said.

'I got guys that can cut a piece out of you every day of your life,' Segura said.

'That sounds like a threat against a police officer,' Clete said.

'I don't play your game, *maricón*,' Segura said.

'You're amateurs, losers. Look behind you. You want to shove people around now?'

Two men had parked their canary-yellow Continental at the end of thc drive and were walking across the grass toward us. Both of them looked like upgraded bail bondsmen.

'Whiplash Wineburger, up from the depths,' Clete said.

'I thought he'd been disbarred for fixing a juror,' I said.

'That was his brother. Whiplash is too slick for that,' Clete said. 'His specialty is insurance fraud and ripping off his own clients.'

'Who's the oilcan with him?'

'Some dago legislator that's been peddling his ass around here for years.'

'I heard you were wired into some heavy connections. These guys need lead in their shoes on a windy day,' I said to Segura.

'*Me cago en la puta de tu madre*,' he replied.

'You hotdogs got two minutes to get out of here,' the lawyer said. He was lean and tan, like an aging professional tennis player, and he wore a beige sports jacket, a yellow open-necked shirt, and brown-tinted glasses.

'We were just on our way. It looks like the neighborhood is going to hell in a hurry,' Clete said.

'By the way, Wineburger,' I said, 'bone up on your tax law. I hear the IRS is about to toss Segura's tax records.'

'Yeah? You got a line to the White House?' he said.

'It's all over the Federal Building. You haven't been doing your homework,' I said.

We walked back to our car and left Segura and his lawyer staring at each other.

We headed back down the lake toward the Pontchartrain Expressway. The palm trees were beating along the shore, and small waves were white-capping out on the lake. Several sailboats were tacking hard in the wind.

'You think we stuck a couple of thumbtacks in his head?' Cletus asked. He drove without looking at me.

'We'll see.'

'That touch about the IRS was beautiful.'

'You want to tell me something, Clete?'

'Am I supposed to go to confession or something?'

'I don't like to see a guy like Segura trying to jerk my partner around.'

'It was three years ago. My wife and I had broke up and I'd been on the shelf for six weeks.'

'You let the girl walk?'

'She was never busted. She was a snitch. I liked her.'

'That's why you put your fist through that guy's stomach?'

'All right, so I don't feel good about it. But I swear to you, Dave, I never got any free action because of my badge, and I never went on the pad.' He looked across at me with his poached, scarred face.

'So I believe you.'

'So buy me a *beignet* and a coffee at the Café du Monde.'

An afternoon thundershower was building out

over Lake Pontchartrain. The sky on the distant horizon had turned green, and waves were scudding all across the lake now. The few sailboats still out were drenched with spray and foam as they pounded into the wind and headed for their docks. It started to rain in large, flat drops when we turned onto the Expressway, then suddenly it poured down on Clete's car in a roar of tackhammers.

The city was soaked and dripping when I went to pick up the social worker, whose name was Annie Ballard, by Audubon Park. The streetlamps lighted the misty trees along the esplanade on St. Charles; the burnished streetcar tracks and the old green streetcar glistened dully in the wet light, and the smoky neon signs, the bright, rain-streaked windows of the restaurants and the drugstore on the corner were like part of a nocturnal painting out of the 1940s. This part of New Orleans never seemed to change, and somehow its confirmation of yesterday on a rainy summer night always dissipated my own fears about time and morality. And it was this reverie that made me careless, let me ignore the car that parked behind me, and let me walk up her sidewalk with the vain presumption that only people like Julio Segura had things happen to them out of sequence.

3

She lived in an old brick rowhouse that was connected to several others by a common porch and a shrub-filled front yard. I heard footsteps behind me, turned and glanced at three men who were joking about something and carrying a wine bottle wrapped in a paper sack, but I paid no attention to them after they turned toward a lighted house where a party was going on.

She smiled when she opened the door. She wore a blue dress with transparent shoulders, and her blond curls stuck out from under a wide straw hat. She was very pretty with the light behind her, and I didn't care whether we made it to the track or not. Then I saw her eyes focus over my shoulder, saw her expression break apart, heard the feet on the porch behind me, this time fast and running. Just as I turned, one of the three men shoved me hard into Annie Ballard's living room and aimed a Browning automatic pistol straight into my face.

'Don't try to pull it, biscuit-eater, unless you want your brains running out your nose,' he said, and reached inside my sports coat and pulled my .38 from my waist holster.

He was tall and angular, his hair mowed into his scalp like a peeled onion, his stomach as flat as a shingle under the big metal buckle on his blue jeans. The accent was Deep South, genuine peckerwood, and on his right arm was a tattoo of a grinning skull in a green beret with crossed bayonets under the jaw and the inscription KILL THEM ALL . . . LET GOD SORT THEM OUT.

The second man was short and olive-skinned, with elongated Semitic eyes and a hawk nose. He went quickly from room to room, like a ferret. But it was the third man who was obviously in charge. His hands rested comfortably in his raincoat pockets; his face looked impassively around the room as though he were standing at a bus stop. He was in his early fifties, with a paunch, a round Irish chin, a small mouth with down-turned corners, and cheeks that were flecked with tiny blue and red veins. The vaguely dissolute edges of his face, with his tangled eyebrows and untrimmed gray hair, gave you the impression of a jaded Kiwanian.

'There's nobody else,' the olive-skinned man said. He spoke with a Middle Eastern accent.

'Do you already know I'm a police officer?' I said quietly.

'We know a lot about you, Lieutenant. You've really spread your name around recently,' the man in the raincoat said.

'I thought Segura was smarter than this,' I said.

'I don't know. I've never met the man. But you're not smart at all.' He took a revolver casually out of his raincoat pocket and nodded to the man with the tattoo, who went into the bathroom, dropped my .38 into the toilet bowl, and started the water in the bathtub. Annie's eyes were wide under her hat, and she was breathing rapidly through her mouth.

'I have friends coming over,' she said.

'That's why you got your hat on,' the man with the tattoo said, smiling from the bathroom door. His hair was cut so close to his scalp that the light made his head glow with an aura. He held a large roll of adhesive tape in his hand.

'I'm going to walk out my door,' she said. Her face was flushed and spotted as though she had a fever, and her voice was filled with strain. 'I have friends next door and out in the yard and over on the next block and they can hear everything through these walls and you're not going to do anything to us – '

'Annie,' I said quietly.

'We're going to leave now and they're not going to hurt us,' she said.

'Annie, don't talk,' I said. 'These men have business with me, then they're going to leave. You mustn't do anything now.'

'Listen to the voice of experience,' the man in the raincoat said.

'No,' she said. 'They're not going to do this. I'm walking outside now. These are weak people or they wouldn't have guns.'

'You dumb cunt,' the man with the tattoo said, and swung his fist into the back of Annie's head. Her hat pitched into the air, and she fell forward on her knees, her face white with shock. She remained bent over and started to cry. It was the kind of crying that came from genuine, deep-seated pain.

'You sonofabitch,' I said.

'Put her in back,' the man in the raincoat said. The other two men pulled Annie's arms behind her and taped her wrists, then her mouth. Her curly hair hung in her eyes, and there were tears on her cheeks. The two men started to walk her to the bedroom.

'Bobby Joe, nothing except what we have to do here,' the man in the raincoat said.

'You wanted her to walk out on the front porch?' said Bobby Joe, the man with the tattoo.

'That's not what I mean. *Nothing except what we have to do*. Do you understand?'

'There's better broads for two bucks in Guatemala City,' Bobby Joe said.

'Shut your mouth, tape her ankles, and get back out here,' the man with the raincoat said.

'Who are you?' I asked.

'You're in way over your head, Lieutenant. I'm just not sure of your own degree of awareness. That's the problem we have to resolve tonight.'

'I'll give you something else to resolve. I'm going to square everything that happens in here.'

'You're presuming a lot.'

'Yeah? We can make New Orleans an uncomfortable place for crackers that beat up on women. Or for over-the-hill spooks.'

He looked amused.

'You think you've made me?' he said.

'You have a strong federal smell.'

'Who knows, these days, employment being what it is? But at least you're professional and you recognize characteristics in people. So you know that Bobby Joe and Erik in there are hired help, not professional at all. They get carried away sometimes. Do you know what I mean? Bobby Joe, in particular. Bad army life, doesn't like authority, certainly doesn't like women. A bad combination for your situation. Tell me where Fitzpatrick is and we'll walk out of here.'

'Who?'

'I was afraid we'd hear that from you.'

The other two men, Bobby Joe and Erik, came out of the bedroom, crossed my wrists behind me, and wound the adhesive tape deep into my flesh. I could feel the blood swelling in my veins. Then the man in the raincoat nodded to Bobby Joe, who jerked my head down with both hands and brought his knee up into my face. I crashed against the coffee table, my nose ringing with pain, my eyes watering uncontrollably. Bobby Joe and Erik picked me up by each arm. Their hands were like Vise-Grips on me. Then Bobby Joe hit me twice in the stomach, and I doubled over and gagged a long string of saliva on the rug.

'Now you're a cooperative biscuit-eater,' Bobby Joe said, and they led me into the bathroom.

The tub was running over now. Erik turned off the taps, and the man in the raincoat lowered the toilet-seat cover, sat on it, and lighted a Camel cigarette.

'In 'Nam we wrapped a towel around Charlie's face and soaked it in water,' he said. 'It was kind of like a portable river to drown in. But it always worked. Even better than calling him up on the telephone crank. Let's have it, Lieutenant, so we don't have to go through this bullshit.'

They had me on my knees, bent over the tub now. My nose was dripping blood into the water. They waited a moment in silence, then shoved my head under.

I fought to get up, but it didn't do any good. My knees felt like they were greased with Vaseline; my stomach was pressed hard over the tub's rim, and Bobby Joe was leaning all his weight on thc back of my neck. My breath bubbled out my nose and mouth, I shook my head violently from side to side with my eyes open, my teeth gritted, then the closure apparatus in my throat broke and I sucked water inside my head and lungs like a series of doors slamming forever.

They pulled me up roaring with water and air, and threw me against the metal legs on the sink.

'This isn't so bad. There's no permanent damage done,' the man in the raincoat said. 'It'd be a lot worse if Segura's people handled it. It has something to do with the Latin tradition. I think they got it from the Romans. Did you know that Nero killed himself because the Senate sent word to him that he was to be executed in "the old way," which meant being whipped to death with his head locked in a wooden fork? If you don't want to say where Fitzpatrick is, you can write it on a piece of paper. It's funny how that makes a difference for people sometimes.'

My heart was thundering, my breath laboring in my throat.

'I never heard of the cocksucker,' I said.

I felt Bobby Joe begin to lift me by one arm.

'Wait a minute,' the man in the raincoat said. 'The lieutenant's not a bad fellow. He just doesn't know what's involved. If he did, he might be on our team. Fitzpatrick probably gave you a patriotic shuck and you thought you were helping out the good guys.'

'I don't know what the fuck you're talking about.'

'You're probably a good cop, but don't tell us you're shaking the bushes all over New Orleans and Cataouatche Parish because of a drowned colored girl,' he said.

'Two minutes this time. He'll tell,' Erik said.

The man in the raincoat leaned down and looked intensively in my face.

'He means it,' he said. 'Two minutes under water. Maybe you'll make it, sometimes they don't. It happens.'

'All he's got to do is nod his head up and down, then he can have all the air he wants,' Bobby Joe said.

He jerked me up half-erect by my arm and started to slide me across the wet tiles to the tub's rim again. But this time I was dripping with water and sweat and I slipped loose from him, fell on my buttocks, and shot one leather-soled shoe like a hammer into his ribcage. He wasn't ready for it, and I felt a bone go like a stick. The blood drained out of his face, his tongue lay pink on his teeth, his skin tightened on his skull as though he were silently absorbing an intolerable pain and rage.

'Oh my, you shouldn't have done that,' the man in the raincoat said.

Erik grabbed my hair and slammed my head against the side of the tub. I kicked at all of them blindly, but my feet struck at empty air. Then Bobby Joe locked his powerful arms around my neck and took me over the rim again, his body trembling rigidly with a cruel and murderous energy, and I knew that all my past fears of being shotgunned by a psychotic, of being shanked by an addict, of stepping on a Claymore mine in Vietnam, were just the foolish preoccupations of youth; that my real nemesis had always been a redneck lover who would hold me upside down against his chest while my soul slipped through a green, watery procelain hole in earth, down through the depths of the Mekong River, where floated the bodies of other fatigue-clad men and whole families of civilians, their faces still filled with disbelief and the shock of an artillery burst, and farther still to the mossy base of an offshore oil rig in the Gulf of Mexico, where my father waited for me in his hardhat, coveralls, and steeltipped drilling boots after having drowned there twenty years ago.

Then Bobby Joe's arms let go of my neck, as though he had tired of me, and I collapsed in a gasping, embryonic heap on the floor. I lay with one eye pressed against the wet tile.

'Get out there and see what it is!' the man in the raincoat said.

Bobby Joe stood erect, stepped over me, and was gone.

'Had a mind-change about Fitzpatrick?' the man in the raincoat said.

I couldn't answer. In fact, at that point I didn't even remember the name. Then I heard Bobby Joe in the doorway.

'His bitch got her feet loose from the bedstead and kicked a lamp through the window. The whole goddamn backyard is full of people from a party,' he said.

'Travel time,' the man in the raincoat said. He stood up and combed his hair as he walked past me. 'You're a big winner tonight, Lieutenant. But let the experience work for you. Don't try to play in the major leagues. It's a shitty life, believe me. Big risks, lot of crazy people running around, few side benefits like the piece you've got in the next room. You've got *cojones*, but the next time around, Bobby Joe and Erik will cut them off.'

Then they went out the front door into the dark like three macabre harlequins who on impulse visited the quiet world of ordinary people with baseball bats.

Three patrol cars from the Second District, an ambulance and a fire truck answered the neighbor's emergency call. Revolving red and blue lights reflected off the trees and houses; the lawn and house were filled with patrolmen, paramedics, firemen in yellow slickers, neighbors drinking beer and sangria, people writing on clipboards and talking into static-filled radios, and all of it signified absolutely nothing. Any candid policeman will tell you that we seldom catch people as a result of investigation or detective work; in other words, if we don't grab them during the commission of the crime, there's a good chance we won't catch them at all. When we do nail them, it's often through informers or because they trip over their own shoestrings and turn the key on themselves (drunk driving, expired license plates, a barroom beef). We're not smart; they're just dumb.

That's why the feds were made to look so bad back in the late sixties and early seventies when they couldn't nail a bunch of middle-class college kids who ended up on the 'Ten Most Wanted' list. Instead of dealing with predictable psychopaths like

Alvin Karpis and Charles Arthur Floyd, the FBI had to second-guess Brandeis and Wisconsin English majors who dynamited research labs and boosted banks and Brinks' trucks and then faded back into the quiet life of the suburbs. For a time, the amateurs ruined crime for everybody.

The last one to leave was the scene investigator whom I'd requested. He dusted the doors, the bedroom, the bath, looked at me with a shrug, and walked out the door without speaking, which was his way of telling me what he thought of the fruitless work I had just created for him.

'Did he find something?' Annie said. She sat at the dining room table with a tumbler of whiskey between her fingers. Her face was wan, her voice and blue eyes listless.

'Everything was probably smeared. Fingerprints never do us much good anyway, not unless we have a body or someone in custody. Even if an examiner has a whole handprint set in blood, he still has to compare it with tens of thousands of file prints, and it's as much fun as threading a needle with your eyes closed. That's why he looked so happy when he left here. Look, I'm sorry I brought all this stuff into your house. I got careless tonight. I should have made those guys when they stepped out of their car.'

'It wasn't your fault.' Her voice was flat, distant.

'I think you should have gone in the ambulance. A concussion can fool you sometimes.'

'It doesn't have anything to do with a concussion.'

I looked at her colorless, depleted face.

'Listen, let me go to my boat and change clothes,

then I'll take you to an Italian restaurant on the lake where they serve lasagna that'll break your heart,' I said.

'I don't think I can go anywhere now.'

'All right, I'll go to that Chinese place on St. Charles and bring us something back. I'll be gone only a few minutes.'

She stared quietly into space for a moment.

'Do you mind not going for a while?' she asked.

'All right, but I tell you what – no booze. Instead, I'm going to fix some hot milk for you, and an omelette.'

I took the tumbler of whiskey from her fingertips. Then her eyes looked desperately into mine, her mouth trembled, and the tears ran down her cheeks.

'He put his hands all over me,' she said. 'He put them everywhere. While the other one watched.'

She started to cry hard now, her chin on her chest, her shoulders shaking.

'Listen, Annie, you're a brave person,' I said. 'You don't know it, but you saved my life. How many people could do what you did? Most people just roll over when violence comes into their lives. A guy like that can't harm a person like you.'

She had her arms folded tightly across her stomach, and she kept her face turned down toward the table.

'You come in the living room and sit on the couch with me,' I said. I put my arm around her shoulders and walked her to the divan. I sat down next to her and picked up her hands in mine. 'What happens outside of us doesn't count. That's something we don't have control over. It's what we do with it, the way that we react to it, that's important. You don't get mad at yourself or feel ashamed because you catch a virus, do you? Listen, I'll be straight-up with you. You've got a lot more guts than I have. I've been in a situation where something very bad happened to me, but I didn't have your courage.'

She swallowed, widened her eyes, and touched at her wet cheeks with the back of her wrist. Her face jerked slightly each time she breathed, but she was listening to me now.

'I was in Vietnam in the early days of the war,' I said, 'a hotshot lieutenant with a degree in English who really thought he could handle the action. Why not? It had never been very rough while I was there. The Vietcong used to pop at us with some old Japanese and French junk that had been heated up and bent around trees. Half the time it blew up in their faces. Then one day we were going through the rubber plantation and we ran into a new cast of characters – North Vietnamese regulars armed with AK-47s. They sucked us into a mined area, then blew us apart. If a guy tried to turn around and crawl out, he'd either set off a mine right under his face or get chopped up in their crossfire. We lost ten guys in fifteen minutes, then the captain surrendered. They marched us through rubber trees down to a coulee where ARVN artillery had killed a bunch of civilians from VC village. There were dead children and women and old people in the water and all along the banks of the coulee. I figured they were going to line us up and blow us into the water with the rest of them. Instead, they stripped off our web gear and tied our hands around trees with piano wire they tore out of a smashed-up piano in the plantation house. Then they ate our rations and smoked our cigarettes and took turns urinating on us. We sat on the ground like kicked dogs while they did it to us. I blamed the captain for surrendering. I even felt pleasure when they urinated on him. But something else happened that really put some boards in my head later on.

'A gunship spotted us, and about ten minutes later a bunch of rangers and pathfinders came through that same mined area to bail us out. We were the bait in the rat trap. I could hear the AKs and the mines going off, hear our guys screaming, even see blood and parts of people explode on the tree trunks, and I was glad that I was out of it, drenched in piss and safe from all that terror out there where those guys were dying, trying to save us.

'I used to pretend to myself that I didn't have the thoughts that I did, that what went through my head didn't have anything to do with the outcome anyway, or other times I just wanted to kill every VC or North Vietnamese I could, but the real truth of that whole scene, before a couple of Hueys turned the place into a firestorm, was that I was glad somebody else was getting shredded into dog-food instead of me.

'That's what I mean about rolling over. You're not that kind of girl. You've got a special kind of courage, and it can't be compromised by some peckerwood dimwit who's going to end up as Vienna sausage if I have anything to do with it.'

'Your feelings were just human. You couldn't help it,' she said.

'That's right, but you were a better soldier

tonight than I was in Vietnam, except you don't want to give yourself any credit.' Then I brushed back her blond curls from her forehead. 'You're a prettier soldier, too.'

Her eyes looked back at me without blinking.

'Pretty and brave. That's a tough combo,' I said.

The blueness of her eyes, the childlike quality in them, made something sink inside me.

'Do you think you'd like to eat now?' I said.

'Yes.'

'My daddy was a wonderful cook. He taught me and my half-brother all his recipes.'

'I think he taught you some other things, too. I think you're a very good man.'

Her eyes smiled at me. I squeezed her hand, which was still cold and formless, then went into the kitchen and heated a pan of milk and cooked an omlette with green onions and white cheese. We ate at the coffee table, and I saw the color come back into her face.

I made her talk about her family, her home, her music, and her work, everything that defined who she was before Bobby Joe had touched her with his probing hands. She told me she had grown up on a wheat and milo farm north of Wichita, Kansas, that her mother was a Mennonite peace worker and her father a descendant of John Brown's people. She described Kansas as a rolling green country traced with slow-moving rivers, dotted with clumps of oak and poplar and cottonwood, a wide, horizonless place under a hot blue sky that would fill with the drone of cicadas on a summer evening. But it was also a country peopled with religious fanatics, prohibitionists, and right-wing simpletons, and on the other side of the equation were the anti-nukers and dozens of vigilante peace groups. It sounded like an open-air mental asylum. Or at least it was to her, because she had gone to Tulane to study music and had not left New Orleans since.

But sleep was stealing into her face now.

'I think it's time for a kiddo I know to go to bed,' I said.

'I'm not tired. Not really.'

'Oh, yes?' I put my arm around her, placed her head on my shoulder, and touched her eyes closed with my fingertips. I could feel her breathing evenly on my chest.

'I'm not a kiddo. I'm twenty-seven,' she said sleepily.

I slipped my other arm under her legs and carried her into her bedroom and laid her down on the bed. I took off her shoes and pulled the sheet over her. She looked up at me from the pillow and put her hand on the back of my neck.

'Don't go,' she said.

'I'll be on the couch in the living room. Tomorrow morning we'll have breakfast at the French Market. If you hear a noise later, it's just me. I walk around a lot at night,' I said, and turned off the light.

It was true, I usually didn't sleep well. Sometimes it was latent memories of the war, but most often I was sleepless simply because I was alone. Even the monastic saints never wrote in praise of nocturnal solitude. I watched three late-hour movies on television, until I saw the light turn gray in the trees outside. When I finally fell asleep, it was with the confidence that the full radiance of day was only a short time away, and that my night's aching celibacy, my battered set of ethics, all my alcoholic dragons would soon resolve themselves in a predictable and manageable way.

The man I sometimes thought of as my father's misplaced seed called me just before noon and told me to come to lunch at his restaurant on Dauphine. Actually, my half-brother, Jimmie, who people said looked like my twin, was a gentleman in his way. He had our father's sense of humor and fairness; he treated his equals as well as his inferiors with respect, and he paid his gambling debts on time; and he had an honorable attitude toward women, one that was almost Victorian, possibly because his mother was supposedly a prostitute from Abbeville, although neither of us remembered her. But he was also locked into off-track betting and trafficking in poker and slot machines, which brought him into a casual but dangerous association with Didoni Giacano.

I often got mad at him because of that association and his cavalier attitude toward it, as well as some of the other things he had continued to do for a lifetime to prove somehow that he was both different from me and at the same time that he was not simply my half-brother and his father's illegitimate son. But I could never stay mad at him long, no more than I could when we were children and he was always devising schemes that invariably went wrong and got us both in trouble.

Even though he was fifteen months younger than I, we did everything together. We washed bottles in the hot-sauce factory on the bayou, plucked chickens for a nickel apiece at the slaughterhouse, set pins at the bowling alley when few white kids would work in those 110-degree pits that were filled with cursing, sweating Negroes, exploding pins, and careening bowling balls that could snap your shinbone in half. But he got us both fired at the hot-sauce factory, since the owner couldn't tell us apart, when he tried to wash bottles en masse by filling a dozen gunny-sacks with them and weighting them down in the bayou's current. We got canned at the slaughterhouse after he decided to streamline the operation and take six dozen chickens out of the cages at one time and herd them into the yard where we were to butcher and then scald them in big cauldrons of water; instead, they panicked and many of them flew into the big window fan and were chopped to pieces in the metal blades.

One hot night at the bowling alley, a group of tough kids who lived down by Railroad Avenue came in and started rolling the second ball before the pin boy could reset the rack. These were kids who went nigger-knocking on Saturday nights with slingshots and marbles and ball bearings. The Negroes in the pits couldn't do much when they were abused by drunks or bad high-school kids, but Jimmie imposed no restraints upon himself and always practiced immediate retaliation. He was picking up four pins at a time in the pit next to me, his T-shirt streaked with dirt, sweat running out of his hair, when a ball sailed past his kneecap and thudded into the leather backstop. A minute later it happened again. He set the rack down to block the alley, went over to one of the other pits, and came back with a spit can filled with chewed Red Man. He poured it into the thumb hole of the bowling ball, packed a wad of bubblegum on top of it, then rolled the ball back down the chute.

A moment later we heard a loud curse, and we looked out from under the racks and saw a big, burr-headed boy staring at his hand with a horrified expression on his face.

'Hey, podna, smear some of it on your nose, too. It'd be an improvement,' Jimmie yelled.

Three of them caught us in the parking lot after the alley closed and knocked us down on the gravel for five minutes before the owner came out, chased them off, and told us we were both fired. Jimmie ran after their truck, throwing rocks at the cab.

'We'll get a paper route,' he said, his face hot and dusty and streaked with dried perspiration. 'Who wants to be a pinsetter all his life? There's a lot of money in paper routes these days.'

Both of us would change a lot when we went to college in Lafayette, and in many ways we would begin to leave our father's Cajun world behind us. Eventually I would go into the army and be sent to Vietnam, and Jimmie would join the national guard, borrow money on the small house and seven-acre farm our father left us, and open a café on Decatur Street in New Orleans. Later he would buy into the first of several restaurants, wear expensive jewelry and Botany 500 suits and learn the manners of the people who lived in the Garden District and belonged to the Southern Yacht Club, primarily because he thought they knew something about money and power that he didn't, and there would be any number of attractive women who floated in and out of his life. But whenever I saw him on Canal or in his restaurant with a group of jocular businessmen, his eyes crinkling good-naturedly at the banal humor, an earlier image would glint briefly in my memory like a small mirror, and I would see again the kid in overalls panicking a swirl of chickens into a window fan or flinging a rock at a pickup truck receding in the darkness.

Didi Gee and my brother were eating in a red leather booth in the back of the restaurant when I walked in. Didi's waistline and stomach had the contours of three inner tubes stacked on top of each other. His hands were as big as skillets, his neck as thick as a fire hydrant, his curly black head as round and hard as a cannon-ball. As a young man he'd been a collector for a group of shylocks across the river Algiers, hence the story about his holding people's hands down in an aquarium filled with piranha. I also knew for a fact that a cop in Gretna shot a plug out of his shoulder the size of an apple core, refused to call for an ambulance, and left him to bleed to death on the sidewalk. Only he lived and got the cop fired from the force, then fired from every job he tried to hold thereafter, until finally he had to go to work for Didi Gee as a numbers runner, a sort of pathetic human exhibit that Didi kept around like a voodoo doll with pins stuck in it.

Jimmie grinned at me with his white teeth, shook hands, and motioned for the waiter to serve me a steak-and-lobster plate from the warmer on the back counter. Didi Gee's mouth was so full of food that he had to put down his knife and fork and continue chewing for almost a half-minute, then drink a glass of red wine, before he could speak.

'How you doing, Lieutenant?' he said flatly. He always spoke as though his nose were clotted with cartilage.

'Pretty good,' I said. 'How's life, Didi?'

'Not so hot, to tell you the truth. I got cancer of the colon. They're going to cut out some of my entrail tract and sew up my hole. I got to walk around with a bag of shit hanging on my side.'

'I'm sorry to hear about that,' I said.

'My doctor says I either get it done or they nail me down in a piano crate. Be glad you're young.' He put a meatball wrapped with spaghetti and half a slice of bread in his mouth.

'We heard some rumors about you,' Jimmie said, smiling. He wore a charcoal suit and gray tie, and his gold watch and rings gleamed in the restaurant's soft light. Ever since he was a kid he had used his grin to hide guilt, to address complexity, or to deny a basic goodness in himself.

'Like they say, you hear a lot of bullshit in the street,' I said.

'Mashing on Julio Segura's nuts is not bullshit,' Jimmie said.

'You have to enrich a guy's day sometimes,' I said.

'Some guys are better left alone,' Jimmie said.

'What did you hear?' I said.

'There's talk about a heavy fall for a homicide cop.'

'It's old news, Jim. I heard it first up at Angola from Johnny Massina.'

'Don't take it lightly,' Jimmie said.

'We're talking about a very low class of people, Lieutenant,' Didi Gee said. 'They're part Indian or colored or something. I bought a nice winter home in Hallendale, Florida, then some Colombians moved in next to me and dug the whole fucking yard into a vegetable patch. Their kids pissed out the second-story window on my car. This is in a neighborhood you don't get into without three hundred thou. They put raw chicken shit on their tomato plants. The smell made your nose fall off.'

'Why are we having this lunch, Jimmie?' I said.

'Julio Segura is real garbage. He doesn't go by anybody's rules. Not yours, not Didi's. There's lots of people that would like to see this guy canceled out. But he's still around and it's because certain other people want him around. I don't want to see you get burned finding out something that's not going anywhere.'

Then Jimmie was silent. Didi Gee stopped eating, lit a cigarette, and dropped the burnt match into his empty plate.

'There's a couple of guys that used to work for me. They don't work for me now,' he said. 'But they hang around my places of business sometimes. They like to talk about what's going on around town. As Jimmie will tell you, I'm not interested in listening to gossip. Also, these are guys that follow their cocks. I don't spend no time thinking of what these kind of young guys got to say. To tell you the truth, Lieutenant, I've been changing my attitudes about people a great deal lately. I think it's my age and this awful disease in my colon. There are classes of people I don't want to have no association with anymore. Like these guys. If you was to ask me their names later, I'd have to honestly tell you I don't remember. I think it's a mental block when it comes to some trashy people that I've been forced to hire in my business.'

'I'm not big on names these days, Didi,' I said.

'Because this story, if it's true, is a horrible one and shows what kind of scum the country has been letting across its border,' he said. 'This colored girl was a parlor chippie for this spick that lives out by the lake. The spick – and I use that word only because he's a genuine lowlife – has got broads on the brain and is always moving them in and out of his mansion, primarily because he's a fucking geek that no normal woman would touch unless she was blind. So the colored girl moved in and the geek really had the hots for her. The girl thought it was going to be hump city from there on out. The spick lets his pet dwarf drive her shopping around town, gives her all the coke she wants, introduces her to a lot of important greasers like she wasn't just another broad with a ten-dollar ass and a five-cent brain. But the girl didn't know this guy went through his own chippies like Jimmy Durante went through Kleenex. One morning after she got drunk and threw up in his pool he told the dwarf to drive her back to the parlor. What the spick didn't figure on was ambition in a colored girl that grew up pulling sweet potatoes out of the ground with her toes.

'Because this broad had ears and a memory like fly-paper. All the time she was poking plastic straws up her nose or balling the geek, she was also getting onto some heavy shit, and I'm talking government, military shit, Lieutenant, that the geek and the other spicks are playing around with.'

'What do you mean "government"?' I said.

'I'm repeating the gossip, I don't analyze. It don't

interest me. I think Immigration ought to take these people to a factory and turn them into bars of soap. The girl tried to put his tit through a wringer. That got her out of the parlor all right. They took her fishing out on the bayou and let her shoot up until her eyes crossed. When she didn't pull it off on her own, they loaded her a hotshot that blew her heart out her mouth.'

'I appreciate the story you've told me, Didi, but I'd be offended if I thought you believed we were in the business of running your competition out of town.'

'You hurt my feelings,' he answered.

'Because we already knew just about everything you told me, except the mention about the government and the military. You're very vague on that. I think we're being selective here. I don't believe that's good for a man of your background who enjoys the respect of many people in the department.'

'I have been candid, Lieutenant. I do not pretend to understand the meaning of everything I hear from people that sometimes lie.'

'You're a mature man, Didi. You shouldn't treat me as less.'

He blew smoke out his nose and mashed out his cigarette in his plate. His black eyes became temporarily unmasked.

'I don't know what he's into. It's not like the regular business around the city,' he said. He paused before he spoke again. 'A guy said the girl was giggling about elephants before they dumped her in the water. You figure that one out.'

A few minutes later Didi Gee picked up his

check and the two hoods who waited for him at the bar, and left. The red leather upholstery he had sat on looked like it had been crushed with a wrecking ball.

'He tips everybody in the place on his way out. Under it all he's a bit insecure,' Jimmie said.

'He's a psychopath,' I said.

'There's worse people around.'

'You think it's cute to mess around with characters like that? You better give it some serious thought if you're fronting points for him. Guys like Didi Gee don't have fall partners. Somebody else always takes the whole jolt for them.'

He grinned at me.

'You're a good brother,' he said. 'But you worry too much about me. Remember, it was always me that got us out of trouble.'

'That's because you always got us into it.'

'I'm not the one that almost got drowned in a bathtub last night. You threw a bucket of shit into a cage full of hyenas, bro.'

'How'd you hear about last night?'

'Forget about how I hear things or what I'm doing with Didi Gee. You worry about your own butt for a change, or those greasers are going to hang it out to dry.'

'What do you think this elephant stuff is?'

'How the hell should I know?'

'You ever hear of a guy named Fitzpatrick?'

'No. What about him?'

'Nothing. Thanks for the lunch. By the way, Johnny Massina told me about you smashing up Didi's rubber machines. The old man would have enjoyed that one.'

'Like they say, you hear a lot of bullshit in the street, Dave.'

I sat out on the deck of my houseboat that evening in the green-yellow twilight with a glass of iced tea and mint leaves, and disassembled my three pistols – my departmental .38 revolver, a hideaway Beretta .25, and a U.S. Army-issue .45 automatic. As I reamed out the barrel of the .45 with a bore brush, I thought about some of the mythology that Southern boys of my generation had grown up with. And like all myth, it was a more or less accurate metaphorical reflection of what was actually going on inside us, namely our dark fascination with man's iniquity. In moments like these I suspected that John Calvin was much more the inventor of our Southern homeland than Sir Walter Scott.

Southern Myths to Contemplate While Cleaning One's Guns – Substitute Other Biographical Names or Geographical Designations to Suit the Particular State in the Old Confederacy in Which You Grew Up:

1. A town in east Texas used to have a sign on the main street that read, 'Nigger, don't let the sun go down on your head in this country.'
2. Johnny Cash did time in Folsom Prison.
3. Warren Harding was part Negro.
4. Spanish fly and Coca-Cola will turn a girl into an instant drive-in-movie nymphomaniac.
5. The crushed hull of a Nazi submarine, depth-charged off Grand Island in 1942, still drifts up and down the continental shelf. At a

certain spot on a calm night, shrimpers out of Morgan City can hear the cries of drowning men in the fog.

6. A Negro rapist was lynched outside of Lafayette and his body put inside a red wooden box and nailed up in a pecan tree as a warning to others. The desiccated wood, the strips of rag, the rat's nest of bones hang there to this day.

7. The .45 automatic was designed as a result of a Filipino insurrection. The insurrectionists would bind up their genitals with leather thongs, which would send them into a maniacal agony that would allow them to charge through the American wire while the bullets from our Springfields and .30-40 Kraigs passed through their bodies with no more effect than hot needles. The .45, however, blew holes in people the size of croquet balls.

There is usually a vague element of truth in all mythology, and the basic objective truth about the .45 automatic is simply that it is an absolutely murderous weapon. I had bought mine in Saigon's Bring-Cash Alley, out by the airport. I kept it loaded with steel-jacketed ammunition that could blow up a car engine, reduce a cinder-block wall to rubble, or, at rapid fire, shred an armored vest off someone's chest.

The darkness of my own meditation disturbed me. My years of drinking had taught me not to trust my unconscious, because it planned things for me in a cunning fashion that was usually a disaster for me, or for the people around me, or for all of us. But by this time I also knew that I was involved with players who were far more intelligent, brutal, and politically connected than the kind of psychotics and losers I usually dealt with.

If I had any doubts about my last conclusion, they were dispelled when a gray, U.S. government motor-pool car stopped on the dock and a redheaded, freckle-faced man in a seersucker suit who could have been anywhere from fifteen to thirty years old walked down the gangplank onto my houseboat.

He flipped open his identification and smiled.

'Sam Fitzpatrick, U. S. Treasury,' he said. 'You expecting a war or something?'

4

'It doesn't look like you believe me,' he said. 'Do you think I boosted the ID and a government car too?' He wouldn't stop grinning.

'No, I believe you. It's just that you look like you might have escaped from "The Howdy Doody Show."'

'I get lots of compliments like that. You New Orleans people are full of fun. I hear you've been taking a little heat for me.'

'You tell me.'

'Are you going to offer me some iced tea?'

'You want some?'

'Not here. You're too hot, Lieutenant. In fact, almost on fire. We need to get you back on the sidelines somehow. I'm afraid it's not going to be easy. The other team is unteachable in some ways.'

'What are you talking about?'

'They have fixations. Something's wrong with their operation and they target some schmoe that's wandered into the middle of it. It usually doesn't do them any good, but they think it does.'

'I'm the schmoe?'

'No, you're a bright guy with stainless steel balls,

evidently. But we don't want to see you a casualty. Let's take a ride.'

'I'm taking a lady to the track tonight.'

'Another time.'

'No, not another time. And let's stop this business of Uncle Sam talking in his omniscience to the uninformed local flatfoot. If the shit's burning on the stove, I suspect it's yours and it's because you federal boys have screwed things up again.'

He stopped grinning. He looked at me thoughtfully for a moment, then wet his lips. He suddenly seemed older.

'You have to have faith in what I tell you, Lieutenant,' he said. 'You're a good man, you've got courage, you've never been on a pad, you go to Mass on Sundays, you treat the street people decently, and you put away a lot of the bad guys. We know these things about you because we don't want you hurt. But believe me, it's dumb for the two of us to be out here in the open talking to each other.'

'Who's this "we" you're talking about?'

'Uh, actually the "we" is more or less just me, at least right now. Come on, I'll explain it. Trust me. Somebody who looks like Howdy Doody has got to be a straight shooter. Besides, I'll buy you a poorboy sandwich on my expense account.'

So this was the state of the art down at the Federal Building, I thought. We didn't see much of the federal boys, primarily because they operated on their own as a rule, and even though they said otherwise, they looked down upon us as inept and uneducated. On the other hand, we didn't have much liking for them, either. Any number of television serials portray the feds as manicured, dapper altruists dressed in Botany 500 suits, who dispassionately hunt down the oily representatives of the Mafia and weld the cell door shut on them. The reality is otherwise. As Didi Gee would probably point out, syndicate gangsters have little fear of any police agency or court system. They own judges, cops, and prosecutors, and they can always get to a witness or a juror.

The Treasury Department is another matter. Law enforcement people everywhere, as well as criminals, consider Treasury agents incorruptible. Within the federal government they are to law enforcement what Smokey the Bear and the U. S. Forest Service are to environmental integrity. Even Joe Valachi, the Brooklyn mob's celebrity snitch, had nothing but admiration for the T-men.

Fitzpatrick drove us across town to a Latin American restaurant on Louisiana Avenue. We sat at an outdoor table in the small courtyard under the oak and willow trees. There were electric lights in the trees and we could see the traffic on the avenue through the scrolled iron gate. The banana trees along the stone wall rattled in the wind. He ordered shrimp and oyster poor-boy sandwiches for us and poured himself a glass of Jax while I sipped my iced tea.

'You don't drink, do you?' he said.

'Not anymore.'

'Heavy sauce problem?'

'You not only look like a kid, you're as subtle as a shithouse, aren't you?' I said.

'Why do you think I brought us to this restaurant?'

'I don't know.'

'Almost everybody working here is a product of our fun in-the-sun policies south of the border. Some of them are legals, some brought their papers from coyotes.'

'That's only true of about five thousand restaurants in Orleans and Jefferson parishes.'

'You see the owner over by the cash register? If his face looks out of round, it's because Somoza's national guardsmen broke all the bones in it.'

He waited, but I didn't say anything.

'The man running the bar is an interesting guy too,' he said. 'He's from a little village in Guatemala. One day the army came to the village and without provocation killed sixteen Indians and an American priest from Oklahoma named Father Stan Rother. For kicks they put the bodies of the Indians in a U.S. Army helicopter and threw them out at high altitudes.'

He watched my face. His eyes were a washed-out blue. I'd never seen a grown man with so many freckles.

'I'm not big on causes anymore,' I said.

'I guess that's why you went out to Julio Segura's and put a hot plate under his nuts.'

'This dinner is getting expensive.'

'I'm sorry I've been boring you,' he said, and broke up a bread stick in three pieces and stood each piece upright. 'Let's talk about your immediate concerns. Let's talk about the three guys who gave you gargling lessons in the bathtub last night. I bet that'll hold your interest.'

'You don't hide hostility well.'

'I get a little emotional on certain subjects. You'll

have to excuse me. I went to Jesuit schools. They always taught us to be up front about everything. They're the Catholic equivalent of the jarheads, you know. Get in there and kick butt and take names and all that stuff. I just think you're a lousy actor, Lieutenant.'

'Look, Fitzpatrick –'

'Fuck off, man. I'm going to give you the scam and you can work out your own options. I'm surrounded by indifferent people and I don't need any more of them. I just don't want you on my conscience. Also, as a matter of principle I don't like another guy taking the heat for me, particularly when he blunders into something he doesn't know anything about. You're damn lucky they didn't blow out your light last night. The girl's too.'

He stopped talking while the waiter put down our plates of oyster and shrimp sandwiches, then he took a bite out of his sandwich as though he hadn't eaten for weeks.

'You don't like the food?' he said, his mouth still full.

'I lost my appetite.'

'Ah, you're a sensitive fellow after all.'

'Tell me, do all you guys have the same manners?'

'You want it straight, Lieutenant? We've got some firemen and pyromaniacs on the same side of the street.'

'Who was that bunch last night?' I said.

'That's the easy part. The one named Erik is an Israeli. He's somebody's little brother back in Haifa and they keep him around to clean up their mess, change toilet-paper rolls, stuff like that. The one you called Bobby Joe in your report is a real cut-up. That's Robert J. Starkweather of Shady Grove, Alabama. The state took away his kid from him and his wife for the kid's own protection. They think he fragged an NCO in Vietnam but they couldn't prove it, so they eased him out on a BCD. How do you like that tattoo about killing them all and letting God sort them out? He's sincere about it, too.'

'How about the guy in charge?'

'He's a little more complex. His name is Philip Murphy, at least we think it is. We've run this guy all kinds of ways and we come up with some blank spots – no addresses, no record of earnings, no tax returns for a couple of years here and there. Or he shows up owning a shoe store in Des Moines. With this kind of guy it usually means protected witness or CIA. He's probably one of those that bounces in and out of the Agency or freelances around. I suspect he's off their leash right now. But it's hard to tell sometimes.'

I picked up my poor-boy sandwich and started to eat. The shrimp, oysters, lettuce, onions, tomato, and *sauce piquante* tasted wonderful. The shadows of the oak and willow leaves moved in etched, shifting patterns across our table.

'I still don't understand the connections. What have these guys got to do with Segura's whores and dope?' I said.

'Nothing directly.' Then he started grinning again. 'Come on, you're a detective. Give me your opinion.'

'Are you sure these guys aren't after you because of what you fancy is a sense of humor?'

'Maybe. Come on, give me your opinion.'

'I have a hard time believing you're a Treasury agent.'

'Sometimes my supervisor does too. Come on.'

'You're with the Bureau of Alcohol, Tobacco and Firearms.'

'Good.'

'Are we talking about guns?' I said.

'Excellento.'

'Nope, not excellento. I still don't see it, and I already told you this meal had gotten expensive.'

'It's simple. I think Segura is putting his dope money back into military equipment for the Contras in Nicaragua. It explains these other guys. The Israelis supplied arms to Somoza for years and they still sell it to right-wing guys like Pinochet in Chile. From what we know about Buffalo Bob, who almost pinched your head off at the shoulders, he's cowboyed for the CIA down on the Honduran border when he wasn't mixing up his phallus with an M-16, and I'll bet Philip Murphy is the tie-in to some arms contractors and military people here in the States. There's nothing new or unusual about it. It's the same kind of unholy trinity we had working for us down in Cuba. Look, why do you think the CIA tried to use some Chicago wiseguys to whack Castro? The mob had a vested interest. They got along very well with Batista, then Castro shut down all their casinos.'

'How did you get onto this current stuff?'

'We had our eye on a paramilitary training camp in Florida and one in Mississippi, then Buffalo Bob left a submachine gun in a Biloxi bus locker. We could have picked him up, but instead we let him keep ricocheting off the walls for a while.

Philip Murphy showed up and it got a lot more interesting.'

He paused for a minute, then looked me flatly in the face again with those washed-out blue eyes that seemed to be immune to both protocol and insult.

'Have you ever had to dust anyone?' he said.

'Maybe.'

'Be straight.'

'Twice.'

'How'd you feel about it?'

'They dealt the play.'

'The next time you see Murphy or Buffalo Bob and Erik, they're going to take you out. You know that, don't you?'

'You said you're an up-front guy. Let me tell you a couple of my own meditations. I don't think you're an up-front guy.'

'Oh?'

'I don't think you want me out,' I said. 'I think you want a partner. I've already got one. He's paid by the city, just like I am.'

'You're a pretty slick cop.'

'I don't like somebody trying to use me.'

'I can't blame you. There's something I didn't tell you. The American priest that was killed in Guatemala was a friend of mine. Our government is into some real bullshit down there, buddy, but everybody who works for the government isn't necessarily on the same team. Some of us still believe in the old rules.'

'Good for you. But if you're into the Boy Scout Manual, don't try to run a game on another cop.'

'Nobody's asking you to sign a loyalty oath. What are you so afraid of?'

'You're genuinely starting to piss me off,' I said.

'I didn't write this script. You got into it on your own. I'll tell you something else, too: you're not going to walk out of it easily. I guarantee it. Guys like Segura and Murphy are just functionary jackoffs for much bigger people. Here's another question for you, too, Mr. Clean. What were you thinking about while you were oiling your guns out on your boat deck? Maybe blowing bone and cartilage all over Buffalo Bob's walls?'

'I think with luck I can still make the fifth race.'

'I'll drive you back.'

'Don't worry about it. The city's got a tab with Yellow Cab.'

'Take this card. My motel's number is on it.'

'I believe the phone is still out of order. See you around,' I said, and walked out of the courtyard onto Louisiana Avenue. Some black children roared past me on roller skates, and heat lightning flickered above the huge oak trees across the street.

I called Annie from the pay phone to try to save part of the evening, but no one was home. It started to rain and I waited a half hour under a leaky awning for my cab to arrive. I made a quiet resolution about accepting invitations from federal employees.

But, as Fitzpatrick had said, I'd written my own script, and the next morning I continued to write it, only with some disastrous consequences that made me wonder if my alcoholic, self-destructive incubus was not alive and well.

I started by looking for Bobby Joe Starkweather. I didn't have many threads, but he was the kind of guy who showed up at certain places. I tried a couple of indoor target ranges, outlaw motorcycle bars, sex shops, and a survivalist store that catered to people who relished the unlimited prospects of living in a post-World War II wasteland. But I struck out.

Then, at noon, while Cletus and I were eating a pizza out of a box on a bench in Jackson Square, I wondered why I was chasing after an unknown quantity like Bobby Joe Starkweather when the primary connection was already available. We sat under a mimosa tree, and St. Louis Cathedral and the square itself were drenched in hot sunlight. There were drops of perspiration and flecks of red pizza sauce on Clete's face while he ate. His eyes were looking abstractedly at the sidewalk artists in Pirates Alley.

'What have you got on the burner for this afternoon?' I asked.

'Not much. Figure out what I'm going to do with my goddamn wife. Get this. She just sent a check for six hundred dollars to the Buddhist priest out in Colorado. I tried to put a stop-payment on it, but it already went through. That's thousands she's given to this guy. When I say anything about it, she says I'm drunk.'

'Maybe y'all should separate for a while.'

'I can't. She's become suicidal. Her psychiatrist says she shouldn't even be driving an automobile.'

'I'm hoping to take a girl out to dinner tonight, if I can get ahold of her. Why don't you and Lois think about coming along? It's on me.'

'Maybe so, Dave. Thanks.'

'I want to go out to Julio Segura's this afternoon.'

'What for?'

'I'm going to roust him and take him in for questioning.'

'He might file a harassment charge this time.'

'He was the last person to see a murder victim alive.'

'Sounds shaky. It's not our jurisdiction.' His eyes smiled.

'You coming or not?'

'Hell, yes.'

We drove in Clete's car along the lakefront road. There was a light chop on the slate-green surface, and pelicans were diving for fish out of the white sun. The palm trees on the esplanade clicked dryly in the wind; and on the right-hand side of the road beyond the pink stucco walls, the long iron pike fences, the impassable hedges and rows of myrtle trees, lay the terraced lawns and mansions of the rich. I knew liberals out at Tulane who would tell me these were the people whom we served. But I didn't like them any better than anybody else did. Actually, they didn't like the police, either, or at least trust us, because they hired their own security, kept attack dogs on the grounds, and maintained floodlight and burglar alarm systems that were an electronic miracle. They lived in fear of kidnappers of their children, sophisticated jewel creeps, minorities who would compromise their property values. The irony was that they were among the most secure people upon earth – secure from disease, poverty, political oppression, virtually everything except death.

'How much you think these places cost?' Cletus asked.

'I don't know, maybe a million bucks.'

'My pop was a milkman in the Garden District, and sometimes in the summer I'd go on the route with him. One morning I was messing around in front of this big house right off St. Charles and this lady came out and said I was the cutest little fellow she'd ever seen and I should come back at three o'clock for some ice cream. That afternoon I took a bath and put on my nice clothes and knocked on her door right at three. At first she didn't remember who I was, then she told me to go around to the back door. I didn't know what the hell was going on. When I got into the backyard I saw the maid handing out ice cream to all these raggedy little colored kids that belonged to the yardmen around the neighborhood.

'This lady had a greenhouse back there. I came back that night with a box full of rocks and broke damn near every pane in it. She got it repaired and three weeks later I came back and broke them again. When my pop figured out I'd done it, he whipped me with a switch till blood ran down my legs.'

Clete turned onto Julio Segura's street, which was filled with trees and blooming shrubs.

'You ever get that mad when you were a kid?' he asked.

'I don't remember.'

'You told me once you and your brother had some rough times.'

'Who cares, Clete? It's yesterday's ball game.'

'So I know that. What's the big deal?' he said.

'You've got a rusty nail sideways in your head. Let it go, quit feeding it.'

'You get a little personal sometimes, Streak.'

'There he goes! Hit it!' I said.

Julio Segura's lavender Cadillac had just bounced out through his front gate onto the street. A dwarf was driving, and a blond woman sat in the front passenger's seat. Segura and another man were in the back. Cletus floored the accelerator until we were abreast of them. The dwarf's face was frightened behind the glass, and he kept driving. I held my badge out at him. He put his foot on the brake, both of his hands on the steering wheel, his chin pointed upward under his purple chauffeur's cap, and scraped the front tire in a long black line against the curb.

'How do you want to play it?' Clete asked before we got out of the car.

'We run up the black flag,' I said.

Clete had stopped our own car in front of the Cadillac, and we walked back on opposite sides of it. I tapped on the passenger's window and on Segura's back window for them to roll down the glass. Later I was to go over this scene again and again in my mind, as well as the careless remark I'd made to Clete about the black flag, and wonder at how differently that afternoon might have turned out if I had approached the driver's side of the Cadillac or if I had kept my own counsel.

Clete reached down into the ignition, pulled the keys, and threw them into a hedge. The dwarf was petrified with fear. His little hands gripped the wheel and his jug head swiveled back and forth between Clete and the back seat.

'You don't have a blowgun hidden in your shorts, do you?' Clete said to him, then sniffed the air inside the Cadillac. 'My, my, what is that aroma I smell? Colombian coffee? Or maybe we've been toking on a little *muta* on our way to the golf course?'

The air was heavy with the smell of marijuana. The blond woman's face looked sick. I saw the cigarette lighter from the dash lying on the floor, and I suspected she'd been snorting the roach off the lighter and had eaten it when we'd pulled them over. She had a nice figure and was dressed in white shorts and heels and a low blouse, but her hair was lacquered with so much hair spray that it looked like wire, and her face was layered with cosmetics to cover the deep pockmarks in her complexion.

I opened the door for her. 'Walk on back home,' I said.

'They lock the gate,' she said.

'Then do the best thing you've done in years and keep on walking,' I said.

'I don't know what to do, Julio,' she said to the back-seat.

'Do what I tell you, hon. Your Latino gumball is going to take a big fall today,' I said.

Her eyes shifted nervously and she bit her lips, then she picked up her purse, eased past me, and clicked hurriedly down the sidewalk.

I leaned down in Segura's window. He and the gatekeeper whom Clete had hit in the stomach the other day sat behind a fold-out bar with vodka drinks in their hands. Rubber bands held the napkins around the drink glasses. Segura wore yellow golf slacks, polished brown loafers, and a flowered white shirt unbuttoned to his stomach. His peculiar triangular face, with the tiny balls of purple skin in the furrows of his forehead, looked up at me in the slanting sunlight.

'What the fuck you think you're doing now, Robicheaux?' he asked.

'Teaching you what a real bad day can be,' I said.

'What do you want? Some kind of action? A piece of something downtown?'

'You're going to give me Philip Murphy, Bobby Joe Starkweather, and the little Israeli.'

'I don't know none of these people. You keep coming around my house talking about things I don't know nothing about.'

'Ole Streak's in a bad mood today, Julio,' Clete said. 'Your friends messed it up the other night and did some real bad things. They're not around now, but you are. You and Paco the barfer here.' He blew his cigarette smoke into the gatekeeper's face.

'You trying to squeeze me? Okay, I'm a realist. I got business arrangements with policemen,' Segura said.

'You don't fly this time, Julio,' I said. 'All the doors are closed. It's just me and you.'

'Call Wineburger,' he said to the gatekeeper.

The other man reached for the telephone that was in a mahogany box inset in the back of the front seat.

'You touch that telephone and I'll stuff it crossways down your throat,' Clete said.

The man sat back in the deep leather of the seat, his face tight, his hands flat on his knees.

'You don't have anything, you don't know anything, you're just a noise like a fart in somebody's pants,' Segura said.

'Try this, my friend,' I said. 'Lovelace Deshotels

was a little black girl from the country who had big aspirations for herself and her family. She thought she'd made the big score, but you don't like broads that slop down your booze and throw up in your pool, so you eighty-sixed her back to the geek circuit. Except you had a badass black girl on your hands that wouldn't eighty-six. On top of it, she developed this fixation about elephants.' I watched his face. It twitched like a rubber band. 'So what does a macho guy like you do when one of his whores gets in his face? He has a couple of his lowlifes take her out on a boat and launch her into the next world with the same stuff she'd already sold her soul for.

'Right now you're wondering how I know all this, aren't you, Julio? It's because the guys that work for you have diarrhea of the mouth. It's information you can get across a lunch table. There are probably only several dozen people we can march by a grand jury right now.'

'Then do it, smart guy.'

'Let me give you the rest of it, just so you'll be fully informed when Wineburger tries to bond you out this afternoon. I'm going to have your car towed in, vacuumed, and torn apart with crowbars. Possession in Louisiana is fifteen years, and all we need is the carbon ash, either off that cigarette lighter or the upholstery.

'Any way you cut it, your ass is busted.'

Then Cletus committed what was probably the stupidest and most senseless act of his career.

'And this little piggy is busted, too,' he said, and reached in the window and caught the gatekeeper's nose between his fingers and twisted.

The gatekeeper's eyes filled with tears; his hand slapped at Clete's, then his hairy, tattooed arm dipped into the leather pouch on the side door.

'*No lo hagas*! *No lo hagas*!' Segura screamed.

But it was forever too late for all of us. The gatekeeper's hand came up with a nickel-plated automatic and let off one round that hit the window frame and blew glass all over Clete's shirt. It was very fast after that. Just as I pulled the .45 from the back of my trousers, I saw Clete rip his nine-millimeter from his belt holster, crouch, and begin firing. I stepped back a foot, to clear the angle away from Segura, and fired simultaneously with my left hand locked on my wrist to hold the recoil down. I fired five times, as fast as I could pull the trigger, the explosions roaring in my ears, and saw not one thing distinctly inside the car. Instead, it was as though an earthquake had struck the inside of the Cadillac. The air was filled with divots of leather, stuffing from the seats, flying shards of glass and metal, splinters of mahogany, broken liquor bottles, cordite, smoke, and a film of blood and vodka that drained down the back window.

There was no place for Julio Segura to hide. He tried to shrink into an embryonic ball away from Clete's line of fire, but his position was hopeless. Then he suddenly leaped up into the window with his hands pressed out toward me like claws. His eyes were pleading, his mouth open with a silent scream. My finger had already squeezed tight in the trigger guard, and the round caught him in the top of the mouth and blew the back of his head all over the jerking body of the gatekeeper.

I was trembling and breathless when I fell back

from the Cadillac and leaned on top of Clete's car, the .45 hanging from my hand. Clete's scarred, poached face was so bloodless and tight you could have struck a kitchen match to it. His clothes were covered with flecks of glass.

'The sonofabitch missed me from two feet,' he said. 'Did you see that? That fucking window glass saved my life. Go back and look inside. We blew them apart.'

Then the dwarf chauffeur climbed down from the driver's seat and ran down the middle of the esplanade on his stubby legs amid a wail of sirens. Clete began to giggle uncontrollably.

5

The next morning Cletus and I sat across from each other at our desks in our small, glass-enclosed office with its smudged yellow walls that made you think of a dressing cubicle at YMCA. Cletus pretended to read a long memo from the superintendent's office, but his eyes were either empty or glazed with the pain of his hangover. He was chain-smoking and eating breath mints, but last night's Scotch was down deep in his lungs. Both of us had already made written reports to Captain Guidry.

'I'm not going to bail you out again, Clete,' I said.

'What do you mean, bail out? I put one through his brisket before you popped your first cap.'

'I'm not talking about that. You provoked it. It didn't have to happen.'

'You're sure about that, huh? What if Paco had come up with the automatic while you were cuffing Segura? There was a nine-round clip in there. He could have cut both of us in half.'

'You provoked it.'

'So what if I did? Scratch two lowlifes that should have been fertilizer a long time ago. Save the hearts and flowers, Dave. Nobody's going to be interested in how Julio Segura bought it. I don't think you could find three people to attend the guy's funeral.'

'Don't bet on it.'

Sergeant Motley came down the corridor and stopped in our doorway. He had just come in from outside, and his round, black head glistened with perspiration. He was eating an ice cream cone, and there were flecks of ice cream in his thick mustache.

'Somebody in the lab said they had to wash Segura's brains off the seat with a hose,' he said.

'Oh yeah? That sounds like it might make a clever Excedrin ad,' Clete said.

'Guess what else I heard?' Motley said.

'Who cares?' Clete said.

'You'll care, Purcel. The lab says the Cadillac was dirty. Reefer on the cigarette lighter, coke in the rug. Who would have thought Segura would let his broads be so careless?' He smiled. 'You guys didn't salt the mine shaft, did you?'

'Why are you so obnoxious, Motley?' Clete said. 'Is it because you're fat and ugly, or is it because you're fat and dumb? It's a mystery to all of us.'

'Except I hear the broad says you told Segura he was going to take a big fall. Not smart of the Bobbsey Twins in homicide,' Motley said.

'Here's to the rapid spread of sickle cell,' Clete said, and toasted Sergeant Motley with his coffee cup.

'My dick in your ear,' Motley said.

'Lay off it,' I said.

'With this guy you've either got to use some humor or a can of insecticide,' Clete said.

A few minutes later Captain Guidry told me to come into his office. I wasn't looking forward to talking with the captain, but I was relieved to get away from Clete.

Captain Guidry scratched the hair implants in his head and looked up at mc from behind his horn-rimmed glasses. My report and Clete's were side by side on his desk.

'The lab found some marijuana ash and grains of cocaine in the car,' he said. His voice was flat and reserved.

'Motley just told us.'

He picked up a pencil and began drumming it on his palm.

'They also said a round fired from inside the car bounced off the window frame and blew glass out into the street,' he said. 'A second round went up through the roof, which would indicate the shooter was hit by that time. A yardman across the street says he heard a sound like a firecracker inside the Cadillac, then he saw you two start shooting. It's all working for you, Dave.'

'What's the dwarf say?' I asked.

'Nothing. All he wants is an airplane ticket to Managua.'

'Something's not getting said here, Captain.'

'I've been over your reports. Very neat stuff. I think they'll get you by Internal Affairs.'

'That's good.'

'My own opinion is they stink. Tell me why a guy with no arrests, who Whiplash Wineburger would have had back on the street in thirty minutes, would throw down on two armed cops.'

I didn't answer.

'Do you think he had a suicidal personality?' the captain asked.

'I don't know.'

'Did Segura tell him to do it?'

'No.'

'Then why did this guy pull his own plug?' His hand closed on the pencil.

'Internal Affairs gets paid to sort that stuff out.'

'To hell with Internal Affairs. I don't like reading a report on two deaths that says "fill in the blanks."'

'I can't tell you anything else, Captain.'

'I can. I think something else happened out there. I think also you're covering Purcel's butt. That's not loyalty. It's stupidity.'

'The essential fact of my report is that somebody pulled a pistol on a police officer and fired it at him.'

'You keep telling yourself that. In the meantime, let me tell you a couple of my observations. The guys in Internal Affairs will mutter around over this stuff, ask you a few hard questions, make you feel uncomfortable a little while, maybe even really try to stick a finger in your eye. But eventually they'll cut you loose and everybody around here will ask you guys out for a beer. But you're going to take the suspicion of a wrongful death with you. It's like a cloud you drag along everywhere you go. Sometimes it even grows into a legend. How about Motley and those guys on the wrist-chain that suffocated to death in the elevator?'

I had to look away from his face.

'It's between Purcel and other people, Captain. I didn't deal the play out there,' I said.

'I'm sorry to see you take that position, Dave.' He opened his palm and dropped his pencil on the top of his desk blotter. 'I'll make one other suggestion before you go. Take Purcel with you to some meetings. Also, if you're going to cover for a partner who's going out of control, you'd damn well better be able to take the consequences.'

It wasn't the best of all possible mornings.

A half hour later the phone in our office rang.

'Guess who,' the voice said.

'The Howdy Doody Show.'

'Guess what I'm doing.'

'I'm not interested.'

'I'm looking at the photographic art on the front page of the *Picayune*,' Fitzpatrick said. 'I underestimated your flair for the dramatic. These are the kinds of pictures we used to see in *The Police Gazette* – grainy black and white stuff, car doors thrown open, bodies hanging out on the street, pools of black blood on the seats. Congratulations, you greased the one solid connection we had.'

'If you want to get on my case this morning, you'll have to stand in line. As far as I'm concerned, your meter is already on overtime. In fact –'

'Shut up, Lieutenant.'

'What did you say?'

'You heard me. I'm mad as hell right now. You've done a lot of damage.'

'You weren't out there, bud.'

'I didn't have to be. I had a real strong tingle down in the genitals that it might go like this, and you didn't disappoint me.'

'You want to explain that?'

'I'm not sure you can handle it. I thought you were a bright guy. Instead, it doesn't look like you can put one foot after another without somebody painting Arthur Murray dance steps on the floor for you.'

I didn't answer. My hand was clenched on the telephone receiver and starting to perspire. Clete was looking curiously at my face.

'Are you where you can talk?' Fitzpatrick said.

'I'm in my office.'

'Who's there with you?'

'My partner, Purcel.'

'Yeah, sure you can talk,' he said irritably. 'I'll pick you up in front of the Acme Oyster Bar on Iberville in ten minutes. I'll be driving a blue Plymouth rental.'

'I don't think so.'

'You either be there or I'll come up to your houseboat tonight and knock out your goddamn teeth. That's a personal promise.'

I waited ten minutes for him in front of the Acme, then went inside and bought a Dr Pepper in a cup of crushed ice with a sliced lime and drank it outside in the sunlight. I could see the spires of St. Louis Cathedral, where I sometimes went to mass, shining in the clear morning air. By the time Fitzpatrick drew up to the curb, my anger had subsided to the point that I was no longer going to pull him out of his automobile by his necktie. But when I sat down in the passenger's seat I did reach across and turn off his ignition.

'Before we go anywhere, let's sort out a couple of things,' I said. 'I don't think you've paid enough dues to be telling people to shut up or making threats to them over the phone. But if you think you're a serious rock-and-roller, we can go over to the Y and slip on the gloves and see what develops.'

He nodded and clicked his fingernails indifferently on the steering wheel.

'Don't worry, they've got a first-aid man there in case you're a bleeder,' I said.

'Okay, you've made your point.'

'You're not too big on hanging tough, are you?'

'I wanted you out of your office. If you'll notice your present geography, you're sitting in my automobile and not at the First District. Is it all right if I start the car now?'

'I think you federal guys just have to do everything with three-cushion shots. Wouldn't it be easier for you and me to go into Captain Guidry's office and talk about this stuff in a reasonable way? We don't want guys like Philip Murphy and his trained psychopaths running around New Orleans any more than you do. The captain's a good man. He'll help you if he can.'

He started the engine and pulled into the traffic. The sunlight fell across his freckled face and candy-striped Arrow shirt.

'Is Purcel a good man?' he asked.

'He's got some problems, but he's working on them.'

'You think he's clean?'

'As far as I know.'

'Six weeks ago we had reason to be in a trick pad. His name was in the girl's book. He was a weekly banger. There was no entry about charge, either.'

I took a deep breath.

'He's had marital trouble,' I said.

'Come off it. We're talking about a compromised cop who started popping caps yesterday on a possible government witness. Which of you nailed Segura?'

'I did. He was trying to get out the door, and he raised up right in front of me.'

'I'll bet one of Purcel's rounds was already in him. What did the autopsy say?'

'I don't know.'

'Great.'

'You're telling me Clete wanted to kill Segura?'

'It's a possibility.'

'I don't buy it.'

'You don't buy lots of things, Lieutenant. But there's people just like you in my bureau. That's why they're sending me back to Boston next week.'

'You're off it?'

'I will be. I haven't made my case and there's other work waiting.'

He looked across at me, and for the first time I felt a liking for him. Under all the invective he was a full nine-inning pitcher. We bought a bucket of fried shrimp and two cartons of dirty rice and ate it in a small, shady part off Napoleon Avenue. A bunch of black and white and Chicano kids were playing a workup game in front of an old chicken-wire backstop. They were rough, working-class boys and they played the game with a fierce physical courage and recklessness. The pitcher threw spitters and beanballs; the base runners broke up double plays with elbows and knees, and sanded their faces off in headlong slides; the catcher stole the ball out from under the batter's swing with his bare hand; and the third baseman played so far in on the grass that a line drive would tear his head off. I thought it no wonder that foreigners were awed by the innocent naïve nature of American aggressiveness.

'Does anything about elephants figure in all this?' I asked.

'Elephants? No, that's a new one. Where'd you get it?'

'I heard Lovelace Deshotels was giggling about elephants when Segura's people shot her up. I dropped it on Segura, and his face twitched like a plumber's helper.'

'Well, we've got a second chance. I found her roommate, a Mexican girl from the same massage parlor, and she wants to stick it to all these bastards.'

'Why is she talking to you instead of me?'

'She seems to think you guys are cretins. Is there a vice sergeant down there named Motley?'

'Yep.'

'She says his zipper's open.'

'Sounds accurate.'

'She's a dancer in a nude bar out by the airport now. For three hundred dollars she says she can turn a couple of interesting people for us, then she wants to take her little girl back to San Antonio and study to be a hairdresser.'

'It sounds like a shuck to me.'

'I think she's straight. Her boyfriend was a Nicaraguan ex-national guardsman who worked for Segura. Then he beat her up and stole her money. They're a class bunch, those guys. Now she wants to blow Dodge. It seems reasonable to me.'

'I think she's selling the same information Didi Gee already gave me.'

'She's hip about Bobby Joe Starkweather. She says he's a latent bone-smoker and can't make it with women. He threw a waitress out of a hotel window, and some local hood got fired for it up at Angola.'

I looked away at the boys playing workup.

'What's the matter?' Fitzpatrick asked.

'I knew him. His name was Johnny Massina.'

'Were you tight with him or something?'

'I tried to help him get off the hooch once. Does she know where Starkweather might be?'

'She's vague on that.'

'I thought so,' I said. 'Write her name and address down for me, would you, but I'm going to pass on her right now. They've got me on a short leash, anyway.'

'Lieutenant, can I broach something personal?'

I started to say 'Why not?' since he had never shown any restraint about anything before, but he kept right on talking before I could speak.

'It's obvious you're a good cop and a private kind of man, but you're a Catholic and you must have feelings about what's going on down there,' he said.

'Where?' I already knew the answer but I wasn't ready to pursue the discussion.

'Central America. They're doing some bad shit to our people. They're killing priests and Maryknoll nuns and they're doing it with the M-16s and M-60 machine guns we give them.'

'I don't think you ought to take all that responsibility on yourself.'

'It's our church. They're our people. There's no way to get around the fact, Lieutenant.'

'Who's asking you to? You've just got to know your limits, that's all. The Greeks understood that. Guys like you and me need to learn from them.'

'You think that's good advice, huh?' he said.

'It beats walking around with a headful of centipedes.'

'Since you're fond of classical metaphors, try this one: Why do we admire Prometheus and have contempt for Polonius? Don't try to tilt with a Jesuit product, Lieutenant. We've been verbally demolishing you guys for centuries.'

He grinned at me the way a high school pitcher would after throwing you a Carl Hubbel screwball that left you twisted in your swing.

That night I drove to the Tulane campus to hear Annie Ballard's string quartet play. She was pretty on the lighted stage in her dark skirt and jacket and frilly white blouse. Her face was both eager and concentrated while she read the music sheet on the metal stand in front of her and drew her bow back and forth on her cello. In fact, her face had a lovely childlike quality in it while she played her music, the kind you see in people who seem to go through a photogenic transformation when they do that private thing that they hold separate for themselves. Afterwards, we were invited to a lawn party in the Garden District. The trees were strung with Japanese lanterns; the swimming-pool lights glowed smokily below the emerald surface; the air smelled of jasmine and roses and the freshly turned, watered dirt in the flower beds; and Negro waiters carrying trays of champagne glasses and cool tropical drinks moved deferentially among the groups of laughing people in evening dresses and summer tuxedoes.

She was having a good time. I saw that her eyes were empty now of the fear and self-loathing that Bobby Joe Starkweather had put in them, and she was doing her best, also, to make me forget what had happened in the back of Julio Segura's Cadillac yesterday. But I was selfish.

I couldn't let go of those ten seconds between the time the gatekeeper pulled the automatic out of the door pouch and the moment when the .45 roared upward in my hand and Segura's head exploded all over the inside of the car. I'm convinced that, unlike most of the hapless and pathetic people whom we usually dealt with, he was truly an evil man, but anyone who has ever fired a weapon at another human being knows the terrible adrenaline-fed sense of omnipotence and arrogance that you feel at that moment and the secret pleasure you take in the opportunity being provided you. I had done it in Vietnam; I had done it twice before as a police officer, and I knew that simian creature we descend from was alive and well in my breast.

I was also bothered by Sam Fitzpatrick and his admonition to me about my religion and my humanity. I wanted to dismiss him. He was a kid, an idealist, a federal hotdog who probably broke a lot of bureau rules and would eventually blow out his doors. If he hadn't become a Treasury agent, he would probably be pouring chicken blood on draft files. A half-dozen like him could have a whole city in flames.

But I couldn't get rid of him. I liked him and he had gotten to my pride.

I genuinely tried to enjoy myself that night. The people at the lawn party came from another world than mine, but they were pleasant and friendly and went out of their way to be courteous to me. Annie was a fine girl, too. When she saw my expression wandering away from the conversation, she would touch the back of my hand with hers and smile at me with her eyes. But it wasn't any good. I gave it up, made an excuse about having to go to work in the morning, and drove her home. On her porch I saw the faint look of hurt in her face when I said I couldn't come in.

'Do you like to be alone, Dave?' she asked.

'No. It's not a good life.'

'Another time, huh?'

'Yes. I'm sorry about tonight. I'll call tomorrow.'

She smiled and then she was gone, and I drove home more depressed than I had been in years.

Why? Because the truth was that I wanted to drink. And I don't mean I wanted to ease back into it, either, with casual Manhattans sipped at a mahogany and brass-rail bar with red leather booths and rows of gleaming glasses stacked in front of a long wall mirror. I wanted busthead boilermakers of Jack Daniel's and draft beer, vodka on the rocks, Beam straight up with water on the side, raw tequila that left you breathless and boiling in your own juices. And I wanted it all in a rundown Decatur or Magazine Street saloon where I didn't have to hold myself accountable for anything and where my gargoyle image in the mirror would be simply another drunken curiosity like the neon-lit rain striking against the window.

After four years of sobriety I once again wanted to fill my mind with spiders and crawling slugs and snakes that grew corpulent off the pieces of my life that I would slay daily. I blamed it on the killing of Julio Segura. I decided my temptation for alcohol and self-destruction was maybe even an indication that my humanity was still intact. I said the rosary that night and did not fall asleep until the sky went gray with the false dawn.

That afternoon I still had Sam Fitzpatrick on my mind. I called the Bureau of Alcohol, Tobacco and Firearms, and was told by the assistant Special Agent in Charge that Fitzpatrick was not in.

'Who is this please?' he asked.

I told him my name and who I was.

'Are you calling from your office?'

I said I was.

'I'll call you there in two minutes,' he said, and hung up.

Sure enough, the phone rang a minute and a half later. They were a very careful bunch down at the Federal Building.

'We're worried about him. He hasn't checked in and he's not at his motel,' he said. 'Are you the guy who smoked Segura?'

'Yes.'

'Bad day at Black Rock, huh?' he said, and laughed.

'Do all you guys have the same sense of humor?'

'We've got an agent out of the nest, Lieutenant. Do you have something we ought to know?'

'He was going to see a Mexican girl, a nude dancer out by the airport. She told him she could turn a couple of Segura's people.'

'We already know about her. What else?'

'That's it.'

'Stay in touch. Drop by and have coffee sometime. We need a better liaison with you people. By the way, Lieutenant, Agent Fitzpatrick has a way of wandering beyond some of our parameters. That doesn't mean that some local authorities should reciprocate by wandering themselves into a federal jurisdiction. You get the picture, don't you.'

There was a pause, then the receiver went dead.

Late that afternoon I went to the Mexican girl's apartment building out in Metairie. No one was home, and the apartment manager said she had not seen the girl, whose name was Gail Lopez, or her daughter in a couple of days. I stuck a small piece of Scotch tape between the bottom of the door and the doorjamb, and drove out to the strip bar by the airport in the fading twilight.

Jet airliners lifted off the runway across the road and roared over the top of the bar into the lavender sky. The building was constructed of cinder blocks that had been painted purple; the door was fingernail-polish red; and the interior smelled of cigarette smoke, refrigerated air, and bathroom antiseptic. Behind the bar was a burlesque runway where a stand-up comic with a face like crinkled parchment went through a lifeless and boring routine that no one at the tables or bar listened to. In the middle of his routine, some bikers in the corner plugged in the jukebox and turned it on full tilt.

The bartender was a big man, about thirty, with a huge granite head that was bald and shining on top with oiled ducktails combed back on the sides. He wore black trousers, a white shirt, and a black velvet vest like a professional bartender, but his thick arms and neck and massive chest and the wooden mallet on a shelf behind him indicated something about his other potential. I asked him about Gail Lopez.

'You don't recognize me, Lieutenant?' he asked, and smiled.

I squinted at him in the smoke and against the glare of lights on the burlesque stage.

'Five or six years ago, right?' I said. 'Something about driving a *Picayune* delivery truck over a Teamster steward.'

'Actually, it's been eight years and I never really got to tell my side of that story, Lieutenant. But it don't matter now. I'm always walking toward something rather than away from something. You know what I mean? Let me ask a little favor of you, though. My PO don't need to know about this situation, does he? He's a good guy and kind of protective and he don't want me working in no shitholes, but some of the guys down at the union hall hold a grudge and don't want to give me my card back and there ain't many places I can make six bucks an hour and tips. Hell, it's degrading to work in a dump like this. I got to pick up cigarette butts from the urinals with my hands and scrub out toilets and mop up the vomit every time one of these fuckers pukes. What do you want to drink? It's on me.'

'Uh, nothing right now. What about Gail Lopez?'

'Well, all these broads get a lot of traffic, you know what I mean? It's a lowlife clientele here, Lieutenant. Greasers, hitters, bull dykes, jerks that like to get in my face till they're way out on the edge, you know what I mean? There's a guy comes in here every night and melts Demerol down in a glass of Wild Turkey, then when I say "Nice weather we're having" or "Hard rain we had this afternoon," he says "no, duh." I ask him if he wants another drink and he says "No duh." "You want some more peanuts?" "No duh." "You want some more peanuts." "No duh." "You're in the wrong place to be a wise-ass." "No duh."'

'No, Charlie, I'm talking about a guy who looks like a human freckle.'

'I haven't seen him. Look around you, Lieutenant. A guy like that in here would stand out like shit in an ice cream factory. Anyway, ask her. She'll be here in an hour.'

I sat through two floor shows that consisted of a half-dozen naked girls dancing to a three-piece band whose instruments could have been tuned to a snare drum. The girls wore thin gold chains around their ankles and stomachs, and their faces seemed lit with some inner narcissistic pleasure that had nothing to do with the world outside them. They undulated and raised their arms above their heads as though they were moving in water, and occasionally their eyes would meet and light with some secret recognition.

During all this the bartender washed glasses indifferently in a tin sink while his cigarette ashes fell into the dishwater. Someone in the back caught his attention and he left the bar for a few minutes, then returned with an uncomfortable look on his face.

'Lieutenant, I got an embarrassing situation here,' he said. 'The manager, Mr. Rizzo, is very happy you're here and he don't want you to pay for anything. But a guy that sits at the bar drinking 7-Up with a piece showing under his coat is kind of like –'

'Anthrax?' I said.

'Well, if you notice, there's nobody else at the bar, Lieutenant, which is not meant as a reflection on you, but on the degenerate pus-bags that drink in here. Even the guy that gets off saying "No duh" to me is sitting way in the back tonight. You got to understand the degenerate mind. See, they all got hard-guy fantasies, but when they take it out too far and step on the nuts of some heavy-metal badass, like some cat that just got out of Angola and has already got a Coke bottle kicked up his ass, I got to bail them out.'

I paid for the 7-Ups I'd drunk and waited another half hour at a small table in a dark part of the room. Gail Lopez didn't show up. I gave the bartender my office card with my telephone number and asked him to call me if she came in. He put down his bar rag and leaned forward and spoke a few inches from my face.

'One of her boyfriends is a tall Nicaraguan dude with a mustache,' he said. 'Don't let him blind-side you, Lieutenant. One night out in the parking lot he cut a guy from his armpit down to his liver. He's the kind of cat if you got to dust him you take him off at the neck.'

I drove back out to the Mexican girl's apartment in Metairie and found the tape still in place between the door and the jamb. I told the building manager that I couldn't ask him to open the apartment, but I suspected that if he did, all he would find would be empty clothes hangers. It took him less than two minutes to get the passkey.

I was wrong, however. She hadn't simply left behind empty clothes hangers. In the wastebasket were several crumpled travel brochures that advertised scenic tours of the Caribbean, not San Antonio and hairdressing school. Fitzpatrick, you poor fish, I thought.

I was tired when I drove home along Lake Shore Drive, past the amusement park with its Ferris wheel lighted against the sky, past the University of New Orleans and its quiet, dark lawns and black trees, and I entered into a self-serving dialogue with myself that almost extricated me from my problems. Let Fitzpatrick's own people take care of him, I thought. Illegal guns and explosives are their jurisdiction, not yours. You took on an obligation about the murdered black girl in the bayou and you fulfilled it, whether you wanted to or not, when you translated Julio Segura's brains into marmalade. If you're interested in revenge against Philip Murphy, Starkweather, and the little Israeli, you're in the wrong line of work. Somewhere down the road they'll step in their own flop and somebody'll be there to put them away. So disengage, Robicheaux, I told myself. You don't have to be a long-ball hitter every time. A well-placed bunt has its merits.

I had almost achieved some tranquility by the time I parked my car on the short, darkened street that dead-ended into a sand dune and three coconut palms and the dilapidated dock where I kept my houseboat moored. A smooth, hard path with salt grass growing on the edges cut through the dune, and the waving palm fronds made shadows on the sand and the roof of my houseboat. I could hear the water slapping against the hull, and the moonlight fell across the lake itself in a long silver band. I walked across the gangplank with the wind cool in my face, the bend of the wood easy and familiar and comforting under my foot, the froth of the incoming tide sliding up on the sand under me. The mahogany and yellowish brown teak and glass panes and brass fittings of my boat were as rectangularly beautiful as metal and wood could be. I opened the hatch, stepped down into the main cabin, and turned on the light switch.

Bobby Joe Starkweather rose up quickly from the floor and swung a short length of pipe at my face. It was crowned on one end with pipe bonnet and wrapped with friction tape on the other. I ducked and put my hands in front of me and took part of the blow on my forearm, but the cast-iron bonnet raked down the side of my face and my ear felt torn loose from my head. I tried to get my .38 out of my belt holster, but someone pinned my arms to my sides from behind and the three of us fell into my rack of musical records on the far wall. My collection of historical jazz, old seventy-eight records that were as stiff and delicate as baked ceramic, shattered in black shards all over the floor. Then a third man was on top of me, a tall man with a pencil mustache and pomade-scented, reddish Negroid hair, and I was covered by their hands, arms, thighs, scrotums, buttocks, knees, their collective weight and strength and visceral odor so powerful and smothering now that I couldn't move or breathe under them. I felt a needle sink into my neck, an unspoken wish clicked dryly in my throat, and my mouth locked open as though the joints of my jaw had been broken. Then my trio of friends squeezed the remaining air out of my chest, the blood out of my heart, the light from my eyes.

6

I awoke in an auto garage of some kind. The roof was made of tin and it was raining outside. I was stretched out on a wooden table, my arms handcuffed around a post behind me, my feet tied to another post at the opposite end. The only light came from a mechanic's portable lamp that was hung on one wall among rows of tools, fan belts, grease guns, and clusters of sparkplug wires. The air was close and hot and smelled of oil and rust. When I turned my head, my neck felt as though it would crack like a dry flower stem.

Then I saw Fitzpatrick in a wooden chair four feet from me. His forearms were tied flush to the arms of the chair, wrapped with clothesline from the elbow to the wrist so that his hands stuck out like broken claws; his clothes were torn, streaked with grease and blood, and his battered and bleeding head hung down in the shadow, obscuring his face. By his feet was a telephone crank, the kind that was used on army field phones.

'Sam,' I said.

He made a sound and moved his head.

'Sam, it's Dave Robicheaux,' I said. 'Where are they?'

He raised his head up into the light and I saw his face. His eyes were swollen shut like a beaten prize-fighter's, his nose broken, his saliva red in his teeth.

'Where are they, Sam?' I said again.

Then he started breathing hard, rattling down in his throat, as though he were trying to generate enough power to speak a solitary line.

'Elephant walk,' he said.

I heard a tin door scrape open on the concrete floor, and the cool smell of the rain blew into the room. Philip Murphy, the little Israeli, and the tall man with the pencil mustache and the kinky reddish hair walked into the light from the mechanic's lamp. They carried paper bags of hamburgers and french fries in their hands.

'You must have a strong constitution,' Murphy said. 'They shot you up with enough Thorazine to knock out a dinosaur.' His wet gray hair was still uncut; he hadn't shaved that day, and stubble grew through the tiny blue and red veins in his cheeks. He took a bite of his hamburger and looked at me while he chewed. His hazel eyes were devoid of either feeling or meaning.

'You're a miserable excuse for a man,' I said.

'Why's that, Lieutenant? You don't like the way things have gone? You didn't have warning about the rules? People have been unfair to you, have they?'

'It takes a special kind of degenerate to torture a defenseless man.'

'People get hurt in wars. Your friend is one of them. You probably don't like that definition, but your sort never does.'

'You're a punk, Murphy. You never fought a war in your life. Guys like you take them off the cattle cars and run the ovens.'

For a moment I saw a flash in his eyes.

'Would you like to live in a communist country, Lieutenant?' he said. 'Would you like Louisiana run by the Sandinistas the way they run things in Nicaragua? You know the Marxists are puritans, don't you? No casinos or horse tracks, no booze or poontang when you want it, no chance for the big fat score that keeps everybody's genitals aglow. Instead, you wait in a sweaty line with a lot of other mediocre people for whatever the government dole is that day. If you lived down there, you'd put a gun in your mouth from boredom.'

'So somehow it's acceptable to tie down a kid and take him apart? What nails me about your kind is that you're always willing to sacrifice half the earth to save the other half. But you're never standing in the half that gets blitzed.'

'You're a disingenuous man, Lieutenant. You remember what Patton said? You don't win wars by giving your life for your country. You make the other sonofabitch give his. I think you're just a poor loser. Look at Andres here. You see the little gray scars around his mouth? He has a right to be bitter but he's not, at least not excessively. Say something for us, Andres. *Que hora es?*'

'*Doce menos veinte,*' the tall man with the mustache replied. His voice was a wheeze, a rasp, as though his lungs were perforated with small holes.

'Andres used to have a regular *puta* in one of Somoza's whorehouses. Then one day he talked a little too casually in front of her about the work his firing squad did. They'd shot a Sandinista girl named Isabella whom they'd captured in the hills. He thought it was a good story, because she'd confessed before she died and turned a couple of dozen other Sandinistas. What he didn't say was that his whole firing squad had raped her before they shot her, and what he didn't know was that Isabella was his *puta*'s sister. So the next time he dropped in for a little dirty boogie between the sheets, it was hotter than the devil's skillet and she fixed him a tall, cool Cuba libre with ice and lime slices and he swallowed it straightaway like the lusty fellow he is. Except she loaded it with muriatic acid, and poor old Andres has been spitting up his insides like burnt cork ever since.'

'You're a piece of shit, Murphy.'

'No, you've got it all wrong, Lieutenant. Some of us serve, others like Fitzpatrick here get in the way, and the majority, such as yourself, go about your games and your self-delusion while we take care of things for you. I don't like to pick on you in your situation, but it's not fair of you to start calling people names, either. Now you're an educated man of some experience, and I want you to answer me something truthfully. You've seen the people who are on the other side of the fence in this country – the peace marchers, the nuke freezers, the out-of-Central-America gang. Who are they?' The down-turned corners of his mouth tugged backwards in a slight smile and his eyes wandered over my face with a sense of merriment. 'Some of them are lesbians, aren't they? Not all of them, but at least some, you've got to admit that. Then there are others that just don't like men. They didn't like their fathers, their brothers, or their husbands, and finally they zero their sights in on any male authority – the President, congressmen, generals, anything with a cock.

'Now we come to the general malcontents,' he continued. 'These are your professional losers who couldn't tell a history book from a Sears, Roebuck catalog, but they do love a parade. I'm sure you got to see a lot of them on television while you were in Vietnam. My favorite bunch, though, is the pussy-whipped contingent. Their wives drag them around to endless meetings that are going nowhere, and if they're good little fellows, Mommy will give them a piece every week or so.

'I don't think that's your kind of group, Lieutenant, but maybe I'm wrong about you. I guess the bottom line is you wanted to be a player. Too bad, because now we've got to take a couple of players off the board.'

'I'll suggest some reading for you,' I said. 'Go down to the *Picayune* morgue and read the clippings on what's happened to people who snuffed New Orleans cops. It's not our finest hour, but the lesson's unmistakable.'

He smiled in a self-amused way, and began eating his hamburger again while his eyes glanced expectantly at the back door. Five minutes later, Bobby Joe Starkweather burst in out of the rain with a paper sack under his arm. His T-shirt and blue jeans were soaked through, and his muscles stood out against the wet cloth like intertwined serpents.

'I got it. Let's put the biscuit-eater under and get it on the road,' he said. 'Did you bring me a hamburger?'

'I didn't think you wanted it cold,' Murphy said.

'You're a great guy to work with, Murphy,' Starkweather said.

'Would you like mine?' Murphy asked quietly.

'I haven't had my rabies shots.'

'Suit yourself, then, and spare us your complaining wit.'

'Look, Murphy, I went after the booze, which you owe me twelve dollars for, and I got rainwater running out my crotch while you guys are in the dry, licking your greasy fingers. Don't provoke me.'

Murphy chewed on his food and looked at nothing. Starkweather wiped his face and arms slick, lighted a Lucky Strike from his Zippo, snapped the lighter shut and stuck it in his watch pocket with a thick thumb, and inhaled the smoke without removing the cigarette from his mouth while he took a fifth of Seagram's whiskey, six-pack of Jax, a capped vial of pills, and a brown medicine bottle from the sack and put them on the table. Then he rummaged around on the workbench until he found a rubber funnel and a glass jar filled with rusty nails. He dumped the nails out on the workbench and walked back to the table with the jar and the funnel. His shaved head was shaped like a question mark.

'You should have been here earlier,' he said. 'We got some real high notes out of your friend. You remember what they used to say in 'Nam. Call up Charlie on the telephone and he always answers.'

He filled the glass jar with beer and whiskey and the liquid from the brown bottle, then poured in the pills and screwed on the cap and shook it all together as though he were making a martini. His saliva was wet on the tip of his cigarette, and he breathed with a mean energy.

'It must be terrible to know you're a lush that can't hold his liquor,' he said.

'I've spilled more in a week than you've drunk in your lifetime, asshole,' I said.

'I'll bet. My first wife was a juicer,' he said. 'She'd do anything for it. She screwed a cabdriver once for a quart of beer. I found out about it, cut me a switch as thick as my finger, and whipped the dress off her back. I took her money and clothes away and locked her in the bedroom and she drank hair tonic. Finally they come and took her off to a crazyhouse in Montgomery.'

'No matter what happens here tonight, I've got some friends who are going to cool out your action, Starkweather,' I said.

'Maybe so, maybe so. But in the meantime I've got a drunkard's dream for you. When those 'ludes hit you, I can pull your teeth with pliers and you won't twitch. The castor oil is just to round out your evening, bring back those old three-day benders when you used to shit your pants. If you're a good boy, we'll let you sit up and drink it by yourself.'

'Get on with it,' Murphy said.

'Stop giving orders for a while, Murphy,' Starkweather said. 'A lot of this mess is yours. We should have taken these guys out the first time they got in our face. Instead, you had to make an intelligence operation out of it to impress Abshire.'

'Why is it in any given situation you never disappoint us?' Murphy said.

'You got a way of letting other people clean the

pot after you get off it. Maybe you ought to do some grunt work yourself. You ought to be there when them Indians close off a village and start pulling them out of the huts. The amusement park really lights up. I don't think you'd have the guts for it.'

'It's not a matter of guts, my friend,' Murphy said. There were small breadcrumbs in the whiskers on his chin. 'Some people are adverbs, others are nouns.'

'It'd be fun watching you hump it.'

'You might not believe this, but I had a role of some minor historical importance at the Bay of Pigs and Dien Bien Phu. The latter was about the time you were trying to figure out the difference between your mother's ovaries and a bowl of grits.'

'You got a great record, Murph. If you'd been at Omaha Beach, we'd be speaking German today.'

Erik, the little Israeli, snickered, and the Nicaraguan looked back and forth hot-eyed at the joke he didn't understand.

'You idiots, he's burning his wrists with the handcuffs,' Murphy said.

'Always the intelligence man,' Starkweather said.

'You do your job and shut your mouth, Starkweather. The lieutenant could operate on one brain cell and outwit you. If you screw something up here tonight, or open your face one more time –'

He stopped and breathed hard through his nose.

'I'm going to bring his car in now. You wrap this package up,' he said. 'We're going to talk later.'

'You heard the bossman,' Starkweather said to me. 'Time to go to work, earn our pay, fetch that barge and tote that bale. Goodbye, fart-breath.'

They forced the spout of the rubber funnel past

my teeth and into the back of my mouth. I gagged and coughed, my eyes filled with water, and I felt my chest convulse under their hands. Then they held my nose and poured the mixture of beer, castor oil, whiskey, and Quaaludes down my throat. The sudden raw taste of alcohol after four years of abstinence was like a black peal of thunder in my system. My stomach was empty and it licked through me like canned heat, settled heavily into my testicles and phallus, roared darkly into my brain, filled my heart with the rancid, primordial juices of a Viking reveling in his own mortal wound.

The light went out of my mind, and in a few moments' time I was caught again in my drunken world of all-night bars, taxi drivers, guiding me through my own front door in the false dawn, the delirium tremens that covered me with sweat and filled the inside of my houseboat with spiders and dead Vietnamese. I heard beer-bottle glass break in my head, saw myself pushed out the back door of a wino bar, saw the contempt in a bouncer's face when he stuffed me in my automobile and threw my hat in after me, felt myself heaving my insides into a public toilet, felt the hands of a pimp and a whore turning my trouser pockets inside out.

Then a strange thing happened. Most of my dreams about Vietnam were nightmares that at one time made me fear sleep. Even before I became a full-blown drunk, I used to drink three beers before bed so I would sleep through to the morning. But now somebody was carrying me in the warm rain and I knew that I was once again in the loving care of the soldiers from my platoon. I had heard the *klitch* under my foot in the dark on the jungle trail;

then, as though I were a spectator rather than a participant, I saw myself covered with cobalt light, my body crawl with electricity, my soul light the trees like an enormous candle.

When I awoke, the smoke was still rising from the rent holes in my fatigues and they were carrying me between them on a poncho while the rain ticked on the trees and the shells from an offshore battery ripped through the sky overhead. In the humid darkness I could hear the labored breathing of the four men carrying me. They were running in a half-trot, the tree branches and vines slapping against their faces and steel pots, their expressions stonelike and heedless of the other Claymores that must have been set on the trail. One of the four was a hillbilly boy from northern Georgia. He had a large American flag tattooed on his flexed, sun-browned arm, and he was so strong and he pulled so hard on his corner of the poncho that he almost tipped me out on the trail. But when a couple of AK-47s went off and they had to set me down suddenly, he crouched close to my face and whispered in his mountain accent, 'Don't you worry none, Lieutenant. If they ain't at the LZ, we'll tote you plumb to Saigon if we have to.'

They carried me the rest of the night. Their faces were exhausted and beaded with pinpoints of sweat and dirt, their fatigues stiff with their own salt. I should have been afraid but I was not. They never faltered, even though their arms and backs ached miserably and their hands were rubbed raw and blistered. The moon broke through the clouds overhead, the mist hung like strips of wet cotton along the jungle trail, and I fell into a deep morphine dream, a prenatal quietness in which the only sound was my own breathing and the labored breath of the four men carrying me, which finally became a collective hum like blood coursing through an umbilical cord. I heard them stop once and set me down gingerly while they changed my serum albumin bottle, but I didn't wake until morning, when I heard the blades of the medevac roaring over the LZ and I looked up out of my black cocoon and saw the boy from northern Georgia lean down out of the light and touch my face with hands that were as tender as a woman's.

But the hands that lifted me out of the trunk of my own automobile on the third level of a parking garage above the river didn't belong to the men of my platoon. In the darkness and the swirling rain I saw the faces of the little Israeli, the Nicaraguan, Philip Murphy, and Bobby Joe Starkweather staring down at me as though I were a loathsome object whose smell made their nostrils dilate and whiten with shock. They lifted me to my feet, then wedged me behind the steering wheel of my car and slammed the door closed. My head felt as though it had been stunned with Novocain, my mouth hung open uncontrollably, my chin and neck were slick with vomit, the sickening sweet stench of excrement rose from my trousers. Through the windshield I could see the green and red running lights of barges out on the Mississippi and clouds of vapor rising from the rain-dented water like a scene out of purgatory.

They propped Sam Fitzpatrick next to me and splashed whiskey and beer on his clothes. I tried to hold my head up straight, to reach out and touch him, but my chin kept falling on my chest and my words became thick bubbles on my lips. His eyes were rolled upward, and when he breathed, fresh blood drained from his nose onto his shirt-front. My face was numb, dead to the touch, stretched tight across the skull the way skin is over a death's head, and I felt my lips splitting apart in a wicked grin, as though I wanted to share an obscene joke with the world about our execution. Then an awful taste rose out of my stomach, my head pitched forward, and I felt something like wet newspaper rip loose inside my chest and then I heard a splattering through the steering wheel onto the floorboards.

Someone had started the car engine now, and a bare arm ridged with muscle like rolls of nickels reached across me and dropped the transmission into gear. The rain was blowing hard on the river.

The car rolled toward the guardrail, gaining speed, as I slapped limply at the door handle and tried to pull the lock free with fingers that felt sewed together with needle thread. At first I could see the river levee, a lighted street down below with cars on it, the black tops of one-story warehouses; then as my car neared the guardrail and the end of the concrete shelf I could see only the sky and the rain twisting out of it and a distant airplane with its wing lights flashing against the blackness.

I heard the rail fold under my bumper, then snap loose altogether from its fastenings just as the front wheels dropped over the edge of the concrete and my car tilted forward and slid out into space like it was beginning the first downward rush of a rollercoaster ride. The back end started to roll over, and I was pressed flat against the steering wheel, watching the street below roar up at me through the windshield, my mouth open wide with a sound that would be caught forever in my throat.

The car hit the corner of another building or concrete abutment of some kind, because I heard metal shear, as though the underside of the car had been surgically gutted, smelled a drench of gasoline briefly, then we crashed upside down in the middle of a sidewalk in a thunderous roar of glass, crumpling metal, and doors exploding off the hinges.

I was outside on the pavement, my clothes covered with oil and glass shards. We had beat it, I thought. The bad guys had done their worst and hadn't been able to pull it off. We were painted with magic, Fitzpatrick and I, and after we had recuperated it would be our turn to kick butt and take names.

But only drunkards and fools believe in that kind of poetic simplicity. The fuel tank was gashed open and the car was soaking in gasoline. I saw wisps of smoke rise from the crushed hood like pieces of dirty string, then there was a *poof* and a burst of light from the engine, and a strip of flame raced along the pavement to the gas tank and the whole car went up in an orange and black ball that snapped against the sky.

I hope he didn't suffer. The inside of the car was a firestorm. I couldn't see anything except flames swirling inside the gutted windows. But in my mind's eye I saw a papier-mâché figure, with freckles painted on its face, lying quietly between the roaring yellow walls of a furnace, ridging and popping apart in the heat.

The next morning the sun was bright through the

windows of my hospital room, and I could see the green tops of the oak trees against the red brick of the nineteenth-century homes across the street. I was only half a block off St. Charles, and when the nurse cranked up my bed I could see the big dull-green streetcar passing along the esplanade.

I had concussion and the doctor took seventeen stitches in my scalp, and small pieces of oily glass were embedded in my shoulder and all down one arm, so that the skin felt like alligator hide. But my real problem was the whiskey and Quaaludes that were still in my system, and the series of people who came through my door.

The first one was Sam Fitzpatrick's supervisor from the Treasury Department. He wasn't a bad guy, I guess, but he didn't like me and I believe he felt it was Fitzpatrick's involvement with me, rather than with Philip Murphy and Central American guns, that had led to his death.

'You keep talking about an elephant walk. There's nothing like that in Fitzpatrick's notes and he never talked about it, either,' he said. He was forty, wore a business suit and a deep tan, and his gray hair was cut short like an athlete's. His brown, green-flecked eyes were steady and intent.

'He didn't have a chance to,' I said.

'You tell a strange story, Lieutenant.'

'Psychopaths and government fuckheads out of control do strange things.'

'Philip Murphy isn't government.'

'I'm not sure about that.'

'Take my word,' he said.

'Then why don't you take mine?'

'Because you have a peculiar history. Because

you keep meddling in things that aren't your business. Because you killed a potential major government witness and because one of our best agents burned to death in your automobile.'

My eyes broke and I had to look away from his face. The trees were green in the sunlight outside and I thought I heard the streetcar clatter on the esplanade.

'Have you heard of a guy named Abshire?' I asked.

'What about him?' he replied.

'I think these guys work for somebody named Abshire.' His eyes looked into space, then back at me. But I had seen the recognition in them.

'Who is this guy?' I asked.

'How would I know?'

'You circling up the wagons?'

'We can't afford to have you around,' he said.

'Too bad.'

'What does it take for you to get the message, Lieutenant?'

'I liked that kid, too.'

'Then make a tribute to his memory by staying out of federal business.'

He left without saying good-bye and I felt foolish and alone in the sunlit whiteness of my room. I was also starting to shake inside, like a tuning fork that starts to tremble at a discordant sound. There was a bottle of Listerine on my nightstand. I walked stiffly to the bath, rinsed my mouth, and spat into the sink. Then I sucked the juice out of my cheeks and tongue and swallowed it. Then I rinsed again, but this time I didn't spit it out. I could feel the alcohol in my stomach like an old friend.

A half hour later, two detectives from Internal Affairs stood over my bed. It was the same two who had investigated the shooting at Julio Segura's. They wore sports clothes and mustaches, and had their hair cut by a stylist.

'You guys are making me nervous. You look like vultures sitting on my bedposts. How about sitting down?' I said.

'You're a fun guy, Robicheaux, a laugh a minute,' the first detective said. His name was Nate Baxter and he had worked for CID in the army before he joined the department. I had always believed that his apparent military attitudes were a disguise for a true fascist mentality. He was a bully, and one night a suspended patrolman punched him headlong into a urinal at Joe Burton's old place on Canal.

'We don't need too much from you, Dave,' his partner said. 'We're just vague on a couple of points.'

'Like what you were doing in that snatch-patch out by the airport,' Baxter said.

'I heard about a girl that wanted to turn a couple of Segura's people.'

'You didn't find her.'

'No.'

'Then why did you have to spend all that time out there watching the gash?' Baxter said.

'I waited to see if she'd come in.'

'What'd you have to drink?'

'7-UP.'

'I didn't know 7-Up caused people to shit their pants,' Baxter said.

'You've read the report. If you don't believe me, that's your problem.'

'No, it's your problem. So run through it again.'

'Stick it up your butt, Baxter.'

'What did you say?'

'You hear me. You get out of my face.'

'Slow down, Dave,' his partner said. 'It's a wild story. People are going to ask questions about it. You got to expect that.'

'It's supposed to be a wild story. That's why they did it,' I said.

'I don't think there's any mystery here. I think you fell off the wagon, got a snootful, and crashed right on your head,' Baxter said. 'The paramedics say you smelled like an unflushed toilet with whiskey poured in it.'

'I keep defending you. No matter what everybody says. I tell them that under that Mortimer Snerd polyester there's a real cop who can sharpen pencils with the best administrators in the department. But you make it hard for me to keep on being your apologist, Baxter.'

'I think your mother must have been knocked up by a crab,' he said.

His partner's face went gray.

'I'm going to be out of here by tomorrow,' I said. 'Maybe I ought to call you up off-duty, meet you someplace, talk over some things. What do you think?'

'You call me up off-duty, you better be asking for the bus fare to an AA meeting.'

'I've got a feeling it won't make much difference if I go out of control here today.'

'I wish you would, wise-ass. I'd love to stomp the shit out of you.'

'Get out of here, Baxter, before somebody pours you out with the rest of the bedpans.'

'Keep popping those Quaaludes, hotshot, because you're going to need them. It's not me that's dropping the hammer on you, either. You blew out your own doors this time. I hope you enjoy the fall, too, because it's a big one.' Then he turned to his partner. 'Let's get out in the fresh air. This guy's more depressing every time I see him.'

They went out the door, brushing past a young Irish nun in a white habit who was bringing in my lunch on a tray.

'My, what an intense pair,' she said.

'That's probably the nicest thing anyone has ever said about them, Sister.'

'Are they after the men who did this to you?'

'I'm afraid they get paid for catching other cops.'

'I don't understand.' Her face was round and pretty inside her nun's wimple.

'It's nothing. Sister, I don't think I can eat lunch. I'm sorry.'

'Don't worry about it. Your stomach will be better by tonight.'

'You know what I'd really like, that I'd give anything to have?'

'What?'

The words wouldn't come. My eyes swept around the brightly lit room and went outside the window to the green tops of the oak trees moving in the breeze.

'Could you get me a big glass of Coca-Cola? With a lot of ice in it, maybe with cherry juice and slices of lime in it?'

'Of course.'

'Thanks very much, Sister.'

'Do you want anything else?'

'No. Just the Coca-Cola. I'm sure that's all I need.'

That afternoon Captain Guidry sat on the foot of my bed, snuffed down in his nose, and wiped his glasses on my bedsheet.

'One time after every newspaper in the country condemned George Wallace as a racist, he told a reporter, "Well, that's one man's opinion,"' Captain Guidry said. 'I was never his admirer, but I always liked that statement.'

'How bad is it going to be?'

'They stiffed you. Indefinite suspension without pay.'

'That's what they give cops who get caught dealing dope.'

'For what it's worth, I argued against it. They dumped on you, Dave, but you've got to see their side of it, too. In a week's time your name has gotten into a lot of paperwork. We're also talking about two people shot to death in one of the richest neighborhoods in New Orleans, and a Treasury agent killed in your automobile that falls three stories in the middle of a city street. That's a tough act to follow.'

'Do you believe my report?'

'You've always been a good cop. There's none better.'

'Do you believe me?'

'How the hell do I know what happened out there? To tell you the truth, I'm not sure you do, either, Dave. The paramedics said you were half crazy when they brought you in here. I saw what was left of your car. I don't know how you survived it. The doctor said you had enough dope and booze in your blood to embalm the Russian army.'

'You want me to resign?'

'Don't let them call the plays for you. You let parasites like Baxter see that you're wounded and they'll try to file a manslaughter charge against you.'

'That special agent, Fitzpatrick's supervisor, knows who this guy Abshire is. I saw it in his eyes.'

'You shake a federal tree, and all you get in your face is birdshit. Secondly, you're suspended. You're out of it. That's absolute.'

'What am I supposed to do, Captain?'

'It's your turn in the barrel. I just hope it passes quick. Tell them all go fuck themselves and take up needle-point if you have to.'

I watched the sunset through the open window that evening. The sky was crimson above the trees and the rooftops, then it turned lavender and finally a deep purple as the sun burned itself out in a crack of brilliant fire on the horizon. I sat alone in the dark awhile, then used the remote television control to switch on the twenty-four-hour cable news. I watched pictures of Salvadoran guerrillas threading their way through a jungle trail at the base of a dead volcano. Their faces were very young, with wispy beards like Orientals, and their bodies were hung with bandoliers and cloth belts of shotgun shells. Each of them had laced his straw hat with long blades of pampas grass.

A moment later the screen showed an unrelated scene of government troops in GI issue moving through a forest of banana trees and enormous clumps of green elephant grass. A Cobra gunship streaked across the glassy sky, hovered at an angle over a deep, rocky ravine, then unloaded a succession of rockets that blew water, powdered coral, and bits of trees and scrub brush out of the bottom of the ravine. The footage closed with a shot of government troops retreating out of the banana trees with their wounded on stretchers. The heat in those trees must have been terrible, because the wounded were covered with sweat and the medics were washing their faces with water from canteens. It all looked very familiar.

Having been raised in Louisiana, I had always thought that politics was the province of moral invalids. But as a gambler I had certain instincts about which side I would wager my money on in certain situations. On one side of the equation were people who had conscripted into the army and were either forced or paid to fight, and who sometimes sold their weapons to the enemy if given the chance. On the other side was a group that lived off the jungle, scavenged guns and ammunition wherever they could buy or steal them, had absolutely nothing of economic value to lose, and who, because they had no illusions about their fate if they were captured, would go down to the last man in a firefight. I doubted there was a bookie in New Orleans who would take a bet on that one.

But my war was over, and maybe my career as well. I turned off the set and looked out the window at the reflection of the lights against the sky. The room was quiet, the sheets were cool and clean, and my stomach didn't feel sick anymore; but the tuning fork was still vibrating inside me. I brushed my teeth, I showered, I rinsed my mouth with Listerine again; then I got back in bed and pulled my knees up in front of me and started to shake all over.

Fifteen minutes later I checked myself out of the hospital and took a cab to my houseboat. It was a dark, hot night and the heat had built up all day in the cabin. My collection of historical jazz records – irreplaceable seventy-eights of Blind Lemon, Bunk Johnson, Kid Ory, Bix Beiderbecke – lay scattered and broken and tattooed with footprints on the floor. I opened the windows wide, turned on my floor fan, picked up the few records that were still hard and stiff in their jackets, cleaned them with a soft cloth, and set them in the wall rack. Then I swept the rest into a paper bag and lay down to sleep on the couch with my clothes on.

Small waves chucked against the hull, and the boat rocked rhythmically under me. But it was no good; I couldn't sleep. I was sweating and trembling and when I took my shirt off I shivered as though I'd been struck with a blast of arctic air. Each time I closed my eyes I felt the earth's surface drop away under me, felt myself spinning end over end inside my automobile toward the distant bottom of a rock-strewn canyon, saw words form like a bubble on the dead lips of Sam Fitzpatrick sitting next to me.

Later, Annie Ballard tapped softly on the cabin door. I unlocked it and went back to the couch in the dark. A sailing yacht out on the lake had a floodlamp lighted on its deck, and it made gold lights in Annie's hair. I saw her feel for the switch on the wall.

'Don't turn it on,' I said.

'Why not?'

'People just out of the hospital don't look good.'

'I don't care.'

'I do.'

'You knew I was coming up there. Didn't you want to leave me a message?'

'I thought I did. Maybe I didn't. There were cops in there all day.'

She walked closer to the couch. She wore a pair of white jeans with a blue denim shirt tucked inside.

'What's wrong?' she said.

'I guess it's malaria. I picked it up in the Philippines.'

'I'm going to turn on the light.'

'No.'

'You don't have to hide anything, Dave.'

'I'm suspended without pay. I don't feel well right now. To tell you the truth, I feel like killing somebody.'

'I don't understand.'

'When they suspend you indefinitely without pay, it means you're probably not coming back. It's the kind of stuff they drop on cops that are about to be indicted.'

She sat down on the edge of the couch and put her hand on my bare shoulder. Her face was a dark silhouette against the glass behind her. She touched my forehead with her fingers.

'I can't believe they would do that to you.'

'It's my past history. You don't know about it. I was a full-blown drunk for years. They figure I'm back into it.'

'They can't hold the past against you.'

'Why the hell not? It makes it easier. Most cops

couldn't think their way out of a wet paper bag. They think categorically about virtually every situation. That's why we don't put a lot of people away. Look, four pieces of human slime that wouldn't even make good bars of soap are out there right now drinking beer, celebrating burning a kid to charcoal, while some of our own people are wondering if they should hang a DUI on me, or a DUI and a manslaughter charge.'

'You're not talking like yourself.'

'Annie, in the real world we fry paupers in the electric chair and send priests to prison for splashing chicken blood on draft files. It's the nature of ritual. We deal with the problem symbolically, but somebody has to take the fall. In this case, a guy that looked like he escaped from a Popsicle wrapper launched a one-man crusade against an entire government policy in Central America. If you were an administrative pencil-pusher, don't you think it would be easier to deal with a drunk-driving fatality than a story about a lot of right-wing crazies who are killing peasant villagers in Nicaragua?'

'Why do you think you're the only person who sees the truth?'

'I didn't say that.'

'But it's the way you feel, Dave. That's too big a burden for a person.' Her face was soft and composed and she looked out the windows across the water for a moment, then stood up and began undressing in the dark.

'Annie, I'm not a charity case. I'm just not doing too good today.'

'If you want me to go away, tell me. But look me

directly in the face and tell me honestly, with no weirdness or bullshit this time.'

'I like you a great deal.'

She sat back on the couch and leaned her face close to mine.

'Loving somebody is being there when nobody else is. When it's not even a choice. You should understand that, Dave,' she said. She bent and kissed me lightly on the mouth.

She was beautiful to look at, and her skin was smooth and warm and I could smell the sun and a perfume like the scent of four-o'clocks in her hair. She kissed me again and blew her breath on the side of my face and slipped her arms around my neck and pressed her breasts tight against me. I sat up in the side of the couch and took off my trousers; then she pressed me back into the cushions, raised herself up on her knees, and with her hand guided me inside her. Her eyes closed, she moaned and her mouth opened wide, and she leaned down over me on her arms with her breasts close to my face. She had ignored all my anger – no, my self-pity – and I felt humbled and dizzy and physically weak when I looked up into the electric blueness of her eyes.

There was a strawberry birthmark on her right breast, and it seemed to grow darker and fill with blood as her breathing became more rapid. I felt her warmth drawing me into her, felt her wet palms slip under me, felt her thighs flex and tighten around me, then her hands held my face and my heart twisted in my chest and I felt an aching hardness crest inside of me and burst apart like a heavy stone ripping loose in a rushing streambed.

'Oh, you fine man,' she said, and brushed the drops of sweat out of my eyes with her fingers, her body still shaking.

She fell asleep next to me, and I covered her with a sheet from the bedroom. The moon was out now, and the light through the glass made her curly blond hair look like it was touched with silver. Just the edge of her strawberry birthmark showed above the sheet.

I knew I was very fortunate to have a girl like this. But the great nemesis of the gambler is that he's never satisfied with just winning the daily double; he'll reinvest his winnings in every race remaining that afternoon, and if he's still ahead when the window closes on the last race, he'll be at the dog track that night and stay with it until he loses everything.

I didn't have a parimutuel window handy, so I left Annie asleep and started walking down the lakefront toward Pontchartrain Beach Amusement Park. The wind had picked up and the waves were cresting against the hard-packed sand of the beach and the palm fronds were rattling dryly against the darkening sky. By the time I reached the amusement park the air was cool and filled with flying grains of sand and smelled of the gale blowing out of the south. Most of the rides were closed, with tarpaulins stretched over them to protect them from the coming rain, and the red neon signs over the empty funhouse looked like electrified blood in the sky.

But I found what I had been looking for all day.

'A double Jack Daniel's with a Pearl draft on the side,' I told the bartender.

'You look like you already lost a fight to a chainsaw, buddy,' he said.

'You ought to see the chainsaw,' I said.

But it was a dark, cheerless place, not given to either humor or protocol, and the bartender poured silently into my shot glass.

7

At five o'clock the next morning the eastern sky was gray and pink beyond the tree line on the far side of the Mississippi. I was in an all-night bar set back from old Highway 90 under the long, black, looming expanse of the Huey Long Bridge. Mist hung in clouds on the river's surface and around the brush-choked pilings of the bridge; the air itself seemed to drip with moisture, and the shale rock in the parking lot glistened with a dull shine as the pinkness of the sun spread along the earth's rim.

A bus loaded with carnival and circus people from Sarasota, Florida, had broken down on the highway, and the bar and the café counter were crowded with a strange collection of roustabouts, acrobats, and sideshow performers. I sat at a table with the Crocodile Boy, the Pencil Man, and a dwarf named Little Mack. The Pencil Man had arms and legs that were so thin and soft that they looked as though all the bone had been surgically removed from them, like rubbery snakes attached to his torso, which in itself could not have been much greater in circumference than a telephone pole. His kinky red hair was waxed and brushed into a conk so that it resembled a pencil eraser. The skin of the Crocodile Boy was covered with hard black bumps like barnacles, and his teeth looked as if they had been filed to points. In rotating order he sipped from his muscatel wine, chased it with beer, smoked a cigar, and ate out of a bowl of pickled hogs' feet. Little Mack sat next to me, his tiny feet not able to touch the floor, his elongated jug face filled with concern at my situation.

I looked at the long-distance number I had written on a damp napkin. My head was filled with a steady buzzing sound, like a neon short circuit.

'You shouldn't call those CIA people again, Lieutenant,' Little Mack said in his high-pitched mechanical voice. 'They're the ones tied in with those UFOs. We saw one once in the desert outside of Needles, California. It was glowing green and orange and it streaked over the top of the bus at maybe a thousand miles an hour. The next day the paper said a bunch of cows on a ranch were all mangled up. Maybe those UFO guys were trying to take some food on board.'

'That could be,' I said, and I motioned to the bartender to bring us two more shots of Jack Daniel's.

'The government will mess you up,' the Pencil Man said. 'Each time you have contact with a government agency, it creates a piece of paper on you. There's people that's got whole rooms of paper on their lives. I don't have any, not even a birth certificate. My mother squatted down just long enough to squirt me out in the back of a boxcar. I been moving ever since. I never had a social security card, a driver's license, a draft card. I never filed an income tax return. You let them get papers on you and they'll jerk you around.'

'You guys are my kind of situational philosophers,' I said.

'What's that?' the Crocodile Boy asked. He had stopped eating a hog's knuckle, and his narrow green eyes were curious and perplexed.

'You deal with the action on your own terms, whether it's a UFO or a bunch of government buttholes. Right?' I said.

'Have you seen a UFO?' Little Mack asked.

'I've heard reports on them,' I said.

I poured a jigger of whiskey into my beer glass, drank it down, then looked at the telephone number on the napkin again. I raked my change off the table into my palm and started toward the pay phone on the wall.

'Lieutenant, don't use dirty words to anyone this time,' Little Mack said. 'I read a story once they even put poison inside a guy's condom.'

I called the number in McLean, Virginia, and asked for a duty officer. My ear felt thick and wooden against the phone receiver. I tried to focus my eyes through the front window on the clouds of steam rising off the river in the soft light. The neon buzz in my head wouldn't stop. Finally the voice of an annoyed man came on the line.

'Who's this?' I asked.

'The same guy you were talking to a half hour ago.'

'Then put somebody else on.'

'I'm all you get, pal.'

'Tell me your name so I can look you up sometime.'

'Let me give you the facts of life, Lieutenant. We traced your call, we know what bar you're in, we ran your sheet, we know everything about you. If you weren't such a pathetic asshole, I'd have your own people pick you up.'

'All right, try this with your morning coffee, motherfucker. I'm the loose cannon on your deck and I'm going to leave blood and shit all over the gunwales.'

'If you didn't have the alcoholic titty in your mouth, I might even take you seriously. Call here one more time and you're going to be sitting in your own drunk tank.'

The line went dead. When I lowered the receiver from my ear, the side of my face felt numb, as though I had been slapped with a thick hand.

'What's the matter? Your face don't look good,' Little Mack said.

'We need some more drinks,' I said.

'They threaten to assassinate you or something? The cocksuckers. You ever read *The Black Star*? There was a story about how the CIA used these Nazi scientists to make clones from Elvis and Marilyn Monroe, then they killed the clones when they couldn't use them to spy anymore. I think they got the idea from this show about these seed-pod people taking over the earth. They put a seed pod under your bed, and when you go to sleep the pod sucks out all your ectoplasm and turns you into a dry shell that just blows away in the wind . . . Where you going?'

'I don't know.'

'Better sit down, get something to eat,' the Pencil Man said. 'You can ride with us when the bus is fixed.'

'Thanks, I need to walk. This last round is on me.'

But when I opened my wallet I had no money.

'You all right, Lieutenant?' Little Mack said.

'Sure.'

'I mean, you're listing pretty bad,' he said.

'I'm okay.'

'You got to be careful out there in the fog and all,' he said. 'There's crazy people on the highway, drunks and such. You going to be safe?'

'Sure,' I said. 'Believe me.'

I started walking in the gray dawn toward the shining black outline of the Huey Long Bridge. I could hear car tires whir on the steel grid of the bridge. The air was cool and damp and smelled of the wet earth along the riverbanks. I began the long walk up toward the apex of the bridge, my breath coming hard in my throat, my heart swelling with exertion. Far down below in the dark waters, a Standard Oil barge was headed north to the refineries in Baton Rouge. The spires, cables, and girders of the bridge seemed to sing and whip and groan in the wind. Then the sun broke through the clouds in a yellow ball, flooding the bridge with light, and for some reason I saw deep down in my mind a black cluster of jungle birds rise clattering into a hot tropical sky.

Late that afternoon I sat under an umbrella on the deck of my houseboat and tried to mend my day and mind back together with a bottle of Jax. I wasn't having much luck. The sun reflected off the water and struck my eyes like broken shards from a mirror. I wanted to call Annie and apologize, but how do you explain that your craving for alcohol can be stronger than your need for someone's love? And in truth, at that moment I didn't have either the courage or the energy to face my own irresponsibility and weakness. Instead, I brooded on the relativity of time, the stark realization that no amount of years could successfully separate me from my nightmarish alcoholic past, that Philip Murphy's cocktail had launched me totally back into a surreal world where the dragons and monsters frolicked.

I also brooded on my drowned father and wondered what he would have done in my situation. He was a big, powerful man, a dark laughing Cajun with white teeth and turquoise eyes who had been raised on *boudin*, *cush-cush*, and garfish balls. He had been a fur trapper on Marsh Island and a derrick man on oil rigs, working high up on the monkey board, and he had done his best to take care of Jimmie and me after my mother ran away with a *bourée* dealer from Morgan City. But when he was out of work he drank hard and sometimes brawled in bars and got thrown in the parish jail; the white streak in Jimmie's and my hair was caused by a vitamin deficiency associated with malnutrition. However, during those bad times he could be imaginative and kind in ways that we would never forget. On a Halloween evening, when the pecan trees stood full and black against the orange sky, he would come home with carved pumpkins, chopped lengths of sugar cane, and blocks of hot gingerbread, or at our birthday breakfasts we would find by our plates of *cush-cush* and *boudin* a dozen Civil War minié balls or rose quartz Indian arrowheads, and one time a rusty Confederate revolver he had dug out of the bank on Bayou Teche.

He usually spoke to us in French, and he entertained us for years with an endless number of admonitions, observations, and folk stories that he said he'd learned from his father but that I think he made up as the situation demanded. An English paraphrase of a few:

- Never do anything you don't want to, you.
- If everybody agrees upon it, it's got to be wrong.
- Rather than the eagle, the crawfish should be the symbol of the United States. If you put an eagle on a rail road track and a train comes along, what's the eagle going to do? He's going to fly, him. But you put a crawfish on that railroad track and what's he going to do? He's going to put up his claws to stop that train, him.

But there was a piece of serious advice that he used to give us, and I could almost hear him whispering it to me now from below the green depths far out in the Gulf: When you've hunted through the whole marsh for the bull 'gator that ate your hog and you come up empty, go back where you started and commence again. You walked right over him.

A cop had never been given a better suggestion.

I slept through the rest of the afternoon and woke in the cooling dusk when the cicadas were loud in the purple haze and the fireflies were lighting in the trees. I showered and felt some of the misery begin to go out of my mind and body, then I took a taxi to the Hertz agency and rented a small Ford.

Because most of the Quarter was closed to automobile traffic at night, I parked the car near the French Market, by the river, and walked back to Bourbon. The street was loud with music from the bars and strip houses, and the sidewalks were filled with tourists, drunks, and street people who were trying to hold on to their last little piece of American geography. My favorite bunch of hustlers and scam artists, the black sidewalk tap dancers, were out in force. They wore enormous iron taps that clipped onto their shoes, and when they danced to the music from the bars, their feet rang on the concrete like horseshoes. A tap dancer would stop a tourist, rivet him in the eyes, and say, 'I bet you a half-dollar I can tell you where you got yo' shoes.' If the tourist accepted the wager, the dancer would then say, 'You got yo' shoes on yo' feet, and yo' feet is on Bourbon Street. You ain't the kind, now, to back out on yo' bet, is you?'

I went inside Plato's Adult Theater, stopped in the men's room, and removed the clip from my .45 automatic. I dropped the empty pistol in one coat pocket, the clip in the other, and opened Wesley Pott's office door without knocking.

'What's happening Wes? Community Outreach here,' I said.

He sat behind the desk in his powder-blue polyester slacks, with his feet up in a chair, watching the baseball game on television and eating fried chicken out of a box propped on his stomach. His pate shone with hair oil, and his eyes looked at me like uncertain blue marbles. He resumed chewing, and swallowed the chicken in his mouth.

'I'm looking for a fellow named Bobby Joe Starkweather,' I said. 'I suspect he's a fan of the Tijuana visual arts.'

His eyes clicked back and forth.

'I hear they pulled your ticket, Lieutenant,' he said.

'You hear a lot of rumors in troubled times.'

'This is more like the *Times-Picayune*.'

'Those are bureaucratic matters that guys like you and me don't need to pay much attention to.'

'I think I already went on the line once for you, Lieutenant. I didn't get nothing for it, either, except my films smashed up by Purcel. I could've got into some real ugly shit because of that.'

'I'm temporarily disconnected from the snitch fund, so we're operating on good faith here.'

'I went through a lot of anxiety because of that day. I think you ought to understand that. No matter what you think about me, I'm not some kind of geek for the mob that hops around in the pan like a piece of popcorn. I got a family, my kids go to Sunday school, I pay a lot of taxes. Maybe my IRS records are a little creative, but how about Nixon's? A guy wants a little respect, a little recognition that he's got his own space, his own problems.'

'I know all that, Wes. That's why it makes me feel bad when I do this to you.'

I took the .45 from my coat pocket, slid back the loading receiver, let it clack back loudly into place, and aimed it at a downward angle between his eyes so he could see the cocked hammer.

He gasped, his face jumped, pinpoints of sweat

broke out on his coarse skin, and his eyes almost crossed as they went out of focus on the pointed pistol. He fluttered his fingers at the barrel.

'Don't point it at me, Lieutenant,' he pleaded. 'I was in the war. I can't take guns.'

'Your sheet says you got a peacetime BCD.'

'I don't care. I hate guns. I hate all violence. God, I'm gonna wet my pants!'

He was trembling badly. The box of fried chicken had spilled to the floor, and he was swallowing dryly, the pulse jumping in his throat, and kneading and rubbing his hands in front of him as though something obscene were on them. Then he began to weep uncontrollably.

'I can't do this to you. I'm sorry, Wesley,' I said, and lowered the .45.

'What?' he said weakly.

'I apologize. I shouldn't have done that. If you don't want to drop the dime on somebody, that's your business.'

He couldn't stop hiccuping and shaking.

'Lighten up. It was empty. Here, look.' I pointed the barrel at my palm and snapped the trigger. His head jerked at the sound.

'I'm gonna have a heart attack. I had rheumatic fever when I was a kid. I can't take high-level stress like this,' he said.

'I'll get you a whiskey from next door. What do you drink?'

'A double Black Jack on ice, with a Tuborg chaser.' He paused and blinked. 'Make sure the beer's cold, too. The Jew that runs that joint is always trying to cut down on his refrigeration bill.'

I went to the bar next door and had to pay eight

dollars for the imported beer and the double shot of Jack Daniel's in a cup of ice. When I got back to Wesley's office the air reeked of marijuana, and his face had the blank, stiff look of somebody who had just eaten the roach.

'My doctor gives it to me for glaucoma,' he said. 'It's a condition I got in the army. A hand grenade blew up in one of the pits. That's how come I'm nervous all the time and can't take stress.'

'I see.'

'The beer cold?'

'You bet. Are you all right now?'

'Sure.' He drank down the whiskey and crunched the ice between his teeth, his close-set eyes narrowing and focusing like BBs. 'Lieutenant, I can give you that fucker.'

'Why is that?'

'He's a creep. Besides, he was muling Mexican brown for Segura. I still live down in the Irish Channel. They hook up neighborhood kids with that stuff.'

'Yeah, the Rotary and the Knights of Columbus have been talking a lot about that lately. Have you been attending some of their breakfasts on that, Wes?'

'I sell dirty fantasies in a dark theater. I don't steal people's souls. You haven't found that tattooed ass-wipe because he don't live in New Orleans. He's got a fish camp over by Bayou des Allemands in St. Charles Parish. He spends his time busting bottles in the backyard with a shotgun. The guy's a walking advertisement for massive federal aid to mental health.'

'Dropping the dime's not always enough.'

'I'm turning him for you. What else you want?'

'You know the rules, Wes. We don't let the customers write the script. Give me the rest of it. Like Didi Gee told me, treat people with respect.'

He drank his beer and looked intently at the wall, his face coloring with remembered anger. I could hear his breath in his nose.

'Segura invited a bunch of guys out to his pool to play cards, have drinks, and fool around with the gash. Starkweather is shooting off his mouth about how he was a Green Beret in 'Nam and how he cut some gooks' throats in their sleep and painted their faces yellow so the other gooks would wake up in the morning and find them like that. Except people are eating their shrimp salad and trying not to puke on the grass, and so I say, 'Hey, give it a break or hand out barf bags with all these sickening war stories.' He stared at me like I was some kind of bedbug. Then, right in front of all them people, with all them broads watching, he jabbed me in both eyeballs with his fingers, the way Moe Stooge was always doing to Shemp and Larry. A broad started laughing real loud, and then he pushed me in the pool.'

'Wes, somehow I believe you,' I said.

I waited until dawn to hit Starkweather's fish camp. Clouds of fog swirled off the bayou through the flooded woods as I banged over an old board that had been cut through the swamp by an oil company. The dead cypresses were wet and black in the gray light, and green lichen grew where the waterline touched the swollen bases of the trunks. The fog was so thick and white in the trees that I could barely see thirty feet ahead of the car. A rotted plank snapped under my wheel and whanged off the oil pan. In the early morning stillness the sound made the herons and egrets rise in a sudden flapping of wings toward the pink light above the treetops. Then to one side of the road, in a scoured-out clearing in the trees, I saw a shack built of Montgomery Ward brick and clapboard, elevated from the muddy ground by cinder blocks and cypress stumps, with a Toyota jeep parked in front. A knobby beagle that looked like it had been hit with birdshot was tied to the front porch.

I cut the car's ignition in the center of the road, opened the door quietly, and walked through the wet trees on one side of the clearing until I was abreast of the porch. The oaks that ringed the clearing were covered with shredded rifle targets; perforated tin cans and shattered bottles dangled from bits of baling wire; the bark on the trunks was ripped and gouged white by bullets.

The screen door to the shack was ajar, but I couldn't see or hear any movement inside. Out back, hogs were snuffing and grunting inside a wood pen.

I pulled back the receiver on my .45 and eased a round from the clip into the chamber. I took a deep breath, then raced across the dirt yard, cleared the porch steps in one jump, almost caused the beagle to break its neck on its rope, and crashed through the screen door.

I crouched and swung the .45 around the room, my heart hammering against my ribcage, my eyes wide in the gloom. The wooden floor was littered with beer cans, bread wrappers, Red Man pouches, chicken bones, bottle caps, and the chewed stuffing from a rotted mattress that was piled in the corner. But there was nobody in the room. Then someone slid back the curtain on the doorway to the single bedroom in the back. I aimed the .45 right at her face, both of my hands sweating on the grip.

'Wow, who the fuck are you?' she said drowsily. She was maybe twenty and wore cut-off blue jeans and only a bra for a top. Her face looked numb, dead, and she had to keep widening her eyes to focus on me. Her hair was the color of weathered wood.

'Where's Starkweather?' I said.

'I think he went out back with that other dude. Are you the heat or something?'

I pushed open the back screen and dropped into the yard. In the mist I could see an outhouse, an upside-down pirogue beaded with dew, a wooden hog pen, a wheelless and rusted-out car body pocked with silvery bullet holes. The sun was lighting the trees now, and I could see the dead green water in the swamp, the levee covered with buttercups, the Spanish moss that was lifting in the breeze off the Gulf. But there was no one back here. Then I heard the hogs grunting and snuffing again, and I realized they were eating something inside the pen.

They were in a circle, their heads dipped down as though they were eating from a trough; then one of them would rattle its head, grunt, crunch something loudly in its jaws, and dip its snout down again. Their faces and mouths were shiny with gore; then I saw one of them tear a long string of blue entrails out of Bobby Joe Starkweather's stomach and run heavily across the pen with it. Starkweather's face was bloodless, the eyes and mouth open, his shaved scalp flecked with mud. Right above one eyebrow was a black hole the size of a dime.

A bucket of kitchen slops was spilled on the ground. His arms were spread out beside him, and he looked as if he'd been shot from the front side of the pen. I looked carefully over the wet ground, which was dented with boot and dog and chicken prints, until I saw the smooth impression of a street shoe in a ridge of mud, and right in the center of it the stenciled outline of a pistol shell that the shooter must have stepped on and then prized up with his finger.

I went back in the shack. The girl was fumbling in a food cabinet.

'Are you heat?' she said.

'It depends on who you talk to.'

'You got any whites?'

'You look like you already did a drugstore.'

'If you had to ball him, you'd be doing Thorazines like M & M's.'

'I hope you got paid up front.'

Her eyes closed and opened and refocused on mine.

'Where is he?' she said.

'Feeding the pigs.'

She looked at me uncertainly, then started out the back door.

'Let it go. You don't want to look back there,' I said.

But she didn't listen. A minute later I heard her make a sound like she had suddenly stepped into an envelope of fouled air. Her face was gray when she came back through the door.

'That's gross,' she said. 'Shouldn't you take him to a funeral home or something? Yuk.'

'Sit down. I'll fix you a cup of coffee.'

'I can't hang around here. I've got an aerobics and meditation class at ten o'clock. The guy I work for enrolls us in the class so we won't build up a lot of tensions. He gets mad if I miss. God, how do I get around all these crazy people? You know what *he* did? He got naked in his army boots and started lifting weights on the front porch. The dog got off the leash and chased a chicken into the privy and he shot the dog with a shotgun. Then he tied it up and gave it a bowl of milk like nothing had happened.'

'Who was the dude he went out back with?'

'He looked like he had a pink bicycle patch on his face.'

'What?'

'I don't know what he looked like. He was big. I was kind of indisposed, you know what I mean?'

'Say it again about his face.'

'His nose and part of his eyebrow were messed up. Like with a scar.'

'What did he say?'

Her eyes seemed to reach out into space. Her mouth was slightly parted, her facial muscles collapsed with thought.

'He said, "They want you to find some new geography. Work on your golf game." Then what's-his-name said, "Money talks and bullshit walks, biscuit-eater. I got to feed my pigs."'

She chewed on a hangnail and her eyes went flat again.

'Look, I got a problem,' she said. 'He didn't pay me. I got to give the guy I work for twenty bucks when I get back to the bar. Will you get his wallet for me?'

'Sorry. I think the hogs got it, anyway.'

'You want some action?'

'I'll drop you where you want to go, kiddo. Then I'm going to call the sheriff's office about Starkweather. But I'll deal you out of it. If you want to tell them something later, that's up to you.'

'You are heat, aren't you?'

'Why not?'

'Why you cutting me loose? You got something in mind for later?'

'They might lock you up as a material witness. That guy out there in the hog lot has killed dozens, maybe hundreds of people. But he was a novice and a bumbler compared to the people he worked for.'

She sat against the far door of my car, her face thick with a drug hangover, and didn't speak during the long ride through the marsh to the parish road. Her yellowed fingers were wrapped tightly in her lap.

Like many others, I learned a great lesson in Vietnam: Never trust authority. But because I had come to feel that authority should always be treated as suspect and self-serving, I had also learned that it was predictable and vulnerable. So that afternoon I sat under my beach umbrella on my houseboat deck, dressed only in swimming trunks and an open tropical shirt, with a shot of Jim Beam and a beer chaser on the table in front of me, and called Sam Fitzpatrick's supervisor at the Federal Building.

'I ran down Abshire,' I said. 'I don't know why you held out on me at the hospital. He's not exactly well concealed.'

There was a moment's silence on the line.

'Have you got wax in your ears or something?' he said. 'How do I get through to you? You stay off federal turf.'

'I'm going to kick a board up his ass.'

'You're not going to do a goddamn thing, except get a warrant filed on you for obstruction.'

'You want in on it or not?' I asked.

'I have a strong feeling you're drunk.'

'So what? I'm going to cool him out. You want to be there for the party, or do you want us local boys to write the story for you in the *Picayune*? It's going to be socko stuff, partner.'

'What the hell is the matter with you? You don't seem to have any bottom. One of my best men is burned to death in your car. Your own people dump you like a sack of dog turds. You're evidently working on becoming a full-time drunk again, and now you're talking about taking out a retired two-star general. You think it's possible you're losing your mind?'

'You're a good man, but don't take up poker.'

'What?'

'It's a terrible vice. It'll lead you to ruin.'

'You bastard, you're not going to get away with this,' he said.

I hung up the phone, knocked back the jigger of Jim Beam, and sipped from the glass of beer. The sun looked like a yellow balloon trapped under the lake's surface. The wind was warm, and sweat ran down my bare chest in the hot shade of the umbrella. My eyes burned with the humidity of the afternoon. I dialed Clete down at the First District.

'Where are you?' he asked.

'At home.'

'There's a bunch of people asking about you. You sure spit in the soup, Dave.'

'I'm not hard to find. Who's curious about me?'

'Who else? Feds. Did you really call up the CIA? Man, that's unbelievable.'

'I have a lot of time on my hands. A guy has to do something for kicks.'

'I don't know as I'd want to fire up these babies. A nasty bunch. They're not our crowd.'

'You think I ought to get lost for a while?'

'Who knows? I just wouldn't pull on their tallywackers anymore.'

'Actually, I called you for a point of information, Clete. In all the shootings you've investigated, how many times have you known the shooter to recover his brass?'

'I don't understand.'

'Sure you do.'

'I don't guess I ever gave it much thought.'

'I've never seen it once,' I said. 'Except when a cop was the shooter.'

'What's the point?'

'It's funny how that can be trained into a guy, isn't it?'

'Yeah. Imagine that.'

'If I was the shooter, I'd rather leave the shell casing than my signature.'

'Maybe some things aren't worth speculating about, Dave.'

'Like I said, I'm idle now. It fills the time. I spent

two hours this morning over at the St. Charles sheriff's department answering questions about Bobby Joe Starkweather. Did they contact you all yet?'

'We heard about it.' His voice was becoming irritated.

'A truly big mess out there. Another hour or so and I don't think there would have been anything left of Bobby Joe except his belt buckle and his boot nails.'

'He's better off as sausage links. A guy finds his proper level after a while. I got to split, partner.'

'Do me a favor. How about punching on the computer and seeing if you can turn up a retired two-star general named Abshire?'

'Stay idle, Dave. Adjust. We'll get out of this bullshit eventually. You'll see. *Adios*.'

The phone went dead in my hand, and I looked at the smoky green surface of the water in the summer haze and poured another jigger of Jim Beam. What did they have on him? I wondered. Whores? Juice from narcotics? It seemed sometimes that the best of us became most like the people whom we loathed. And whenever a good cop took a big fall, he could never look back and find that exact moment when he made a hard left turn down a one-way street. I remembered sitting in a courtroom when an ex-major-league baseball pitcher from New Orleans was sentenced to ten years in Angola for extortion and trafficking in cocaine. Seventeen years earlier he had won twenty-five games, had thrown fastballs that could destroy barn doors, and now he weighed three hundred pounds and walked as though a bowling ball were slung between his thighs. When asked if he had anything to say before sentencing, he stared up at the judge, the rings of fat on his neck trembling, and replied, 'Your Honor, I have no idea how I got from *there* to *here*.'

I believed him, too. But as I sat in the warm breeze with the drowsy heat of the whiskey working in my head, my concern was not for Clete or an ex-baseball pitcher. I knew that my own fuse was lit, and it was only a matter of time before my banked fires would roar out of control in my life. I had never felt more alone, and I uttered a prayer that seemed a contradiction of everything I had learned back at the Catholic School: *Dear God, my higher power, even though I've abandoned You, don't abandon me.*

8

Late that afternoon I fixed a poor-boy sandwich of oysters, shrimp, lettuce and *sauce piquante*, then drove through the cooling, tree-shaded street toward the *Times-Picayune*, where a night editor sometimes let me use their morgue.

But first I wanted to make amends to Annie for deserting her at the houseboat the other night. Afternoon Jim Beam always endowed me with that kind of magical power.

I bought a bottle of Cold Duck and a box of pralines wrapped in orange cellophane and yellow ribbon, kept my freshly pressed seersucker coat on, and strolled up her sidewalk in the dusky light. The air smelled of lilac and spaded flower beds and clipped lawns and water sprinklers clicking across hedges and the trunks of trees.

When she didn't answer the bell, I walked around the back and found her barbecuing steaks on a portable grill on a brick patio under a chinaberry tree. She wore white shorts and Mexican straw shoes and a yellow shirt tied under her breasts. Her eyes were watering in the smoke, and she stepped away from the fire and picked up a gin gimlet from a glass tabletop that was set with plates and silverware. The gimlet glass was wrapped in a paper napkin with a rubber band around it. Her eyes lighted briefly when she saw me, then she looked away.

'Oh, hello, Dave,' she said.

'I should have called. I caught you at a bad time.'

'A little bit.'

'I brought these pralines and some Cold Duck,' I said.

'That was nice of you.'

'I'm sorry I left you the other night. It's something you won't understand very well, I'm afraid.'

The light came back in her blue eyes. I could see the red birthmark on the top of her breast.

'The best way to end a conversation is to tell somebody she can't understand something,' she said.

'I meant there was no excuse for it.'

'There was a reason. Maybe you just don't want to look at it.'

'I went after liquor. I was drunk all night. I ended up in a bar on Old 90 with a bunch of sideshow performers. I called up the CIA and cussed out the duty officer.'

'I guess that prevented you from finding a telephone for two days.'

'I tried to find Bobby Joe Starkweather. Somebody canceled him out in a hog lot.'

'I'm not interested, Dave. Did you come by to screw me?'

'You think I'm giving you a shuck?'

'No, I think you're singleminded and you're bent

on revenge. I made the overture the other night and complicated things for you. Now you're feeling a gentleman's obligation. Sorry, I'm not in the absolution business. I don't have any regrets. If you do, that's your problem.'

She began to poke the meat on the grill with a fork. The fire flared up and her eyes winced in the smoke. She poked at the meat all the harder.

'I'm truly sorry,' I said. 'But you're right about my being singleminded. There's only one girl I'm interested in.'

I wanted to put my arms around her waist and take her out of the smoke, hold her against me and feel her curly hair under my hands.

'You just can't leave a woman alone in the night, Dave.'

I looked away from her face.

'I woke up and you were gone and I thought maybe those defective people had come back. I drove up and down the beach looking for you until dawn,' she said.

'I didn't know that.'

'How could you, if you were with some sideshow people?'

'Annie, I'd like another chance with you. I can't make you many promises, except I won't deliberately hurt you again. That's probably not very adequate, but it's all I have.'

She turned her face away from me, and I saw her brush her eye with the back of her wrist.

'Another night. There's someone coming over now,' she said.

'All right.'

'Are those people out there worth all this?'

'They'll find me if I don't find them. You can bet on it.'

'My great-grandparents were part of the Underground Railway. Quantrill's Raiders tore down their sod houses and burned their cornfields. Long after Quantrill and Bloody Bill Anderson and Jesse James were dead, they were raising children and Russian wheat in a free state.

'But somebody canceled Quantrill and Company's action first, namely, federal cavalry.'

I smiled at her, but her face suddenly looked wan in the electric light that was hung in the chinaberry tree. I didn't care about propriety or restraint or the fact that her friend would arrive any minute now; I set the Cold Duck and the pralines on the glass tabletop and put my arms around her and kissed her curly hair. But she didn't respond. Her shoulders were stiff, her eyes turned down, her arms angular and dead.

'Call me tomorrow,' she whispered.

'Sure.'

'I want you to.'

'I will. I promise.'

'Things just aren't right with me tonight. I'll be all right tomorrow.'

'I'll leave the pralines. I'll call early. Maybe we'll have breakfast at the Café du Monde.'

'That sounds nice,' she said. But her eyes were veiled, and I couldn't read them. Under all her fascination with weirdness, she had the sensitive heart of a small-town Midwestern girl.

On my way down the front walk I passed a young man who looked like a graduate student at Tulane. He wore cream-colored slacks, a pale blue shirt, and a striped tie, and his smile was good-natured and his face very handsome. I asked him if he was having dinner with Annie Ballard.

'Why, yes,' he said, and smiled again.

'Here, take this,' I said, and handed him the bottle of Cold Duck. 'It's on the fuzz tonight.'

It was an *old* thing to do, and a moment later I felt foolish and rude. Then I remembered an axiom taught me in Vietnam by a line officer who used to cut through Gordian knots with a sentence: Fuck it. Who wants to be a good loser?

That night as I sat in the morgue of the *Times-Picayune* and turned the yellowed pages of old newspapers or flipped the strips of microfilm up on the viewing screen, I reflected upon the ambiguous importance of the past in our lives. In order to free ourselves from it, I thought, we treat it as a decaying memory. At the same time, it's the only measure of identity we have. There is no mystery to the self; we are what we do and where we have been. So we have to resurrect the past constantly, erect monuments to it, and keep it alive in order to remember who we are.

For some, even our darkest past moments are preferable somehow to those few interludes of peace and sunshine in the world. Why? God only knows. I thought about the followers of Pancho Villa who found his assassination and the end of his violent era so unacceptable that they dug up his corpse, sawed the head from the trunk, sank it in a huge glass jar of white rum, and brought it in a Model T Ford to the Van Horn Mountains outside of El Paso, where they entombed it under a pile of orange rocks. At night for years thereafter, they would remove the rocks and drink mescal and smoke marijuana in the hot wind and talk to his bloated, leering face floating against the glass.

But I was looking at another kind of dark history now. The retired two-star general had not been hard to find. His full name was Jerome Gaylan Abshire, and he lived right here in New Orleans, in the Garden District off St. Charles Avenue. He was a West Point graduate, and he'd had a distinguished combat record in World War II and Korea. A 1966 color photograph showed him eating out of a GI mess kit with his men in an LZ cut out of the elephant grass in the central highlands of Vietnam. He wore an automatic pistol in a shoulder holster over his bare, leathery chest; his face was deeply tanned, his eyebrows and hair very white, his eyes the intense blue of a butane flame. A creative journalist had called him 'The Happy Warrior' in the cutline.

But I ran across another Jerome Gaylan Abshire in the newspaper files, this one a junior, a U.S. Army lieutenant, obviously his son. His name first appeared in a 1967 story when he was listed as missing in action; then I found a second clipping dated November 1, 1969, that described how two American prisoners held by the Vietcong in an area called Pinkville had been tied to posts with their heads inserted in wooden cages filled with rats. The article said one of these soldiers may have been Lieutenant Jerome Abshire of New Orleans.

The word 'Pinkville' leaped off the page like a sin not confessed and deliberately forgotten. It was the name that GIs called the area around My Lai.

Then, as though the newspaper librarian had

made the same associations as I, he or she had attached a crossreferenced Xerox copy of an article about some testimony at the court-martial of Lieutenant William Calley, when he was tried for ordering the My Lai massacre. One of the grunts who had taken the stand said in a parenthetical aside that some captured Vietcong had told him that two American prisoners had helped them string mines through a rice field, the same field in which his company had been blown apart.

I was tired. My system was beginning to crave alcohol again, and the place names, the dates, a photograph of villagers executed on a trail, filled me with a sadness and despair that made me close the file, flick off the viewing screen, walk to the window, and stare out into the darkness for a full minute, hoping that no one in the room saw my eyes.

I never saw an American atrocity, at least not a deliberate one, so I did not have those kinds of memories from the war. Instead, if there was one experience that encapsulated my year in Vietnam, it was a strange incident involving two men in my platoon and a drowning water buffalo.

They were almost all Southerners, from textile and cannery and cotton-gin towns where young people seldom expected more than Saturday nights at the drive-in movie with others like themselves who would wear their high school jackets years after their graduation. We had walked twenty miles out of Indian country into a secured area by a tree-lined, milky brown river, and the men had dropped their packs and rifles and undressed, and were splashing around in the shallows like boys. The late-afternoon sun was warm through the trees and dappled the ground with shadow. I hadn't slept in a day and a half, and I lay down in the cool, short grass under a banyan tree, put my arm across my eyes, and in seconds I was asleep.

I awoke a half hour later to giggling and laughter and the drowsy smell of marijuana. Somebody had scored some Cambodian red, and the whole platoon was getting loaded. I got up stiffly from under the tree, walked down the bank, and realized they were all being entertained by a scene taking place in the middle of the river. A water buffalo had wandered out into the hard current, had become stuck in the silt on the bottom, and was now floundering and barely able to keep its nostrils above the surface. Its eyes were wide with terror, its horns webbed with debris from the river. The owner of the buffalo, who wore a French legionnaire's flop hat on his pointed head and who was so thin and bony that he looked like he was made of coat hangers, ran up and down the bank, waving his arms and shouting at us in Vietnamese and scraps of French.

Two cousins from Conroe, Texas, had waded in after the buffalo with a lariat they had fashioned from a rope they had taken out of the back of a Marine Corps six-by. Their brown backs were wet and ridged with muscle and vertebrae, and they were grinning and laughing and flinging out their lariat with all the stoned confidence of nineteen-year-old cowboys.

'There's dropoffs out there,' I said.

'Watch this, Lieutenant,' one of them called

back. 'We'll slide this honker out slicker than a hog's pecker.'

Then suddenly out of the brown current I saw the gnarled, black roots of a floating tree break through the surface and reach into the air like an enormous claw.

It hit them broadside with such force that their faces went white. Their mouths gasped open, then spat water. They tried to push away from the roiling, yellow foam around the tree and the roots that spiked their eyes and twisted their faces into contortions. The tree spun around in the current, shining with mud, caught new momentum, and pressed them under. We waited for them to surface on the other side, to pop up in a calm place, rattling water and light from their hair, but we never saw them again.

We probed the river with poles and dragged it with a grappling hook for three hours. Instead of our own people, we dredged up belts of French machine-gun ammunition, a box of unexploded Japanese potato mashers that leaked rust and green slime on the bank, American soda-pop cans, and a cargo net filled with Vietcong dead that must have been dropped by one of our helicopters. When the hook pulled the net tautly from the water's surface, we saw arms and heads draped through the webbing like those of prisoners long since tired of their eternal sentence.

I wrote letters to the families of the two boys in Conroe, Texas. I said they had given their lives in trying to help others. Their lives had not been *taken*; they were *given*. I did not say I regretted there were no medals for innocence and the trusting courage it took to keep being a Texas country boy in a land that seemed created for jaded and transient colonials.

An hour later I was in a wonderful old bar on Magazine Street, which separated the Garden District from a huge black residential area of paintless, wooden nineteenth-century houses whose sagging galleries and dirt yards reminded me of the Negro quarters on the plantations in Iberia Parish. The bar, like many buildings along Magazine, had a wooden colonnade in front, big windows and screen doors, and inside was a long mahogany counter with a brass rail, overhead fans, walls filled with Hadacol and Dixie 45 and Dr. Nut signs, and Earl K. Long political posters, and a blackboard with the name of major-league teams and ball scores chalked all over it. The owner used to be a submarine pitcher for the Lafayette Bulls in the defunct class-C Evangeline League, and he had never been quite able to extricate himself from yesterday. He sold loose-string Virginia Extra tobacco and cigarettes out of cartons on the shelf, covered the pool table with oilcoth on Thursday nights and served free chicken gumbo as bar owners often did back in the bayou country, never called the cops to settle a beef, kept hard-boiled eggs in big pickle jars on the bar, and made hot *boudin* that would break your heart. It was always cool and softly lighted inside, and the jukebox was full of *zydeco* and Cajun records, and workingmen shot pool in the back under a red Jax sign and a tin-shaded swinging light.

Archie, the owner, picked up my empty *boudin* plate and wiped under it with a rag. He was a dark Cajun with a big round face and a small mouth. His arms were covered with black hair. I motioned with my shot glass for a refill.

'You know why they call them boilermakers, Dave?' he asked. 'Because they put pieces of foundry plate in your head, like broken metal teeth.'

'Sounds like bad stuff.'

'Then one day it chews its way through your brain.'

'Can I have another shot of Beam?'

'I don't like to argue against my own profits, but I hate to see you sit on the porch and listen to your liver rot.'

'Would it make you feel better if I told you I'm not enjoying it?'

'Ease up tonight. You can have a shithouse of misery any day you want.'

I looked away from his face. He was a friend and an honest man, and because I had no defense, I knew I was capable of insulting people, even an old friend, to save my situation.

'I got another problem, too. Your slip's showing,' he said.

'What?'

'Wearing a pistol as big as a cornbread pan on your hip gives anxiety to some people.'

'Here,' I said, unsnapping the holster from my belt. 'Stick it under the bar till I leave.'

'What the hell is wrong with you, Dave? Are you trying to take a big fall? Why invite more trouble in your life?'

'It came free of charge.'

'I'm talking about tonight. They took your badge. That means you can't walk around like Wyatt Earp.'

'Do you know anything about a retired general named Jerome Abshire over on Prytania?'

'A little bit. His kid used to come in here.'

'Is he a right-wing crazy?'

'No, I don't think so. I always heard he was a kind of classy guy. His kid was a hell of a fine boy, though. He used to come in here with his baseball team when he went to Tulane. He was a big, blond boy with a pitching arm like a whip. He was always arm-wrestling and tussling and having fun. It was a shame he disappeared over there in Vietnam.'

'Does anybody know what happened to him?'

'Just a lot of stories. He was captured, he was missing, the Vietcong executed him or something. My boy was over there, but he came back home all right. I tell you the truth, Dave, if I'd lost him, I'd be afraid what I'd do.'

'I've got to cruise. We'll see you around, Archie.'

'I hope so. Don't crowd the plate when you don't have to, podna.'

I drove into the Garden District. The neighborhood was filled with homes that had been built during the 1850s. They were pillared and scrolled, marked with widow's walks and latticework, wide porches and second-story verandas, with brick courtyards and gazebos on the lawns. The streets were lined with oaks and the yards themselves seemed to explode with every type of Southern flower and tree: blooming myrtle, azalea, bamboo, umbrella and banana tree, elephant ears, hibiscus, tangles of red and yellow roses. I could smell barbecue fires and hear people diving in swimming pools. It was a neighborhood of historical security and endless summer parties that flowed from one thick, clipped lawn onto the next.

Jerome Gaylan Abshire's home was no exception. The brick walk was lighted by burning candles placed inside paper bags in the flower beds, and through the tall windows beyond the front porch I could see the guests crowded in a large living room lighted by chandeliers. The loud conversation reached all the way to the street. A band was playing on the lawn somewhere in the back.

Why not? I thought. I had on a coat and tie. Archie was right. Why crowd the plate when it was just as easy to throw the bat at the pitcher's head?

I parked the car up the street and walked back to the party. The sidewalk was buckled and peaked by the enormous roots that grew under the concrete. I buttoned my coat so my .45 wasn't apparent, combed my hair, flattened my tie with the palm of my hand, and walked up the brick entrance with my eyes fixed steadily on the face of the man checking invitations at the door.

He probably worked for a security service and was not accustomed to handling anybody more serious than college party-crashers.

'I don't have an invitation. I'm the New Orleans heat,' I said.

'May I see your identification?'

'Here's a quarter. Call the First District and tell them Lieutenant Dave Robicheaux is here.'

'I think you're drunk, sir.'

I brushed past him, went to the bar, and picked up a glass of champagne off a tray. The rooms were furnished with French antiques, gold and silver grandfather clocks, deep purple divans with scrolled walnut frames, oil portraits of a Southern military family that went back to the War of 1812. The blond hardwood floors were waxed to a shine that looked like clear plastic. Every tabletop, brass candelabra, ashtray, glass light chimney, and polished strip of seamed woodwork gleamed as though it had been rubbed incessantly with soft rags.

The people in the room were an older crowd, undoubtedly wealthy, confident in themselves and their friends and the world of manners and success in which they lived. The women had bluing in their hair and wore glittering evening dresses, and their throats and wrists dripped with jewelry. In their white tuxedo coats, the men gave you the impression that age was no more a physical problem in their lives than the remote struggles of the poor. It was obvious that I didn't belong there, but they were too polite to look directly at me.

But the security man at the door was talking with two others who looked like rent-a-cops, and all three of them were staring at me. I put down my empty champagne glass, picked up another, and walked out the French doors onto the back patio, where a half-dozen black cooks in white jackets were making mint juleps and barbecuing a pig impaled on a roasting spit. The wind rustled through the oaks, the banana trees, the bamboo border of the lawn, and ruffled the unlit water in the swimming pool that was as dark as burgundy wine. One of the elderly black cooks fanned the barbecue smoke away from his face with his hand.

'Where's the general gone to?' I asked.

'He having his julep in the library with the other gentlemens,' he said.

'I don't want to go back through that big crowd. Is there another way I can get to the library?'

'Yes suh. Go back through the kitchen. The girl tell you where it's at.' I walked across the clipped lawn, went through a huge Colonial-style kitchen with brick in the walls, where three black maids were making hors d'oeuvres, and came out in a hallway. I could see the library door partly open and two men with highball glasses in their hands talking to somebody who sat in a chair with his legs crossed. I recognized one of the standing men immediately. I pushed the door, sipped out of my champagne glass, and smiled at the three of them.

The general had gained weight since the newspaper photograph was taken, but his skin was still deeply tanned and glowing with health, the white hair was cut GI, and his acetylene-blue eyes looked at you with the unflinching clarity of a man who was never inhibited by complexity or moral doubt.

'How are you doing, General?' I said. 'It's amazing who might drop in on a cocktail party these days. I'm speaking about myself, of course. But what are you doing with a character like Whiplash Wineburger? Most people call the Orkin Company if they see this guy anywhere near their neighborhoods.'

'I'll take care of it,' Wineburger said, and moved his hand to the table phone.

'It's all right,' the general said.

'I don't know about that,' I said. 'I think some of your cadre are starting to unravel. I've got a couple of Polaroids of Bobby Joe Starkweather lying out behind his fish camp. You can have them for postcards.'

'You'll be treated as a guest in my home, even though you came here uninvited. You can go back to the bar, or you can leave.'

'I'm comfortable here.'

'You've had too much to drink, or perhaps you're simply obsessive,' he said. 'But there's no point in your being here.'

'You should have stuck with regular army, General. These guys working for you wouldn't even measure up to Mafia standards. Wineburger here is a jewel. One time a naïve cop down at the First District asked him to defend some indigent Haitians, and he said, "I'm full up on food stamps." It's the amateurs that kill the IPs.'

'What do you know about IPs?'

'I was in Vietnam, too, except my outfit went out of its way to protect innocent people. I don't think you can say the same.'

'How dare you!' he said.

'Cut the gentlemanly rancor. You've got Sam Fitzpatrick's blood painted all over you, and I'm going to nail you for it.'

'Ignore him. He's a lush,' Wineburger said.

'I'll give you something else to work on, too,' I said. 'I visited the father of that nineteen-year-old girl that Segura's people murdered. I wonder if you'd like to confront him and explain why she had to lose her life over some elephant game you and your cretins are playing.'

'Get out.'

'You lost a son in Vietnam. I think if he were alive he'd consider you a disgrace.'

'You leave my home. Don't you ever enter it again.'

'You'll get no rest from me, General. I'm going to be the worst thing in your life.'

'No, you won't, Robicheaux,' Wineburger said. 'You're a motormouth and you smell bad. You're just a jitterbird that everybody is bored with.'

'Whiplash, how do you think you got in here? Because you're a brilliant attorney? Most of these people don't like Jews. They're paying for your ass right now, but when they don't need you anymore, you might end up like Bobby Joe or Julio. Think about it. If you were the general, would you keep a lowlife like yourself around?'

'Turn around. Some of your colleagues want to talk with you,' Wineburger said.

Two uniformed street cops stood behind me. They were young, and they had their hats off and were uncomfortable at their situation. One of them tried to smile at me.

'Bad night, huh, Lieutenant?' he said.

'Don't worry about it,' I said. 'I'm wearing my rock-'n'-roll cassette, though. Just unbutton my coat and pull it out.'

His hand brushed across my stomach, almost like a caress, and eased the .45 out of my belt holster.

'Walk this way with us. We'll go out the side door,' he said. 'But we'll have to cuff you in the car.'

'It's all right,' I said.

'Hey, Robicheaux, call that colored bondsman on Rampart. He gives credit,' Wineburger said.

I glanced back at the general, whose tanned brow was webbed with wrinkles as he stared intensely into space.

They booked me into the drunk tank downtown. I

woke up with the first gray light on an iron bunk whose gray paint was covered with scratched and rusted names and obscenities. I sat up slowly, holding the bunk on each side of me, and smelled the rancid odor of stale sweat, cigarette smoke, alcohol, urine, vomit, and the seatless and caked toilet in the corner. The floor and all the bunks, which were suspended from wall chains, were filled with snoring drunks, demented street people, barroom brawlers still flecked with blood, a few genuine badasses, and anxiety-ridden, middle-class DUIs who later would expect to be treated with the courtesy due good Kiwanians.

I walked in my socks to the toilet and leaned over it. Names had been burned into the yellow paint of the ceiling with cigarette lighters. My eyes watered from the reek of the toilet, and my hangover had already started to tighten the veins in my head like a hatband. Ten minutes later a guard and a trusty in white fatigues opened the barred door and wheeled in a stainless-steel food cart loaded with powdered scrambled eggs, grits, and black coffee that tasted like iodine.

'Hors d'oeuvres time, gentlemen,' the guard said. 'Our accommodations are humble, but our hearts are warm. If you're planning to stay for lunch today, we're having spaghetti and meatballs. Please do not ask for doggy bags. Also, even though it's a temptation, don't try to take the food home in your pockets.'

'Who the fuck is this guy?' asked a soldier sitting on the floor. His tie hung loose around his neck, and the buttons were torn off his shirt.

'He's a pretty good guy,' I said.

'Some place for a fucking comedian,' he said, and flipped his cigarette butt off the wall above the toilet.

I waited until the trusty had passed out the paper plates of eggs and grits and he and the guard had gone back out the door, then I went to the bars and clicked my ring against the metal to get the guard's attention. He looked at me without expression, blinking his eyes to hide either recognition or his embarrassment.

'Is arraignment at eight?' I asked.

'They'll put you on the wrist-chain then. I don't know what time they'll get to you.' He almost said 'Lieutenant,' but he clamped his lips tightly.

'Who's on the bench this morning?'

'Judge Flowers.'

'Oh boy.'

'You want a lawyer with you?'

'No, not just yet. Thanks, anyway, Phil.'

'You bet. Hang tough. It's going to be all right. Everybody's got a right to a hard night sometimes.'

An old man with a wild, tobacco-stained beard sat down beside me on the iron bunk. He wore plastic cowboy boots, jeans that fit him like balloons, and a denim shirt cut off at the armpits.

'You ain't gonna eat your food?' he said.

'No. Go ahead.'

'Thanks,' he said, and began putting the dry eggs in his mouth with a plastic spoon. 'The spiders starting to crawl around in your head?'

'Yep.'

'Look down in my boot,' he said. 'The hack missed it when they shook me down. Take a snort. It'll swat them spiders right back into their nest.'

I looked down at the pint bottle of whiskey inside his boot. I breathed deeply and ran my tongue over my cracked lips. My own breath was stronger than the smell of the drunk tank. It wouldn't be long before I would start sweating and shaking, maybe even going into the dry heaves. I wondered what I would look like in front of Judge Flowers, a notorious morning-court jurist who could put the fear of God into a drunk with his gavel.

'I'll pass right now, but I appreciate it, partner,' I said.

'Suit yourself. Don't let them shake you up, though, son. I been up in front of this court so many times they don't even mess with me. The judge gives me thirty days and tells me to get out. That ain't nothing. We got them by the short hairs.'

A half hour later, Sergeant Motley stood at the tank door with the guard. He smoked a cigar and looked on quietly while the guard turned the key in the lock. He wore his shirt lapels pressed back so the hair on his black barrel of a chest stuck out like wire.

'Come with us, Robicheaux,' he said.

'Zoo visitors aren't allowed in until this afternoon,' I said.

'Just come along,' he said.

I walked between him and the guard to the far end of the jail corridor. A trusty was damp-mopping the floor, and our shoes left wet imprints where he had cleaned. Sunlight came through the windows high up on the corridor wall, and I could hear traffic out on the street. The guard turned the lock on an individual cell. Motley's weight made him breathe as though he had emphysema.

'I got you transferred to a holding cell,' he said.

'What for?'

'You want somebody in that tank to make you?'

I stepped inside the cell, and the guard locked me in. Motley remained at the door, his cannonball head beaded with perspiration from the heat outside.

'What are you up to?' I asked.

'I've been in your shoes. I think they're putting a RotoRooter up your hole, and all you've got going for you is your own balls. That's okay, but after a while they get ground down to the size of marbles.'

'I have a hard time buying this.'

'Who asked you to? We never got along. But I'll tell you a story, Robicheaux. Everybody thinks I let those seven guys die in that elevator to save my own buns. I was responsible, all right, but not because I was afraid. I didn't have the key to the chain. I didn't have the fucking key. I climbed up out of the shaft to find somebody with a master. When we pried the doors open, they looked like smoked oysters in there. Whether you believe me or not, that's some hard shit to live with.'

'Why don't you tell that to somebody?'

'You know why I didn't have the key? I got a freebie that morning from one of Julio Segura's broads and she rolled me. The key was in my billfold.'

'You tried to get them out, Motley.'

'Tell that to everybody in the courthouse and the First District. Tell it to Purcel. He's always got clever things to say to a black man.'

'What's he been doing?'

'I don't like those guys in Internal Affairs any more than you do. In my opinion, Purcel is operating in their area. I don't drop the dime on other cops, not even racists, so I don't comment on Purcel.'

'He's not a racist.'

'Wake up, Robicheaux. You got to get hit in the face with it? The guy's got a hard-on all the time. Quit the Little Orphan Annie routine.'

'You're determined to make people love you, aren't you?'

'Read it like you want. I hope you get out of this crap. I don't think you will.'

'You're a breath of fresh air, buddy.'

'They stiffed you on the charge. I'd get out of town if I were you. I think they're going to put you away.'

I touched the side of my face to the bar and looked at him silently. I could feel the pulse working fearfully in my throat.

'They charged you with carrying a concealed firearm,' he said, and looked back at me with his knowing, hard brown eyes. It was a lowball morning. I went to court on a chain with four other drunks, a street dealer, a psychotic exhibitionist, and a black kid who had murdered a filling-station attendant for sixty-five dollars. Judge Flowers was what we called at AA a white-knuckler. He had gotten off the booze on his own, but he'd stayed dry only by redirecting his intense inner misery into the lives of others, particularly those who stood before him blowing alcohol in his face. He set my bond on the concealed firearm charge at ten thousand dollars.

I didn't even have the thousand I would need to pay the bondsman's ten-percent fee. I sat on the bunk of the holding cell and stared at the scatological words scratched all over the opposite wall. It was the lowest morning of my life, except perhaps for the day my wife left me for the Houston oilman. We had gone to an evening lawn party out by the lake, and he had been there and did not even make a pretense about the affair they were having. He touched shoulders with her at the drink table, brushed his palm across the down on top of her arm, smiled good-naturedly at me with his rugged good looks, as though we enjoyed an intelligent understanding of our situation. Then a lesion snapped open somewhere behind my eyes; I felt color rise into my vision, the way a glass might fill with red water, then a woman screamed and I felt men's arms lifting me up from the lawn, pulling me away from his stunned, terrified face.

In the morning I found her note on the table under the big umbrella where we ate breakfast while the sun rose across Lake Pontchartrain.

> Dear Dave,
>
> I don't know what it is you're looking for, but three years of marriage to you have convinced me I don't want to be there when you find it. Sorry about that. As your pitcher-bartender friend says, Keep it high and hard, podjo.
>
> Nicole.

'What are you doing with your clothes off?' the guard asked through the bars of the holding cell.

'It's hot.'

'There's people that walk through here.'

'Don't let them.'

'Jesus Christ, Dave, get your act together.'

'I got it solidly together. I'm very copacetic at the moment.' I opened and closed my palms. I watched the way the veins in my forearms filled with blood.

'Unless you bond out, I got to move you. You got to go into the main population unless you want lockdown.'

'Do what you need to do, Phil.'

'I can't put you in lockdown if you don't request it. Dave, there's some real badasses upstairs.'

I fingered the *pungi*-stick scar on my stomach. Somebody was shouting hysterically in a cell down the corridor, then a cop's baton rang on the bars.

'I'm going to get the doctor. You're going into lockdown whether you like it or not,' he said.

I heard him walk away. My head felt as if piano wire were twisted around it. I closed my eyes and saw balloons of orange flame erupt out of a rain forest, GIs locked up to their knees in a muddy shimmering rice field while the shards of Claymores sang through the air with the edges of boiler plate, the souls of children rising like gunsmoke from the ditch where they lay, Sam Fitzpatrick's boyish face lighted in the purgatorial fire of a holy card. The sweat leaked out from under my palms and ran down my naked thighs.

At three o'clock that afternoon, another guard walked down the corridor of the isolation unit, called 'Queen's Row,' where I was in lockdown with the snitches, pyschotics, and roaring homosexuals. The door of my small cell was made of metal grillwork, with a slit and an iron apron for the trusty to pass in the food tray. The guard was having trouble with the key in the lock, and the light behind him made his body seem to jerk and disconnect itself through the squares in the door.

'Pack it up. You're going all the way,' he said.

'What happened?'

'Somebody went bail for you. Strip your sheets and throw them into the corridor. Pick up that plastic spoon off the floor and drop your soap in the toilet.'

'What?'

'You still drunk or something? Clean out your cell if you want to leave here today.'

We walked down the corridor to the hydraulically operated double-barred doors that gave onto the booking room, where two black women were being fingerprinted. I signed at the possessions desk for the large brown envelope tied with string that contained my wallet, car keys, pocket knife, and belt.

'Happy motoring,' the trusty clerk said.

Out in the visitors' area I saw Annie sitting on a wooden bench with her hands pinched together in her lap. She wore blue tennis shoes, Clorox-faded jeans, and a print shirt covered with purple flowers. The tables in the rooms were filled with inmates and their families who had come to visit them, and each group tried to isolate themselves in their intimate moment by bending their heads forward, never focusing their eyes beyond their own table, holding one another's forearms tightly in their hands. Annie tried to smile at me, but I saw the nervousness in her face.

'Are you all right?' she asked.

'Sure.'

'My car's right at the curb. We can go now.'

'Sure, let's get out of here.'

'Dave, what's wrong?'

'The bastards took my piece. I ought to get a receipt for it.'

'Are you crazy?' she whispered.

'Forget it. Let's go.'

We went through the glass doors onto the street, and the afternoon heat hit me like somebody opening a furnace door next to my skin. We got into her car and she started the engine, then looked across at me with a cloud in her face. My arm jerked when it touched the burning metal on the window.

'Dave, are you okay? Your face is white,' she said.

'I'm running on some weird fluids. Just consider the source and don't take everything I say to heart today. How did you know I was in jail?'

'Your partner, what's his name, Clete, called. He said something strange, but he told me to tell it to you just like he said it – "You still own yourself, Streak. That's a big victory. Disconnect from this dogshit while there's time." What's he talking about?'

'It means part of him is still intact. I'm not sure if the same is true of me. I think I felt all the stitches pop today.'

She steered into the traffic. The yellow haze, the heat off the concrete, the hot leather against my back, the acrid gasoline fumes around me, filled my head with a sensation that was like breathing over a tar-roofer's pot on a summer day.

'I don't know much about alcohol and drinking problems, Dave. Do you want to stop for a beer? I don't mind. Isn't it better to taper off sometimes?'

She had made it very easy, and at that moment I

think I would have cut my fingers off one at a time with tin snips for a frosted quart of Jax beer.

'I'd just appreciate it right now if you'd drive me to my houseboat. Did you have to put up a thousand for the bondsman?' I said.

'Yes.'

'I'll make it good tomorrow. I'm suspended from the credit union, but I'm going to take a loan out on the boat.'

'I'm not thinking about that. Last night you tried to make amends, and I sent you away.'

'You had someone coming for dinner.'

'He was just a friend from the music school. He would have understood.'

'Let me explain something. My getting thrown in jail doesn't have anything to do with you. I had four years of sobriety, and I blew it in.'

'You can stop again.'

I didn't answer. We were on Elysian Fields Avenue, headed out toward the lake. My seersucker suit was rumpled and stained with tobacco juice from the jail, and the skin of my face felt grimy and unshaven under my hand.

'Pull in by that eating place, will you?' I said.

She parked next to a café that had an open-air counter and tables under shade trees where people ate poor-boy sandwiches and bleeding slices of watermelon. I ordered two Dr. Peppers in paper cups packed with crushed ice and asked the waiter to add a handful of candied cherries and cut limes. I sat in the car and drank out of the cup with both hands, and the slide of ice and bruised cherries and syrupy soda ached wonderfully all the way down my throat and into my stomach.

'When I was a kid in New Iberia, we had a drink called Dr. Nut. It tasted just like this,' I said. 'My father always bought my brother and me a Dr. Nut when we went to town. That was a big treat back then.'

'How do you think of the past, Dave?' she asked. Her curly hair blew in the wind through the window while she drove.

'What do you mean?'

'What feelings do you have when you remember your father?'

'I think of him with fondness.'

'That's right, you do, even though your family was poor and sometimes your father wasn't there when you needed him. You didn't take any anger toward him into your adult life. You forgave him and you remember what was best about him. Why not do the same for yourself.'

'It's not that simple with some people's metabolisms.'

'Today is Saturday, and it's Saturday all day long, and I don't care about what happened yesterday, at least not about the bad things. I like being with you and remembering good things and knowing it's going to get better all the time. Don't they teach something like that at AA?'

'That's pretty close.'

'Will you take me to the horse races tonight?'

I touched the damp, curly hair at the nape of her neck and brushed the smoothness of her cheek with my fingers. She smiled at me with her eyes and patted me on the thigh, and I felt a weakness drain through my body like water and then settle and swell in my loins.

When we got to Lake Pontchartrain it was like walking out from under a layer of steam into a slap of cool, salt-smelling air. Pelicans dove for fish out of the blue sky, plummeting downward with their wings cocked behind their heads as though they had been dropped from a bomb rack, exploding in the smoky green water and rising suddenly with silvery fish flipping helplessly in their beaks. Far out on the horizon the water was capping in the sunlight, and a long, gleaming white yacht with red sails was dipping into the troughs and sending geysers of foam bursting into the air.

I showered and shaved in my tin stall and felt the smell of the jail, its physical touch was like an obscene hand, go out of my body. I washed carefully around the stitches in my scalp, then I pulled off the old dressing on my shoulder and arm, where the chips of glass had been embedded, and let the water run warmly on the crusted skin. Annie was cooking bass fillets and spinach with hard-boiled eggs on my small stove, and for the first time that day I felt hunger. I dried off, sat on the side of the bed with the towel wrapped around my waist, and opened the plastic first-aid box in which I kept the bandages and ointment to dress my shoulder and arm. I could have done it myself. Pride and a larger measure of self-respect actually required it. I looked at the closed curtain and heard Annie turn the pots down on the stove.

'Annie, I need you to help me,' I said.

She slid back the curtain on the door.

'I have a little trouble getting these bandages into place,' I said.

She sat beside me, wiped ointment on my cuts

with a piece of cotton, snipped adhesive tape into strips with the scissors, and taped down two big, folded squares of gauze on top of the ointment. Then she rubbed her hands over my skin, down my shoulders and back, across my chest, her eyes looking over my body without embarrassment, as though she were discovering me for the first time. I leaned her back on the bed and kissed her mouth, her neck, unbuttoned her flowerprint blouse and placed my head against the red birthmark on her breast. I felt her body stretch out against mine, felt the confidence, the surrender that a woman gives in that moment when she no longer hides her hunger and instead blesses you with a caress that is always unexpected and heart-rushing and humbling in its generosity.

This time I wanted to give her more than she gave me, but I wasn't able. In seconds I was lost inside her, her hands tight against my back, her legs wrapped in mine in almost a maternal way, and when I tried to tense and stop because it was too soon, she held my face close to hers, kissed my cheek, ran her fingers through the back of my hair, saying, 'It's all right, Dave. Go ahead. It's all right.' Then I felt all the anger, the fear, and the heat of the last two days rise inside me like a dark bubble from a well, pause in its own gathered energy and momentum, and burst away into light, into the joy of her thighs, the squeeze of her arms, the blue tenderness of her eyes.

That night at the track, while heat lightning danced in the western sky, we strolled among the flower gardens by the paddock, watched the hot-walkers cool out the thoroughbreds that had already run, smelled the wonderful odors of freshly raked and dampened sod and horse sweat and manure and oats in the stables, and looked with genuine wonder and admiration at the rippling sheen of the roans and black three-year-olds walking onto the track under a halo of electric arc lights.

We cashed the daily double, a perfecta, two win, and three place tickets. The palm trees were purple against the flickering sky; the lake in the center-ground caught the stars and the moon, and when the surface shuddered in a gust of wind off the Gulf, the water streaked with quicksilver; I could smell oak trees and moss and night-blooming flowers. Gamblers and lovers pay big dues and enjoy limited consolations. But sometimes they are enough.

9

The sky was pink over the lake at dawn the next day, and I put on my running shoes and tennis shorts and ran five miles along the lakefront with the wind cool in my face and the sun warm on my bare back. I could feel the sweat glaze and dry on my skin in the wind, and the muscles in my chest and legs seemed to have a resiliency and tension and life in them that I hadn't felt in weeks. Seagulls drifted on the air currents above the water's edge, their wings gilded in the sunlight, then they would dip quickly down toward the sand and peck small shellfish from the receding foam. I waved at families in their cars on the way to church, drank orange juice at a child's street stand under a palm tree, and pounded down the asphalt with a fresh energy, my chest and head charged with blood, my heart strong, the summer morning part of an eternal song.

I could have run five more miles when I got back to the houseboat, but my phone was ringing. I sat on the edge of a chair and wiped my sweating face with a towel while I answered it.

'Why don't you trust your own family a little bit?' my brother Jimmie asked.

'What are you talking about?'

'I understand you bopped into an interesting scene the other night. Very stylish. There's nothing like crashing a Garden District party with a .45 on your hip.'

'It had been a dull night.'

'Why didn't you call me? I could have bonded you out in fifteen minutes. I might even have had a little influence on that concealed-weapons charge.'

'This is one you can't oil.'

'The point is, I don't like my brother being taken apart by some pencil-pushers.'

'You'll be the first to know the next time I'm in the bag.'

'Can you get somebody over there that speaks Spanish in the next half hour?'

'What for?'

'I told Didi Gee I'd get him in the Knights of Columbus. He likes me. Who else would eat lunch with a character like that except at gunpoint?'

'What are you doing, Jimmie?'

'It's already done. Presents come in strange packages. Don't question the fates.'

'Anything Didi Gee does has ooze and slime all over it.'

'He never said he was perfect. Stay cool, bro,' he said, and hung up.

I called a Cuban horse trainer I knew at the Fairgrounds and asked him to come to the houseboat. He arrived there ten minutes before a Cadillac limousine with tinted windows pulled up on the dead-end street by the sand dune and palm trees where my boat was moored, and two of Didi Gee's hoods, dressed in slacks, loafers, and shades, with flowered shirts hanging over their belts, got out and opened the back door with the electric motions of chauffeurs who might have been delivering a presidential envoy. Instead, an obviously terrified man sat in the gloom of the backseat with a third hoodlum next to him. He stepped out into the sunlight, swallowing, his face white, his pomade-slicked, kinky red hair and grease-pencil mustache like a parody of a 1930s leading man's. He held one palm around the fingers of his other hand.

'This guy asked us for a ride. Begged us to bring him here,' the driver said. 'We can't shut him up, though. All he wants to do is talk.'

'But give him something for his breath. It smells like sewer gas. The guy must eat dog turds for breakfast,' the other hood said.

'Hey, serious, he's got an interesting story,' the driver said. 'If somehow he don't remember it, tie a shirt on your TV antenna. I got to pick up a loaf of bread at the corner store a little later. We can help him fill in the empty spaces. We're just out for the morning air, anyway.'

I couldn't see either one of them well behind their shades, and Didi Gee's hired help tended to run of a kind – slender young Sicilians and Neapolitans who would blow out your lights as easily as they would flip away a cigarette – but I thought I'd seen the driver in a lineup two years ago after we'd prized parts of a bookie out of his own kitchen garbage compactor.

They drove off in their Cadillac, the white sun bouncing off the black-tinted glass in the rear.

'Andres, I wouldn't hang round with that bunch if I were you,' I said.

★

But you still can't accept gratuities when they're given to you on other people's terms, particularly when they came from somebody like Didi Gee. Besides, the fingers of the Nicaraguan's left hand were wrapped in tape, and I had an idea where they had been earlier. He sat at my kitchen table, rigid, his brown eyes riveted fearfully on me as though the lids were stitched to his forehead. I put a tape recorder, a Polaroid camera, and a pint of white rum on the table.

'I don't have a tank full of piranha here, and I'll take you to the hospital if you want to go,' I said to him through my Cuban friend, whose name was Jaime.

He did not need a hospital; the injuries were not serious; but he would very much appreciate a glass of Bacardi, no ice, please.

I opened the morning newspaper, pulled my chair around next to him, held up the front section between us so the headline and date were visible, and told Jimmie to take our picture with the Polaroid. The Nicaraguan's breath was awful, as though there were something dead in his lungs. He drank the rum and wiped his lips, and the wispy gray scars around his mouth shone like pieces of waxed string.

'I want you to understand something,' I said. 'You're going to be a cooperative person, but not because of Didi Gee's hoods and the business with your fingers. Those guys will not get to you again, at least not because of me. If you want, you can file assault and kidnapping charges against them. I'll drive you to either the police station or the FBI.'

He watched me carefully as Jaime translated.

The thought of reporting Didi Gee's people to the authorities was evidently so absurd to him that his eyes didn't even register the proposal.

'But our photograph here is another matter,' I said. 'I'll make copies, many of them, and circulate them around town for those who might be interested. Maybe you have the trust of your friends, and this will be of little consequence to you. Maybe you are in command of your situation and this is childishness to you.'

His face clouded, and his eyes flicked meanly at me for a moment, the way an egg-sucking dog might if you pushed it inside a cage with a stick.

'*Qué quiere?*' his voice rasped.

It was a strange tale. It was self-serving, circumventive, filled in all probability with lies; but as with all brutal and cruel people, his most innocent admission and most defensive explanations were often more damning and loathsome in their connotations than the crimes others might accuse him of.

He had been a sergeant in Somoza's national guard for seven years, a door gunner on a helicopter, and he had flown in many battles against the communists in the jungles and the hills. It was a war of many civilian problems, because the communists hid among the villages and posed as workers in the rice fields and coffee plantations, and when the government helicopters flew too low they often took hostile fire from the ground, where the peasants denied there were any Sandinistas or weapons. What was one to do? Surely Americans who had been in Vietnam could understand. Those who fought wars could not always be selective.

The soldiers went forth in uniform, as men, in plain sight, while the communists threaded their way among the poor and fought with the methods of cowards and homosexuals. If I did not believe him, witness his eye, and he pulled down the skin on one side of his face and showed me the dead, puttylike muscle under the retina. Their gun-ship had come in low over a secured area, and down below he could see Indians stacking green hay in the field, then a rocket exploded through the armored floor of the helicopter, blew one man out the door, and left a steel needle quivering in Andres's eyeball. The American journalist who visited the army hospital in Managua did not seem interested in his story, nor did he take pictures of Andres as the journalists did of the communist dead and wounded. That was because the American press's greatest fear was to be called rightist by their own membership. Like the Maryknoll missionaries, they kept their own political vision intact by compromising the world in which others had to live.

If I was offended by his statement, I must remember that he did not choose exile in this country any more than he chose the ruination of his vocal cords and lungs.

'I heard his regular punch gave him some special gargle water,' I said.

'What?' Jaime said.

'He and some other guys gang-raped a girl before they executed her. Her sister poured muriatic acid in our friend's drink.'

'This is true?' Jaime asked. He was a small and delicate man with a sensitive face. He always wore a New York Yankees baseball cap and rolled his own cigarettes from illegal Cuban tobacco. His toylike face looked from me to the Nicaraguan.

'Our man from Managua is a big bullshitter, Jaime.'

The Nicaraguan must have understood me.

The story about the execution and the acid was a lie, he said, a fabrication of Philip Murphy and the *maricón* Starkweather. They took pleasure in the denigration of others because they were not real soldiers. Murphy was a morphine addict who made love to his own body with syringes. He pretended courage but was flaccid like a woman and could not bear pain. Did I really want to know how he, Andres, had his throat and lungs burnt out, how this terrible odor came to live in his chest like a dead serpent?

'I was blind in one eye, but I could not stop in the fight for my country,' Jaime translated for him. 'Just as they posed as priests and labor organizers, I went among them as a radical who hated the Somoza family. But a diseased *puta*, a worthless army slut, betrayed me because she thought I had given her the foulness of her organs. The Sandinistas cocked a pistol at my head and made me drink kerosene, then they lighted matches to my mouth. I suffered greatly at their hands, but my country has suffered more.'

'Where are Philip Murphy and the Israeli?' I asked.

'Who knows? Murphy lives in airports and pharmacies and finds people when he needs them. Jews stay with their own kind. Maybe Erik is with the rich Jew who owns the warehouse. They're a close and suspicious people.'

'What Jew? What warehouse?'

'The warehouse where the weapons to free Nicaragua are kept. But I don't know where it is, and I don't know their Jew. I'm only a soldier.'

His face was empty. His eyes had the muddy, stupid glaze of someone who believed that the honest expression of his ignorance was an acceptable explanation to those who had the power to make judgments.

'I'll give you an easier question, then,' I said. 'What did you all do to Sam Fitzpatrick before he died?'

Jaime translated, and the Nicaraguan's face became as flat as a shingle.

'Did you wire up his genitals?' I asked.

He looked out at the lake, his mouth pinched tight. He touched the rum glass with his fingers, then withdrew them.

'Murphy gave the orders, but I suspect you and Bobby Joe carried them out with spirit. Your experience stood you well.'

'I think this one has a big evil inside him,' Jaime said. 'I believe you should give him back to the people who brought him here.'

'I'm afraid they're not interested in him, Jaime. The man they work for just wanted to knock his competition around a little bit.'

His small face was perplexed under the brim of his baseball cap.

'We use them. They use us. It keeps everybody in business,' I said.

'If you don't need more of me, I'll go. Sunday is a bad day with this type of man. I've smelled that odor before. It comes out of a great cruelty.'

'Thank you for your help. I'll see you at the track.'

'Send him away, Dave. Even a policeman should not look into the darkness of this man's soul.'

I reflected upon Jaime's statement after he had gone. Yes, it was about time that the Nicaraguan became somebody else's charge, I thought.

I locked a handcuff on one of his wrists, walked him out to my rental car, and hooked the other end through the safetybelt anchorage on the back floor. I went back inside the houseboat, dropped the tape cassette in my pocket, and looked up the number of Nate Baxter, from Internal Affairs, in the phone book.

'I've got one of the guys that killed Fitzpatrick,' I said. 'I want you to meet me down at the office.'

'You've got who?'

'I've got the Nicaraguan in cuffs. I'm going to bring him in.'

'You're suspended, Robicheaux. You can't bring anybody in.'

'I can't book him, but I can sign a complaint.'

'Are you drinking?'

'Maybe I ought to drop by your house with him.'

'Listen, I can deal with you personally on any level you want. But you better not drag your bullshit into my life. If you haven't figured it out by this time, there's a lot of people that think you should be locked up in a detox unit. These are your friends I'm talking about. Other people think you're a candidate for a frontal lobotomy.'

'The last time you talked to me like this, I was in a hospital bed. Don't take too much for granted, Baxter.'

'You want to clarify that, make it a little more formal?'

I looked out at the sun beating on the water.

'I've got the man that helped kill a federal agent,' I said. 'He can clear me, and I'm bringing him in. If you want to ignore this phone call, that's your choice. I'm going to call Captain Guidry now, then I'm going down to the First District. Are you going to be there?'

He was silent.

'Baxter?'

'All right,' he said, and hung up.

Then I called Captain Guidry. His mother said he had gone to a band concert in the park. I poured out the rum remaining in the Nicaraguan's glass and started to wash the glass in the sink. Instead, I threw it as far as I could into the lake.

I could see the Nicaraguan's hot eyes looking at me in the rearview mirror. He had to bend forward because of the way his wrist was handcuffed to the floor, and his face was flushed and deaded with sweat in the seat.

'*Adónde vamos*?' he said.

I didn't answer him.

'*Adónde vamos*?'

I wondered which he feared most: Didi Gee's people, the city police, or Immigration. But, regardless, I wasn't going to help him about our destination.

'*Hijo de puta! Concha de tu madre*!' he said.

'Wherever it is, I don't think it's Kansas, Toto,' I said.

I parked in front of the First District headquarters

on Basin, cuffed both of the Nicaraguan's wrists behind him, and led him by the arm into the building.

'Is Nate Baxter back there?' I asked the sergeant at the information desk.

'Yeah, he's sitting in your office. What are you doing, Dave?'

'Give Purcel a call for me. Tell him I have some freight he ought to check out.'

'Dave, you're not supposed to be down here.'

'Just make the call. It's not a big deal.'

'Maybe you should make it yourself.'

I set the Nicaraguan down on a wooden bench and used the phone on the sergeant's desk to call Clete at home. I don't know what I had in mind, really. Maybe I was still pulling for him. Or maybe like a jilted lover I wanted to deliver a little more pain in a situation that was beyond bearing it.

'I can't come down there now. Maybe later. Lois is going apeshit on me,' he said. 'She took all the beer bottles out of the icebox and busted them all over the fucking driveway. On Sunday morning. The neighbors are watering their lawns and going to church while beer foam and glass are sliding down my drive into the street.'

'Sounds bad.'

'It's our ongoing soap opera. Drop around sometime and bring your own popcorn.'

'Clete?'

'What is it?'

'Get down here.'

I led the Nicaraguan through the traffic squad room, which was filled with uniformed cops doing paperwork, into my office, where Nate Baxter sat on the corner of my desk. His sports clothes and two-toned shoes and styled hair gave you the impression of a Nevada real-estate salesman who would sell you a house lot located on an abandoned atomic test site.

I threw the tape cassette into his lap.

'What's this?' he asked.

'His confession. Also some information about gun smuggling.'

'What am I supposed to do with it?'

'Listen to it. I've got an interpreter on the tape, but you can get your own.'

'You taking coerced statements from suspects?'

'He had his options.'

'What the hell are you doing, Robicheaux? You know this isn't acceptable as evidence.'

'Not in a courtroom. But you have to consider it in an IA investigation. Right?'

'I can tell you now it's got about as much value as toilet paper.'

'Look, you're supposed to be an impartial investigator. There's a murder confession on that tape. What's the matter with you?'

'All right, I'll listen to it during working hours tomorrow. Then I'll tell you the same thing I told you today. But let's look at your real problem a minute. An unverifiable tape-recorder statement brought in by a suspended cop is worthless in any kind of investigation. You've been here fourteen years and you know that. Secondly, while you were on suspension you got yourself busted with a concealed weapon. I didn't do that to you. Nobody else around here did, either. So why not quit pretending

I'm the bad actor that kicked all this trouble up your butt? You got to deal with your own fall, Robicheaux. That's real. Your rap sheet is real, and so is your drinking history.'

'How about Andres here? Does he look like something I made up?'

My office enclosure was half glass, and the door was open and our voices carried out into the squad room.

'Is he going to make a statement?' Baxter asked.

'Is he go –'

'That's right. You got a tape. You got a guy. Now the tape's no good, so is the guy going to talk to us?'

I didn't answer. The backs of my legs were trembling.

'Come on, tell me,' Baxter said.

'He did it. He tortured a Treasury agent with a telephone crank, then burned him to death in my automobile.'

'And he's going to waive his rights and tell us all that? Then he's going to put his signature on it?'

'I'm still signing the complaint.'

'Glad to hear it.'

'Baxter, you're a sonofabitch.'

'You want to call names, be my guest.'

'Ease off, Lieutenant,' the desk sergeant said quietly in the doorway behind me.

I took my handcuff key from my pocket and unlocked one of the Nicaraguan's wrists, then hooked the loose end to the radiator pipe on the wall.

'Your trouble is you been making love to your fist so long you think you're the only guy around here with any integrity,' Baxter said.

I swung from my side, hard, with my feet set solidly, and caught him square on the mouth. His head snapped back, his tie flew in the air, and I saw blood in his teeth. His eyes were wild. Uniformed cops were standing up all over the squad room. I wanted to hit him again.

'You want to pull your piece?' I said.

'You've finished yourself this time,' he said, holding his hand to his mouth.

'Maybe so. But that doesn't get you off the hook. You want to do something?'

He lowered his hands to his sides. There was a deep purple cut, the shape of a tooth, in his lower lip and it was starting to swell. His eyes watched me carefully. My fist was still clenched at my side.

'Don't you hear well?' I said.

His eyes broke, and he looked at the uniformed cops watching him from the squad room.

'Use some judgment,' he said almost in a whisper, the threat and insult gone from his tone.

'Go on home, Lieutenant. It's no good for you here,' the sergeant said behind me. He was a big man, built like a hogshead, with a florid face and a clipped, blond mustache.

I opened my hand and wiped the perspiration off my palm on my slacks.

'Put my cuffs in my desk drawer for me,' I said.

'Sure,' the sergeant said.

'Look, tell Purcel –'

'Go home, Lieutenant,' he said gently. 'It's a nice day out. We can handle it.'

'I'm signing the complaint against this guy,' I said. 'Get ahold of Captain Guidry. Don't let anybody kick this guy loose.'

'It's no problem, Lieutenant,' the sergeant said.

I walked woodenly through the squad room, the skin of my face tight and dead against the collective stare of the uniformed officers. My hand was still shaking when I filled out the formal complaint of assault with a deadly weapon, kidnapping, and homicide against the Nicaraguan.

Outside, the glare of the sun was like a slap across the eyes. I stepped into the shade to let my eyes adjust to the light and saw Clete walking toward me in yellow and purple LSU T-shirt cut off at the armpits and a pair of red and white Budweiser shorts. The shadow of the building fell across his face and made him look like he was composed of disjointed parts.

'What's happening, Dave?' His eyes squinted at me out of the glare, but they didn't actually meet mine. He looked as though he were focusing on a thought just beyond my right ear.

'I brought in the Nicaraguan. Didi Gee's people dumped him on my dock.'

'The fat boy is rat-fucking the competition, huh?'

'I thought you might want to check him out.'

'What for?'

'Maybe you've seen him before.'

He lit a cigarette and blew the smoke out into the sunlight.

'You know you got blood on your right hand?' he said.

I took out my handkerchief and wiped my knuckles with it.

'What went on?' he said.

'Nate Baxter had an accident.'

'You punched out Nate Baxter? Jesus Christ, Dave, what are you doing?'

'Why'd you do it, Clete?'

'A lowlife is off the board. What do you care?'

'A bad cop would have used a throwaway. He would have just said Starkweather came up in his face with it and he had to smoke him. At least you didn't hide behind your badge.'

'You once told me yesterday is a decaying memory. So I got no memory of yesterday. I don't care about it, either.'

'Confront it or you'll never get rid of it, Clete.'

'You think all this bullshit is political and involves principles and national integrity or something. What you're talking about is a bunch of perverts and heroin mules. How you take them out is irrelevant. Bust 'em or smoke 'em, all anybody cares about is they're not around anymore. My uncle used to walk patrol in the Irish Channel back in the forties. When they caught some guys creeping the place, they broke their arms and legs with baseball bats and left one guy to drive the rest of them out of town. Nobody complained then. Nobody would complain if we did it now.'

'These guys don't hire part-time help.'

'Yeah? Well, I'll worry about that when I have the chance. Right now my home life is like living inside an Excedrin ad. I got a little heat rash and Lois thinks it's the gon.'

'Don't you think you've been working that domestic scam a long time?'

'Sorry to tire you with it, Streak.'

'I'm going to take those guys down. I hope you're not there when I do.'

He flipped his cigarette off the back of the passing truck. A sign showing a woman in a bathing suit was on the side.

'Why would I be?' he said. 'I'm just the guy that carried you two flights down a fire escape while a kid tried to notch our ears with a .22 rifle.'

'You can't win on the game you pitched last Saturday.'

'Yeah? Sounds like an AA meet. I'll see you around. Stay off the booze. I'll drink it for both of us. It's a lousy life.'

He walked back toward his automobile, his sandals flopping on the pavement, a big, lumbering man whose boiled, stitched face reminded me of a bleached melon about to explode in the sun.

I pretended to be a pragmatist, a cynic, a jaded war veteran, a vitriolic drunk, the last of the Louisiana badasses; but like most people I believed that justice would be done, things would work out, somebody would show up with the Constitution in his hand. That afternoon I kept the phone on the deck table while I washed down the boathouse, polished the brass and windows, and sanded and revarnished the hatch. I put on flippers and goggles and cooled off in the lake, diving down into the yellow-green light, feeling the power in my lungs and chest that were now free of alcohol, bursting to the surface with a ringing in my ears that was never the telephone.

Finally, at six-thirty Captain Guidry called and said that the Nicaraguan remained in custody and that he would question him himself in the morning and also contact Fitzpatrick's supervisor at the Federal Building.

I invited Annie over for a late supper, and we cooked steaks outside on my hibachi and ate under the umbrella in the cooling evening. The western horizon was aflame with the sun's afterglow, then the clouds became pink and purple and then finally you could see the city light the night sky.

The next morning I did one hundred sit-ups, worked out with light barbells for an hour while I listened over and over to the old original recording of Iry Lejeune's 'La Jolie Blonde,' made out a grocery list, then asked a college kid who lived down the beach to listen for my phone while I went to a loan company and borrowed three thousand dollars on my houseboat.

The sun was straight up and white in the sky when I got back. Captain Guidry had called a half hour earlier. I dialed his extension at the First District and was told he was in a meeting and would not be out for two hours. Then I called Fitzpatrick's supervisor at Alcohol, Tobacco and Firearms.

'What did you expect me to tell you this morning?' he asked. I could almost see his hand clenched on the receiver.

'I thought by this time maybe you'd questioned the Nicaraguan.'

'You must get up in the morning and brush your teeth in the toilet.'

'What's that supposed to mean?'

'You finally nail one of them and you turn him over to the same people who're letting you twist in the wind. They put him upstairs in the tank. Last night a couple of strungout blacks didn't like the way his breath smelled and they stuffed his head down the flooded floor drain and broke his neck.'

10

That afternoon I repaid Annie the one-thousand-dollar bail fee she had put up for me, then I searched in the Jefferson, Orleans, and St. Bernard parish courthouses for commercial property deeds with Whiplash Larry Wineburger's name on them. I discovered that he was a slumlord of large proportions; but if he owned a warehouse in one of those three parishes, it was deeded under another name.

I went to an AA meeting that evening and later took Annie to dinner at the track. It was hot that night, and I slept on the deck of my houseboat, possibly a careless thing to do, but I felt so discredited by this time that I doubted if my now often-repeated story was a threat to anyone. The wind blew across the lake all night, and I slept so soundly in my hammock that I didn't wake until the sun was hard in my eyes.

I went to an early-morning AA meeting in the Quarter, then bought *beignets* and coffee from the Café du Monde and sat on a bench in Jackson Square and watched the sidewalk artists paint and sketch the tourists. It was still cool in the shade, and the breeze blew off the river. It smelled of coffee and pastry, shrimp in bins of ice, the trees and flowers in the Square, damp stone, the water sprinklers knocking through the banana leaves that grew over the top of the iron piked fence enclosing the park. I went inside St. Louis Cathedral and bought a small book that narrated the history of the building and read it on the bench while a Negro street musician played a bottleneck guitar a few feet away from me.

I was ready to give up my pursuit. I knew I wasn't a coward or a quitter, but at some point reason had to reestablish itself in my life. I couldn't afford any more attrition. I had already had one slip, had progressed within minutes from one drink to a full-blown bender (as they say at the meetings, you pick it up where you left it off), and if I slipped again I wasn't sure I'd ever get back from it.

After I'd struck out at the courthouse, I'd even thought about creeping Wineburger's house or his law office. I knew people who would help me pull it off, too – thieves who worked in car washes, where they made impressions of the house keys on the automobile key ring; a very slick second-story man who ran a wrecking service and would pull the distributor cap off a car owner he wanted to burglarize, then tow the car around the block, cut duplicate keys on a machine he kept in the truck, return the car with a fraudulent bill for repairs, and clean out the house a week later.

But it wasn't worth it. Wineburger, the little Israeli, Philip Murphy, and the general were out there malfunctioning in society because others much more important and powerful than I allowed them to. When these guys ceased to fill a need for somebody else, they would be taken off the board. That sounds like a cynical conclusion for a man to arrive at while sitting on a shady stone bench on a cool morning under banana trees, but most honest, experienced cops will tell you the same thing. It's facile to blame the Supreme Court for the pornographic bookstores and the live sex shows. They usually exist because somebody on the zoning board is getting greased. Kids don't do dope because their parents and teachers are permissive. They do it because adults sell it to them. No psychological complexities, no sociological mysteries.

When people become tired of something, it will end. In the meantime, Dave Robicheaux isn't going to make much difference in the scheme of things. My brother Jimmie knew that. He didn't contend with the world; he dealt in electric poker machines and off-track betting, and I suspected that he sold whiskey and rum that came in from the Islands without tax stamps. But he was always a gentleman and everybody liked him. Cops ate breakfast free in his restaurant; state legislators got pig-eyed drunk at his bar; judges introduced him to their wives with expansive courtesy. His transgressions had to do with licences, not ethics, he used to tell me.

'The day those people don't want to gamble and drink, we'll both be out of jobs. In the meantime, go with the flow, bro.'

'Sorry,' I'd answered. '"Flow" somehow suggests "effluent" to me. I guess I'm just imaginative.'

'No, you just believe in the world that should be, rather than the one that exists. That's why you'll always be the driven guy you are, Dave.'

'Is there any change for that?'

'What do I know? I'm just a restaurateur. You're that guy that fought the wars.'

As irony would have its way, my reverie was broken by a maroon Cadillac convertible with an immaculate white top that pulled to the curb twenty feet from my bench. Two of Didi Gee's hoods got out on each side. They were young, lithe, dressed in summer slacks and open-necked shirts with gold medallions around their necks. Their mirror sunglasses and tasseled Nettleton shoes were almost part of a uniform. What always struck me most about lower-level Mafia hoods were the insipid expressions, as though their faces had been glazed with tallow, and the lifeless speech patterns that they believed passed for sophistication. The only political regime that ever dealt with them effectively was Mussolini's. The fascists tore out their hair and fingernails with pliers, shot them, or sent them to fight against the Greeks. The Mafia welcomed the Allied liberation in 1943 with great joy.

'Good morning, Lieutenant. Mr. Giacano would like to invite you out to his house for brunch,' the driver said. 'You can drive out with us if you want. The road's tore up by Chalmette.'

'I'm not sure I place you with the sunglasses on. Is it Joe Milazzo?' I said.

'That's right. I used to run my uncle's pizza place right across from your office.'

But that wasn't why I remembered his name. He had been a runner for his uncle's book, and he used to lay off bets at the parimutuel when his uncle took on an overload. But I'd also heard a rumor a year ago that he and his uncle had doped a thoroughbred with a speedball that literally exploded the animal's heart on the far turn at the Fairgrounds.

'What's on Didi Gee's mind?' I said.

'He just said ask you out, Lieutenant.'

'I'm kind of tied up today.'

'He said if it's too far for you to drive, he'd like to have you as his guest for lunch at Mama Lido's.'

'Thank him for me just the same.'

'I think it's about these people that's been giving you all this trouble. If you want, you can use the phone in the car to talk with him.'

'I appreciate the help he tried to give me Sunday. But as he probably knows, it didn't do much good. In other words, take the Nicaraguans to the First District.'

He looked away toward the Pontalba Apartments on the corner, his face quietly exasperated.

'I'm kind of in a hard spot, Lieutenant,' he said. 'Mr. Giacano is a nice guy to work for. He paid off my old man's hospital bills, he give my little boy a bicycle for Christmas, he don't let nobody pay for anything when we go to the club. A lot of guys would pay a lot to buy my job. But he don't like to hear words like "maybe" or "no" from a guy that waxes his cars and drives people around. If you ain't coming, I'd really appreciate you calling him up and telling him that.'

'I'm afraid you'll have to live with it, podna.'

'All right, I don't know from shit about Mr. Giacano's business dealings. I'm not an ambitious person. I don't care about what don't concern me. But I got ears. I'm human. I can't turn into a potted plant just because people are talking around me. It's about some guy named Murphy. You're interested, Lieutenant, that's okay. But I done my job.'

I closed my book and took a bite of my *beignet.* I watched a woman sweeping out her storefront under the colonnade on the corner. Rolls of sausage and cheese were hung in the window, and a little black boy was spraying the boxes of grapes and plums along the front wall with a hose.

'Tell Didi Gee I'll meet him at Mama Lido's at noon,' I said.

Joe Milazzo smiled behind his sunglasses and put an unlit cigarette in his mouth.

'Don't get the wrong idea, Joe. I'm just an impulsive guy. Next time save the shuck for a Fuller Brush route,' I said.

His face went dead.

Didi Gee had reserved a private dining room at the back of the restaurant. It was hung with pink and lavender curtains that were tied back to give the illusion of windows on the walls, which were painted with wispy Venetian canal scenes, gondolas, boatmen in striped T-shirts with flat hats and mandolins. The baseboards and woodwork around the doors were painted with grapevines that wound their way up the corners to the ceiling, which was hung with clusters of green plastic grapes.

There must have been fifteen people at the long white table that was filled with bottles of red wine in wicker casks, bowls of spaghetti and meatballs, lasagna, shrimp cooked in some kind of tomato sauce that made your eyes wince, loaves of Italian bread that people broke apart with their hands and ate loudly with a shower of crumbs on the tablecloth.

What a crew to be seen with, I thought. Some of them were aging soldiers who had survived any number of gang wars and jolts in Angola and Lewisburg since the 1950s, now thick-bodied and flatulent, with cigarette-and-whiskey throats and hair growing out of their ears and nostrils. Then there were the young ones like Joe Milazzo, who might have been raised in a vacant lot. There was always a hidden thought in their eyes that they couldn't quite conceal. They would hit anybody, even their own kind, just to earn a chair closer at the table to Didi Gee. They all ate like troglodytes, made the waitresses take the food back if it wasn't warm, complained about the chipped glass or a fork with dishwasher spots on it. The hostess who wandered in every ten minutes to ask if everything was all right looked as though she had swallowed a mouthful of bumblebees.

Didi Gee had saved the seat next to him for me. He wore a white suit and an orange-flowered shirt with the shirt lapels on the outside of his coat. A gold St. Christopher's medal rested on the black hair that grew up to his throat. His chest and stomach were so huge that he had to keep his chair pressed back almost to the wall.

'You want wine?' he asked.

'No, thanks.'

'I heard you were drinking again. I say that only because it don't matter to me. Everybody's got a vice. It's what makes us human.'

'I'm not drinking today. Put it that way.'

'That's the one-day-at-a-time stuff, huh? I wish I

could do that. I worry about stuff all the time I don't have control over.'

It was amazing, I thought, how the true indicators of a sudden change in your social status worked. Didi Gee no longer used the deferential 'Lieutenant' when he spoke to me, and his hoods were eating as though I were not there.

'I worry all the time about this operation I got to have,' he said. 'The longer I wait, the more they got to cut out of my hole. I just can't bring myself to face it. Maybe there're some things you're not supposed to accept. It ain't natural for a person to be leaking shit into a bag strapped to his side. Look what I got to sit on now. That's bad enough.'

He rose a little from his chair and exposed an inflated rubber cushion that was shaped like a toilet seat in a public restroom.

'I'm going over to Baylor Hospital in Houston and see what they say. All the best surgeons in New Orleans are Jews. A guy my size walks through the door and they start looking at my parts like they got meat prices stamped on them.'

'Maybe they'll find another way to help you, Didi.'

'That's right. Maybe I get the right doctors over there at Baylor and I'll just retire there. My brother died and left me an office building in San Antonio three blocks from this Alamo place. They got an amusement park there or something?'

'It's a historical –'

'Because even though I was born and grew up in New Orleans, I'm tired of people dumping on me, and nickel-and-dime legal farts trying to make a name by cutting off my cock.'

His voice had intensified suddenly, like heat building down in a furnace system, and the others at the table stopped talking and moved their knives and forks softly in their plates.

'I'm not sure what we're talking about,' I said.

'I got subpoenaed by the grand jury. Me and some people I'm associated with.'

'I didn't know that.'

'Businesses I run for thirty years somehow start bothering some people. Their little noses start twitching like there's a bad smell in the air. I'm talking about people that were at my children's baptisms, that always come around at election time for donations. Suddenly I'm like some kind of disease.'

'You're a professional, Didi. It comes with the geography.'

'They're serious this time. I got it straight from the prosecutor's office. They want me in Angola.'

'Like you said, maybe it's time to retire.'

'They're not cutting no deals on this one. That means I'm gonna have to break my own rules. I'm gonna have to do some stuff I don't like.' His dark eyes were flecked with black electricity.

'I guess I'm not following you.'

And I didn't want to follow him, either. The conversation had already grown old. I didn't care about his troubles with the grand jury, and his vague references to violating his own ethical system seemed at the time like another manifestation of the self-inflated grandiosity that was characteristic of his kind.

'You're right. It's personal,' he said. His glare went from me to the men around the table. They started eating and talking again. 'You want this guy Philip Murphy?'

I tapped my fingers on my water glass and looked away from his face.

'No games, partner,' I said.

'You think I play games? A guy that ran Orleans and half of St. Bernard Parish when you were a schoolboy? You think I brought you out here for games?'

'How is it you have a string on this guy?'

'He's an addict. An addict's one day away anytime you want him. This guy used to be a joy-popper. Now he's a two-ballon-a-day regular. You want him, try this restaurant.' He dropped a matchbox on the tablecloth. On the cover was a palm tree and the words GULF SHORES. FINE FOOD. BILOXI, MISSISSIPPI. 'His connection's the guy that runs the valet parking.'

'What do you care about Philip Murphy, Didi?'

'I got my reasons, a bunch of them maybe.'

'He plays in a different ballpark. He's not a competitor.'

'He's screwing up some things over in Fort Lauderdale. There's some people there want him out of the way.'

'I know this guy. He's not your crowd.'

'That's right, he ain't. But he messes with it. What you don't understand is south Florida's not New Orleans. Miami and Fort Lauderdale are open cities. Nobody's got a lock on the action, nobody gets cow-boyed down there. Everybody always respected that. Now there's coloreds, Cubans, and Colombians in everything. They're fucking animals. They'll cowboy you for fifty bucks, they kill each other's children.

Then guys like Murphy come around and make political deals with them – plots against Castro or some bullshit down in Central America. People that's cannibals, that was born in a chicken yard, end up working for the government. In the meantime, guys like me are in front of a grand jury.'

I picked up the matchbox and put it in my shirt pocket.

'Thank's for the information, Didi. I hope things turn out better for you over at Baylor,' I said.

'You ain't eat your lunch. You don't like Italian food?'

'You know how us old-time boozers are, scarred stomach and all that.'

'Maybe you don't like eating as my guest, huh?'

'I've appreciated your hospitality. You're always a generous man. We'll see you, Didi.'

'Yeah, sure. You're welcome. Keep one thing in mind, though. I never did time. Not in thirty years. You can tell that to any of those farts you know in the prosecutor's office.'

It was boiling when I got back to the houseboat. Heat waves bounced off the roof, and every inch of metal and wood on the deck was hot to the touch. I put on my trunks and snorkel mask and swam out into the lake. The surface was warm, but I could feel the layers of coldness below me grow more intense the farther I swam from the shoreline. I watched three pelicans floating in the groundswell in front of me, their pouched beaks swollen with fish, and tried to figure out what Didi Gee was up to. I hadn't accepted his explanation about Murphy creating complication for the mob in southern

Florida, and his anger at the government's support of Cuban political gangsters seemed manufactured for the moment. But who was to say? In terms of law enforcement, south Florida was the La Brea Tar Pits East.

The real problem was that nobody knew what went on in the mind of Didi Gee except Didi Gee. Most cops categorize criminals as dimwits and degenerates, or we assume that the intelligent ones think more or less in the same logical patterns as we do. The truth is that absolutely no one knows what goes on in the mind of a psychopath. Didi Gee was a vicious, sentimental fat man who could just as easily tip a waitress fifty dollars as put an icepick in her husband's stomach. When he was a collector for the shylocks across the river in Algiers, his logo had been a bloodstained baseball bat that he kept propped up in the back seat of his convertible.

But somehow he and his kind always had their apologists. Journalists would treat them as honorable men who lived by an arcane private code; television documentaries dwelt on their families, their attendance at Mass, their patriotism – and made only fleeting reference to their connections with semiacceptable forms of organized crime, such as numbers and union takeovers. They were simply businessmen who were no more unethical than large corporations.

Maybe so. But I'd seen their victims: some grocers and dry cleaners who borrowed money from them and who became employees in their own stores; nightclub entertainers, beer and meat distributors, horse jockeys who couldn't move out of town without permission; addicts who were always looking for more mules to pull their wagons; and those who became object lessons, their faces blown all over a car windshield with double-ought buck-shot.

Maybe the deeper problem was that the Didi Gees of the world understood us, but we did not understand them. Were they genetically defective, or evil by choice? I took a breath through the snorkel and dove down to the bottom of the lake and glided above the gray, rippling sand while small fish scurried away in the green-yellow light. The salt water I swam in contained the remains of people who symbolized to me the greatest possible extremes in human behavior. They were created by the same Maker. The similarity ended there.

Three years ago a small plane with a family on board from Tampa hit a bad headwind over the Gulf, used up all its gas, and pancaked into the lake ten miles out. They got out with only one life preserver. Both the father and mother were strong swimmers and could have struck out for the shore or the causeway, but they stayed with their three children and kept them afloat for two days. One by one the parents and the two oldest children slipped under the waves. The smallest child survived because their father had strapped him in the life preserver and tied his shirt around the child's head to protect it from the sun.

Some miles to the west and just south of Morgan City was the crushed and barnacle-encrusted hull of a German U-boat that an American destroyer had nailed in 1942, when Nazi submarines used to lie in wait for the oil tankers that sailed from the refineries in Baton Rouge and New Orleans. Shrimpers in

New Iberia told stories of the orange fires that burned on the southern horizon late at night, and of the charred bodies they pulled up in their nets. I didn't understand then who the Nazis were, but I imagined them as dark-uniformed, slit-eyed creatures who lived beneath the water and who could burn and murder people of goodwill whenever they wished.

Years later, when I was in college, I dove down to that wreck with an air tank and a weight belt. It was in sixty feet of water, lying on its side, the deck railing and forward gun shaggy with moss, the painted identification numbers still visible on the conning tower. The stern was tilted downward into deeper water, and I thought I could see the frenetic turning movements of sand sharks near the screws. My heart was clicking in my chest, I was breathing oxygen rapidly from my tank, and actually sweating inside my mask. I determined that I wasn't going to be overcome by my childhood fears, and I swam down to the dark, massive outline of the conning tower and knocked against the steel plate with the butt of my bowie knife.

Then the strangest occurrence of my life took place as I hovered above the wreck. I felt a cold current blow across me, a surge from the darkness beyond the submarine's screws, and air bubbles rose from under the hull. I heard the metal plates start to grate against the bottom, then there was a crunching, sliding sound, a dirty cloud of moss and floating sand, and suddenly the sub trembled almost erect and began sliding backwards off the continental shelf. I watched it, horrified, until it disappeared in the blackness.

The sand sharks turned like brown minnows in its invisible wake.

I learned that this particular wreck moved several miles up and down the Louisiana coastline, and it was only coincidence that its weight had shifted in a strong current while I was on top of it. But I could not get out of my mind the image of those drowned Nazis still sailing the earth after all those years, their eye sockets and skeletal mouths streaming seaweed, their diabolical plan still at work under the Gulf's tranquil, emerald surface.

A navy destroyer broke the spine of their ship with depth charges in 1942. But I believed that the evil they represented was held in check by the family who sacrificed their lives so their youngest member could live.

The phone was ringing when I climbed the ladder onto my deck. I sat in the hot shade of the umbrella and wiped my face with a towel while I held the receiver to my ear. It was Captain Guidry.

'Dave, is that you?' he said.

'Yes.'

'Where've you been? I've been calling you for two hours.'

'What is it?'

'I hate to have to call with bad news. It's your brother, Jimmie. Somebody shot him twice in a public rest room by the French Market.'

I squeezed my hand on my forehead and looked out at the heat waves hammering on the lake's surface.

'How bad is it?' I asked.

'I won't kid you. It's touch-and-go. It looks like

the guy put two .22 rounds in the side of his head. Look, Jimmie's a tough guy. If anybody can make it, he will. You want me to send a car for you?'

'No, I have a rental. Where is he?'

'I'm here with him at Hotel Dieu Sisters. You drive careful, hear?'

The traffic was bad all the way across town. It was a half hour before I got to the hospital and found a place to park. I walked hurriedly up the tree-shaded walkway into the building, my sandals clacking on the tiles, my sweaty, unbuttoned print shirt hanging outside my slacks. I had to swallow and breathe quietly for a moment before I could ask the receptionist where Jimmie's room was. Then I turned and saw Captain Guidry standing behind me.

'He's in recovery on the fifth floor, Dave. They got the bullets out,' he said.

'What's it look like for him?'

'Better than it did when I talked with you. Let's walk down to the elevator.'

'What happened?'

'I'm going to tell you everything we know. But slow down now. There's some real good docs taking care of him. We're going to ride this one out all right.'

'Tell me what happened.'

The elevator door opened, and a nurse pushed out a wheelchair in which sat a pretty woman in a pink nightgown. She was smiling and she held a spray of flowers in her lap. We stepped inside and the doors closed behind us.

'He walked down to the Café du Monde for *beignets*, then stopped at the public restroom next door. The one that's under the levee. A black kid that was taking a piss in the wall urinal said Jimmie went into one of the stalls and closed the door. A minute later a guy came in, kicked open the door, and fired twice, point-blank. The kid says the gun had something on the barrel and it made a spitting sound. It sounds like a professional hit.'

'What'd the guy look like?'

'The kid was scared shitless. He still is. We got him looking in mug books, but don't expect anything.'

I clenched and unclenched my fists. The elevator was a slow one, and it kept stopping at floors where no one was waiting.

'Maybe this is the wrong time to tell you this, but some people are starting to think twice about your story,' the captain said.

'How's that?'

'Maybe they were after you instead. Jimmie looks like your twin. There might be other explanations, but the local talent tends toward shotguns and car bombs.'

'It's damn poor consolation to be believed because your brother was shot.'

'People are human. Give an inch.'

'I don't have that kind of charity. That's my whole family up there.'

'I can't blame you. But for what it's worth, we've got uniforms all over the floor. Nobody'll get to him here.'

'If he doesn't make it, you might be arresting me, Captain.'

'I hate to hear you talk like that, Dave. It brings me great worry,' he said.

Jimmie remained three more hours in the recovery room before they brought him into intensive care on a gurney. I wanted to go inside, but the surgeon wouldn't let me. He said both rounds had hit Jimmie at an angle, which was the only factor that saved his life. One had caromed off the skull and exited the scalp at the back of the head, but the second round had fractured the skull and put lead and bone splinters into the brain tissues. The surgeon's concern was about paralysis and loss of sight in one eye.

Captain Guidry had already gone back to the office, and I spent the rest of the afternoon alone in the waiting room. I read magazines, drank endless cups of bad coffee from a machine, and watched the light fade outside the window and the shadows of the oak trees fall on the brick-paved street down below. At eight o'clock I went downstairs and ate a sandwich in the cafeteria. I wanted to call Annie, but I thought I had already caused her enough traumatic moments and should spare her this one. Upstairs again, I talked with nurses, made friends with an elderly Cajun lady from Thibodaux who spoke English poorly and was afraid for her husband who was in surgery, and finally I watched the late news on television and went to sleep in a fetal position on a short couch.

In the morning a Catholic sister woke me up and gave me a glass of orange juice and told me it was all right to see my brother for a few minutes. Jimmie's jaws and head were wrapped thickly with bandages, almost like a plaster cast. His face was white and sunken, both eyes were hollow and blackened as though he had been beaten with fists.

An IV needle was taped down to the blue vein inside his right arm; an oxygen tube was attached to his nose; his bare chest was crisscrossed with curlicues of electronic monitoring wires. He looked as though all the life had been sucked out of him through a straw and the lighted machines around him had more future and viability than he.

I wondered what my father would think of this. My father brawled in bars, but he always fought for fun and he never bore a grudge. He wouldn't carry a gun for any reason, even when he played *bourée* with gamblers who were known as dangerous and violent men. But this was a different world from the New Iberia of the 1940s. Here people with the moral instincts of piranha would pump two bullets into the brain of a man they didn't know and spend the contract money on cocaine and whores.

There were small lights in Jimmie's dark eyes when he looked at me. His eyelids looked like they were made of paper, stained with purple dye.

'How you doing, boy?' I said. I rubbed the back of his arm and squeezed his palm. It was lifeless and felt like Johnny Massina's had when I shook hands with him the night of his execution.

'Did you see who it was?'

His throat swallowed and his tongue made small saliva bubbles on his lower lip.

'Was it this guy Philip Murphy?' I asked. 'A late-middle-aged, frumpy-looking guy with glasses? Like somebody who'd be selling dirty postcards around a schoolyard?'

His eyes looked away from me, the lids fluttering.

'How about a dark little guy?'

Jimmie started to whisper, then choked on the fluids in his throat.

'All right, don't worry about it now,' I said. 'You're safe here. There's three uniformed cops with you, and I'll be in and out of here all the time. But while you get well, I'm going to find out who did this to us. You remember what the old man used to say – "You pull on dat 'gator's tail, he gonna clean your kneecaps, him."'

I smiled at him, then I saw his eyes flicker with an urgent light. His mouth opened and clicked dryly.

'Not now, Jim. There'll be time later,' I said.

He worked his hand off the bed onto my chest. Then his fingers began to trace lines against my skin, but he was so weak that the frail pattern he made was like a cobweb spread across my breastbone. I nodded as though I understood, and placed his hand back on the bed. The energy and effort in his eyes were now used up, and he looked at the ceiling with the expression of those who are suddenly forced to deal in a very different and dark dimension.

'I've bent your ear too long. You sack out now. I'll be back a little later,' I said.

But he was already disconnected from our conversation. I left the room quietly, with the sense of both guilt and relief that we feel when we're allowed to walk away from the bedside of someone who reminds us of our mortality.

The two uniformed cops on the door nodded to me. At the end of the corridor I saw Captain Guidry walking toward me with a potted geranium wrapped in green and silver foil. The implants in his scalp had grown, and his head looked as though a badly made wig had been grafted to it.

'I'm going to leave this at the nurses' station. How's he doing?' he asked.

'He's a tough little brother.'

'You look like hell. Go home and get some sleep.'

'I slept all right on the couch last night. I just need a shower and a change of clothes.'

Captain Guidry's eyes stared into mine. 'What did he tell you in there?'

'Nothing.'

'Don't jerk me around, Dave.'

'He didn't say anything.'

'I've worked with you a long time. You don't hide things well.'

'Ask the nurse. He can't talk. I'm not sure he even knows how he got here.'

'Listen, I think you're about to get out of all this trouble you've been in. Don't blow it now with an obstruction charge.'

'Do I get my badge back?'

His lips pinched together, and he looked down the corridor.

'You shouldn't have hit Baxter,' he said.

'So nothing is changed.'

'We do it one step at a time. Have some patience, will you? Trust people a little bit.'

'I'm out on ten thousand dollars' bond. I'm going to have to go to trial unless I can negotiate a misdemeanor plea.'

'You're a reader. You know about Saint John of the Cross and the long night of the soul. So this is your long night. Why make it longer?'

At the houseboat I took my Remington twelve-gauge pump out of its sheepskin-lined case. The blueing shone with the thin layer of oil that I kept on it. My father had given me the twelve-gauge when I went away to college in Lafayette, and I had knocked down mallards and geese with it from Cypremont Point to Whiskey Bay almost every year since. I rubbed my fingers along the polished, inlaid stock, then wrapped the barrel with a rag and locked it in the machinist's vise that I kept anchored to one end of the drainboard. I made a pencil mark three inches in front of the pump, then sawed through the barrel with a hacksaw. The end of the barrel clanged to the floor. I picked it up and started to drop it in the garbage but, instead, ran a piece of Christmas ribbon through it and hung it on the wall over what was left of my historical jazz collection.

I sat at the kitchen table and rubbed the sawed edges of the gun's muzzle smooth with emery paper and removed the sportsman's plug from the magazine so that it would now hold five shells instead of three. I went to the closet and took out my duffel bag of decoys, my army-surplus bandolier I used when the hunting weather was too warm for a coat. I emptied everything out on the table and stood all my shells up in an erect row like toy soldiers. Then I selected out the street cop's buffet – deer slugs and double-ought buckshot – slipped them one at a time into the magazine with my thumb until the spring came tight, slid the breech shut, and clicked on the safety.

In my mind were images that I didn't want to recognize. I looked out the window and saw a man turning a raw steak on a barbecue fire, saw the two kids trying to burn each other out in a pitch-and-catch game, their faces sweaty and narrow, saw a waxed red car parked next to a sand dune under the murderous white sun.

Annie ate lunch every day in a delicatessen by Canal and Exchange, not far from where she worked at the social welfare agency. I sat in a wooden chair across the street and read the *Times-Picayune* and waited for her. Just after noon I saw her coming down the sidewalk in the lunchtime crowd, wearing sunglasses, her wide straw hat, and a pale yellow dress. She could live in New Orleans the rest of her life, I thought, but she would always be from Kansas. She had the tan of a farm girl, the kind that never seemed to change tone, and even though her legs were beautiful and her hips a genuine pleasure to look at, she walked in high heels as though she were on board a rocking ship.

I watched her sit by herself at a table, her back to me, remove her sunglasses, and give her order to the waiter while she moved both her hands in the air. He looked perplexed, and I could almost hear her ordering something that wasn't on the menu, which was her habit, or telling him about some 'weirdness' that she had seen on the street.

Then I heard the metal-rimmed wheels of a huge handcart on the pavement and an elderly black man's voice crying out, 'I got melons, I got 'loupes, I got plums, I got sweet red strawberries.' His cart was loaded with tiers of fruit and also with boxes of pralines, roses wrapped in green tissue paper, and small bottles of grape juice shoved down in an ice bucket.

'How you doing, Cappie?' I said.

'Good afternoon, Lieutenant,' he said, and grinned. His head was bald and brown, and he wore a gray apron. He had grown up in Laplace next door to Louis Armstrong's family, but he had sold produce in the Quarter for years and was so old that neither he nor anyone else knew his age.

'Is your wife still in the hospital?' I asked.

'No suh, she fit and fine and out do'-popping again.'

'I beg your pardon.'

'She do'-popping. She pop in dis do', she pop out dat do'. You want your grape drink today?'

'No, I tell you what instead. You see that pretty lady in the yellow dress eating across the street?'

'Yes suh, I think so.'

'Give her some of these roses and a box of pralines. Here, you keep the change, Cappie.'

'What you want me to tell her?'

'Just tell her it's from a good-looking Cajun fellow,' I said, and winked at him.

I looked once more in Annie's direction. Then I turned and walked back to where I had left my rented car parked on Decatur Street.

The beach outside of Biloxi was white and hot-looking in the afternoon sun. The palm trees along the boulevard beat in the wind, and the green surface of the Gulf was streaked with light and filled with dark patches of blue, like floating ink. A squall was blowing up in the south, and waves were already breaking against the ends of the jetties, the foam leaping high into the air before you heard the sound of the wave, and in the groundswell I could see the flicker of bait fish and the dark, triangular outlines of stingrays, almost like oil slicks, that had been pushed in toward shore by the approaching storm.

I found the Gulf shores restaurant, but the man who ran the valet parking service wasn't there. I walked a short way down the beach, bought a paper plate of fried catfish and hush puppies from a food stand, and sat on a wooden bench under a palm tree and ate it. Then I read a paperback copy of *A Passage to India*, watched some South American teenagers play soccer in the sand, and finally walked out along the jetty and skipped oyster shells across the water's surface. The wind was stiffer now, with a sandy bite in it, and as the sun seemed to descend into an enormous flame across the western sky, I could see thin white streaks of lightning in the row of black clouds that hovered low on the watery horizon in the south. When the sun's afterglow began to shrink from the sky, and the neon lights of the amusement rides and beer joints along the beach began to come on, I walked back to my car and drove to the restaurant.

Two black kids and a white man in his thirties were taking cars from under the porch at the entrance and parking them in back. The white man had crewcut brown hair and small moles all over his face, as though they had been touched there with a paintbrush. I drove up to the entrance, and one of the black kids took my car. I went inside and ate a five-dollar club sandwich that I didn't want. When I came back out, the white man walked up to me for my parking ticket.

'I can get it. Just show me where it is,' I said.

He stepped out of the light from the porch and pointed toward the lot.

'The second-to-last-row,' he said.

'Where?'

He walked farther into the dark and pointed again.

'Almost to the end of the row,' he said.

'My girlfriend said you can sell me some sneeze,' I said.

'Sell you what?' He looked me up and down for the first time. The neon light from a liquor store next door made his lips look purple.

'A little nose candy for the sinuses.'

'You got the wrong guy, buddy.'

'Do I look like a cop or something?'

'You want me to get your car, sir?'

'I've got a hundred bucks for you. Meet me someplace else.'

'Maybe you should talk to the manager. I run the valet service here. You're looking for somebody else.'

'She must have told me about the wrong place. No offence,' I said, and I walked to the back of the lot and drove out onto the boulevard. The palm trees on the esplanade were crashing in the wind.

I drove through a residential neighborhood away from the beach, then circled back and parked on a dark street a block inland from the restaurant. I took my World War II Japanese field glasses from the glove compartment and focused them on the lighted porch where the man with the moles was parking cars.

In the next three hours I watched him go twice to the trunk of his own automobile before he delivered a car to a customer out front. At midnight the restaurant closed, and I followed him across town to an unpaved neighborhood of clapboard houses, open drainage ditches, and dirt yards littered with rusted engine parts and washing machines.

Most of the houses on the street were dark, and I left my car a block away and walked to a sandy driveway that led up to the lighted side door of a boxlike wooden house surrounded by unwatered and dying hedges. Through the screen I could see him in his undershirt, with a beer in his hand, changing the channels on his television set. His shoulders were as white as a frog's belly and speckled with the same brown moles that covered his face. He sat back in a stuffed chair, a window fan blowing in his face, salted his beer can, and sipped at it while he watched television. The first raindrops clicked flatly on the roof.

I slipped my hand through the screen-door handle, then jerked it backward and tore the latch loose from the jamb. He sat erect, his eyes wide, the beer can rolling across the floor in a trail of foam.

'Some customers are persistent as hell,' I said, stepping inside.

But I should have come in holding the .25 Beretta that was in my pocket. He reached behind him on a workbench, grabbed a ball-pen hammer, and flung it into my chest. The steel head hit me just to the right of my breastbone, and I felt a pain, a breathlessness, shoot through my heart cavity as though I had been stunned with a high-voltage wire. Then he charged me, his arms flailing like a kid fighting on a school ground, and he caught me once on the eye and again on the ear before I could get my guard up. But I had been a good boxer at New

Iberia High, and I had learned long ago that either in the ring or in a street fight there was nothing to equal setting your feet square, tucking your chin into your shoulder, raising your left to guard your face, and coming across with a right hook aimed somewhere between the mouth and the eyes. I got him right across the bridge of the nose. His eyes snapped straight with shock, the light glazed in them, and I hit him again, this time on the jaw, and knocked him over his chair into the television set. He looked up at me, his face white, his nose bleeding on his upper lip.

'You want to do it some more?' I said.

'Who are you, man?'

'What did you care, as long as you come out of this all right?'

'Come out of what? What you want with me? I never saw you before tonight.'

He started to get up. I pushed him down on the floor.

'You come here to rip me off, you're going to deal later with a couple of bad dudes. That's no joke, buddy,' he said.

'You see this in my hand? I'm not going to point it at you, because I don't think you're up to it. But we're upping the stakes now.'

'You come in my goddamn house and attack me and wave a gun around, and *I'm* in trouble? You're unbelieveable, man.'

'Get up,' I said, and pulled him erect by his arm. I walked him into the bedroom.

'Turn on the light,' I said.

He flicked the light switch. The bed was unmade, and dirty clothes were piled on the wood floor. A jigsaw puzzle of Elvis Presley's face was half completed on a card table. I pushed him through the hallway into the tiny kitchen at the back of the house.

'You forget where the light switch is?' I said.

'Look, man, I just work for some people. You got a problem with the action around here, you take it up with them, I'm just a small guy.'

I felt the wall with my hand and clicked on the overhead light. The kitchen was the only clean room in the house. The drainboards were washed down, the dishes put away in a drying rack, the linoleum floor waxed and polished. A solitary chair was placed at the large Formica-topped table in the center of the room, and on the table were three black plastic bags closed with masking tape, an ether bottle, and boxes of powdered milk and powdered sugar.

He wiped his nose on his hand. The moles on his face looked like dead bugs. Beyond the drawn window shades I could hear the rain falling in the trees.

'It looks like you've been watering down the stock,' I said.

'What do you want? You're looking at everything I got.'

'Where's Philip Murphy?'

He looked at me curiously, his brow furrowed.

'I don't know the guy,' he said.

'Yes, you do. He's a two-poke-a-day regular.'

'That's lots of people. Look, if I could give you the dude and get you out of my life, you'd have him.'

'He's in his fifties, wears glasses, tangled gray hair

and eyebrows, talks a little bit like an Englishman sometimes.'

'Oh, that fucker. He told me his name was Eddy. You out to pop him or something?'

'Where is he?'

'Look, this dude has a lot of money. Around here we piece off the source. Everybody gets along that way.'

'Last chance,' I said, and moved towards him. His back bumped against the sink and he raised his hands up in front of his chest.

'All right,' he said. 'The last stucco duplex on Azalea Drive. It's straight north of Jefferson Davis's house. Now get the fuck out of here, man.'

'Do you rent or own this place?'

'I own it. Why?'

'Bad answer,' I said, and I unscrewed the cap from the ether bottle and poured it over the black plastic bags on the kitchen table.

'What are you doing?' he said.

'Better get moving, partner,' I said, and folded back the cover on a book of matches.

'Are you crazy? That stuff's like napalm. Don't do it, man.'

He stared at me wild-eyed, frozen, waiting until the last second to see if I was serious. I lighted the whole book, and he broke for the window, put one foot through the shade, balanced for a moment on the sill like a clothespin while he stared back at me incredulously a last time, and then crashed to the ground outside with the torn shade dangling behind him.

I backed out the door and threw the flaming match-book at the table. The air seemed to snap apart with a yellow-blue flash like lightning arching back on itself. Then the Formica tabletop erupted into a cone of flame that was absolutely white at the center. Within seconds the paint on the ceiling burned outward in a spreading black blister that touched all four walls.

When I walked away from the house, the fire had already cracked through the shingles of the kitchen roof and I could see the rain turning in the red light.

I drove along the beach boulevard next to the sea wall in the dark. The surf was loud, the waves crashing hard on the sand, and the shrimp boats that were moored in their slips were knocking against the pilings. I passed Beauvoir, the rambling, one-story home of Jefferson Davis, set back on a dark lawn under spreading oak trees. The wide veranda was lighted, and in the darkness and the sweep of rain through the trees, the building seemed like an inverted telescopic vision into that spring of 1865 when Davis watched his failed medieval romance collapse around him. If the grass in that same lawn was a darker green than it should have been, perhaps it was because of the two hundred Confederate soldiers who were anonymously buried there. The road to Roncevaux lures the poet and the visionary like a drug, but the soldier pays for the real estate.

I turned north and followed the road to a pink stucco duplex at the end of an unfinished subdivision. There was no moon, the sky was totally black now, and I parked my car down the street under a dripping oak tree. Murphy wasn't going to be easy, and I had to make some decisions. My father used to say that an old armadillo is old because he's smart, and he doesn't leave his hole unless you give him an acceptable reason. I had packed a change of clothes and a raincoat and a rain hat in a small suitcase before I had left New Orleans. I put on the hat and coat, slipped the shotgun out of its sheep-lined cover, and hung it through the trigger guard from under my armpit with a coat hanger. I buttoned the coat over the shotgun and walked to the duplex, which was set apart from the other houses by a vacant lot filled with construction rubble.

Both sides of the duplex were dark, but the driveway on the far side was empty and newspapers moldered on the lawn. I went behind the apartment closest to me, cut the telephone wire at the box with my Puma knife, and unscrewed the lightbulb on the porch. The rain beat against my hat and coat, and the shotgun knocked against my side and knee like a two-by-four. I pulled my hat low on my eyes, put a pencil between my teeth, then hammered on the door with my fist and stepped back out into the rain.

A light went on in back, and a moment later I saw the curtain move behind the door glass.

'Who is it?' a voice called.

'Gulf Coast Gas and Electric. We got a busted main. Turn off your pilot.'

'What?' the voice asked from behind the door.

'The main's busted. We can't get it shut down at the pump station. If you smell gas, go to the National Guard armory. Don't light no matches, either,' I said, and walked into the darkness as though I were headed toward another house.

But instead I cut behind a pile of bulldozed fiberboard in the vacant lot next door, circled through a stand of pines along a coulee, and came out in back of the duplex. I suspected that Murphy had stayed at the window until he gave up trying to locate me in the darkness and rain, then had gone to the telephone. I was right. As I eased under the window I heard him dialing, a pause, then the receiver rattling in the cradle. I stopped and walked quickly along the side wall toward the front porch, trying to keep the barrel of the shotgun out of the mud. At the corner I stopped and listened. He unlocked the deadbolt and opened the door on the chain.

Come on, you've got to prove you have *cojones*, I thought. Big boys wear them on the outside of their pants. You kicked gook ass with the Legionnaires, crouched in the bottom of an LST at the Bay of Pigs, hung parts of Sandinista farmers in trees like Christmas-tree ornaments. What good is life if you're not willing to risk it?

Then I heard him slide the chain and let it swing back against the door. I raised the shotgun in front of me, my body pressed tightly against the stucco wall. He stepped out into the slanting rain, his pajama top unbuttoned over his white pot belly, a flashlight in one hand and a blue two-inch .38 in the other.

I clicked off the safety and came around the corner and aimed the twelve-gauge's barrel at the side of his head in one motion.

'Throw it away! Don't think about it! Do it!' I said.

He was frozen, the flashlight's glow illuminating his face like a piece of dead wax. But I could see thought working in his eyes.

'I'll cut you in half, Murphy.'

'I suspect you would, Lieutenant,' he said, and he bent his knees, almost as though he were going to genuflect, and set the revolver on the porch slab.

I pushed him inside, turned on the light switch, and kicked the door closed behind me.

'Facedown on the floor, arms straight out,' I said.

'We don't need all this street theater, do we?' He looked again at my face in the light. 'All right, I don't argue. But there's nobody else here. It looks like you've won the day.'

The inside of the duplex looked like a motel room. An air-conditioning suite hummed in one window and dripped water on the shag carpet; the wallpaper had been roller-painted a pale green; the furniture was either plastic or made of composite wood; the air smelled of chemical deodorizer. I looked quickly in the bedroom, the bath, the small kitchen and dinette.

'It's a simple place,' he said. He had to turn his head sideways on the rug to talk. The pink fat around his hips was striped with gray hair. 'No women, no guns, no mysteries. This might be a disappointing bust for you, Lieutenant.'

'Take off your shirt and sit in that chair.'

'All right,' he said, and a smile flickered around the corner of his lips.

'Do I amuse you for some reason?'

'Not you. Just your attitude. I told you once before you had puritan sympathies. At some point in your career, you need to realize that nobody cares about these things. Oh, they say they do. But they really don't, and I think you know it.'

He dropped his pajama top on the arm of a

stuffed chair and sat down. His chest was small and gray, and his stomach pushed up high on his breastbone.

'Turn them up,' I said.

He shrugged his shoulders and turned up his forearms so I could see the flat, gray scar tissue along the veins. The scars were so thick they could have been traced there with a barber's razor.

'I heard you were just a two-pop-a-day man. I think you've worked up to the full-tilt boogie,' I said.

'Does that somehow make you feel better?' The smile was gone, and I could see the contempt, the cynicism, the glint of evil in his eyes.

'If I allowed myself to have feelings about you, I would have blown you up on the porch.'

'And we thought you were a professional.'

'I hope you shot up a lot of dope tonight. You're going on a long dry. Figure what it's going to be like after two days in lockdown.'

'I'm trembling already. See the cold sweat on my face. Oh Lawsie, what's I going to do?'

At that moment I felt a genuine rush of hatred in my chest.

'If my brother dies and you somehow get back on the street, God help you,' I said.

'Your brother?'

I watched his face carefully.

'He's still alive, and he saw the guy you sent to do it,' I said.

'You think we tried to kill your brother?'

I watched the head of light in his eyes, the curve of his palms on the arm of the chair.

'That's what all this bullshit is about? Somebody

hit your brother and you think we were behind it?' he said.

He widened his eyes, pursed his lips with his own question. He started to smile but glanced at my face and thought better of it.

'I'm sorry to tell you this, old boy. It wasn't us,' he said. 'Why would we want to hurt your brother?'

'He looks like my twin.'

'Ah yes, I heard something like that. Give us our innings, though. We don't make those kinds of mistakes, at least not as a rule. Actually, we'd marked you off, thought you'd be working on some of your own problems for a while.'

'Get back on the floor.'

'What are we doing now, Lieutenant?'

'You go well with the rug.'

I cut the light cord, tied his wrists behind him, pulled his bare feet up in the air, and wrapped the cord tightly around his ankles. Then I emptied all the drawers on the floor, went through all the clothes in his closets, dumped his suitcases on the bed, looked in his mailbox, went through everything in his wallet, and poured his garbage can out on the kitchen table. There was nothing in the duplex that would indicate that he had any life at all outside of Biloxi, Mississippi. There wasn't a matchbook cover, a canceled check, a credit-card receipt, an unpaid bill that would indicate he had even been out of the duplex. Almost everything in the apartment could have been purchased yesterday at K-Mart. The exception was a box of Trojan rubbers in the drawer of his nightstand, and his works – a very clean syringe, two shining hypodermic needles, a spoon with a bent and tape-wrapped handle and three packets of high-grade scag, all kept lovingly in a velvet-lined, zippered leather case.

'My, my, we do like to probe after a man's vices, don't we?' he said. He was on his side in the middle of the living room rug. 'Give you a little rush, doesn't it, like watching a dirty movie? Your secret sins aren't so bad after all.'

I closed the leather case and tapped my fingers on it a moment.

'What to do, what to do, he thinks,' Murphy said. 'He can drop the dime with the locals and have the depraved old junkie locked up in a county slam. But then there's the problem of breaking into a man's house with a shotgun, isn't there?

'Or maybe a trip back to New Orleans. But, zounds, that's kidnapping. The worries of our chivalric detective seem endless. It's a great burden, being one of the good guys, isn't it? There are so many lofty standards to uphold. Your little piece of tail from Kansas isn't so discriminating.'

'What?'

'We checked her out. She has a file.'

'You are a CIA, then.'

'Are you so dumb you think the government is one group of people? Like the U. S. Forest Service in their Smoke Bear suits? Even your regular punch knows better than that. Ask her. She's had some interesting experiences as a peace groupie back in the land of Oz. Except she was so committed she balled everything in sight and got herself knocked up. So she took a little horseback ride across the prairie and bounced the little fellow right out of there. Almost as messy as a coat hanger. But fortunately for you they have good doctors in

Wichita, and they took out the baby carriage and left the playpen intact.'

I flipped the leather case through the kitchen door onto the pile of garbage I had poured over the table, then I went into the bedroom and picked up a shirt and a pair of slacks and shoes from the closet floor. Lightning splintered the sky outside, and thunder reverberated through the house. The rain was hitting hard against the windowpanes. I dropped the clothes next to him, untied his hands, and picked up the shotgun again.

'Put them on,' I said.

'Travel time?' he said, and smiled.

'Get dressed, Murphy.'

'I don't think this is going to be a pleasant trip.'

'Think of your alternatives. This is Mississippi.'

'I suspect I'll be riding in the trunk.' He sat on the floor and put on his shirt. 'Do you mind if I use the bathroom? I was headed there when you knocked.'

'Leave the door open,' I said.

He walked flatfooted to the toilet, like an old man, in his pajama bottoms and unbuttoned shirt. He looked back at me while he took out his penis and urinated loudly in the water. His face was composed, pink in the fluorescent light, as though he had surrendered both to the situation and the release in his kidneys. Out of decency or revulsion, I suppose, I looked away from him. The trees were thrashing against the windows, and through the edge of the shades I could see the lawn flicker whitely as lightning leaped across the sky. I was tired, my hands thick with fatigue so that they didn't want to curve around the stock and pump of the shotgun.

He might have pulled it off if he hadn't scraped the ceramic top of the toilet tank when he lifted it up to get the Walther 7.65 millimeter that was taped inside. But he had gotten his hand securely around the handle just as I snapped off the safety on the trigger guard, lifted the sawed-off barrel from the hip, and fired at his chest. The angle was bad, and the explosion of buckshot blew the side of the doorjamb away in a shower of white splinters and tore the shirt off his shoulder and streaked a long pattern of blood on the wallpaper, as though it had been slung there by a paintbrush. Later, I would never be able to decide whether the second shot was necessary. But the Walther was in his hand, the black electrician's tape hanging loose from the barrel, the broken ceramic top lying in the toilet bowl. I ejected the spent shell from the magazine, pumped the next round into the chamber, smelled the smoke and cordite in the air, and almost simultaneously pulled the trigger. It was a deer slug, and it caught him just below the heart and blew him backwards, his arms outspread, his face filled with disbelief, through the glass shower doors into the bathtub.

I picked up the warm shells off the rug and put them into my pocket. I looked down at Murphy in the tub. The deer slug had flattened inside him and had made an exit hole in his back the size of a half-dollar. His eyes were open and staring, and his face was absolutely white, as though the wound had drained every drop of his blood out of him. One hand still twitched convulsively on his pot belly.

But I took no joy in it.

I hung the shotgun on the hanger under my arm,

buttoned my raincoat, and walked back out in the storm. The air was cool and smelled of wet trees and torn leaves blowing in the wind and the sulfurous odor of lightning that licked across the black sky over the Gulf. The rain sluiced off my hatbrim and blew in my face, and I walked through the dark puddles of water on the sidewalk as though they were not there. In a few more hours it would be dawn, the eastern sky would be pink with the new day, the palm trees and the beach and the fingers of surf sliding up on the sand would light slowly as the sun climbed in the sky, and I would be back in New Orleans with this night in my life somehow arranged in the proper compartment.

But my thought processes of convenience and my attempts at magic were seldom successful. The storm blew all night and well into the next day, and back on my houseboat I didn't feel better about anything.

11

That afternoon I visited Jimmie in the hospital. He was still in intensive care, his condition unchanged, his voice still locked inside his chest. His hands and face looked as though they had been painted with wet ash.

At five-thirty I drove over to Annie's place. The sky had cleared and the air was suddenly blue and gold when the sun broke through the clouds, but the wind was still loud in the oak trees along the lane, and torn leaves were scattered across the lawns. She fixed both of us iced coffee, tuna sandwiches, and deviled eggs, and we took them out on the back porch and ate on the glass table under the chinaberry tree. She wore white Levi's, a pink pull-over blouse, and gold hoop earrings that made her look like a flower child of the sixties. I hadn't told her about Jimmie, or anything about Biloxi, but she had caught my mood when I came through the door, and now as I sat with my food half eaten, her anxiety and incomprehension in having to deal with a representative of a violent and unfathomable world stole back into her face.

'What is it, Dave? Can't you trust me a little? Are

we always going to stake out our private areas that we don't let the other one into?'

So I told her about Jimmie.

'I thought it was probably in the newspaper,' I said. 'He's a well-known guy in the Quarter.'

'I don't –' she began.

'You don't read those kinds of stories.'

She looked away, her eyes hurt.

'I'm sorry. Jimmie might not make it, and I might not be around to help him, either. I'm in some very big trouble right now.'

Her blue eyes looked intently into mine.

'The roses and the pralines in the delicatessen,' she said. 'That's why you didn't want to see me. You were going somewhere, and you thought I'd try to stop you.'

'There's no reason I should bring all my problems into your life. Loving a girl shouldn't include making her miserable.'

'Dave, why do you think you're the only person who can bear hardship? A relationship is more than just sleeping with somebody, at least it is with me. I don't want to be your part-time lover. If you really want to do some damage, keep treating me like somebody who can't take it, who has to be protected.'

'I'm going to hurt you tonight, and I don't have any way around it.'

'I don't understand.'

'I had to kill Philip Murphy last night in Biloxi.'

Her face jumped, and I saw her throat swallow.

'He didn't give me a choice,' I said. 'I guess I wanted to do it when I went over there but wanting to do something and deliberately choosing to do it are two different things. I was going to take him back to New Orleans. I got careless, and he thought he could drop me.'

'Was he the one who shot your brother?' Her voice was quiet, the knowledge I had given her an enormous pain behind her eyes.

'I don't think so.'

'What are you going to do?'

'I'm not quite sure yet. Somebody'll find the body soon. In this weather, even with the air conditioning on –'

I saw her mouth form a tight line and her nostrils dilate slightly.

'The point is, sooner or later I'll be arrested,' I said.

'You did it in self-defense.'

'I broke into somebody's house with a shotgun, with no legal authority. Then I left the scene of a homicide. It'll take them a while, but they'll run my prints and eventually get a warrant out.'

'We have to talk with somebody. It isn't fair,' she said. 'Everything you do turns back on you. You're an innocent man. It's these other people who should be in jail. Doesn't anybody in that police department see that?'

'I've told you all this for another reason, Annie.' I let out my breath. 'Murphy said some things I have to ask you about. He was an evil man who tried to make others think the world was as evil as he was. But if any part of what he said is true, he had connections with a government agency or somebody in one.'

'What –'

'He said you were a peace groupie back in

Kansas. He said you got pregnant and lost the child riding a horse.'

I waited. Her face flushed and her eyes filmed with tears.

'They reach far into your life, don't they?' she said.

'Annie –'

'What else did he have to say?'

'Nothing. Don't let a man like that wound you.'

'I don't care about him. It's you. Do you think I aborted my own child on a horse?'

'I don't think anything.'

'You do. It's in your face. Is she the person I thought she was? Was she an easy piece for those weird people back in Kansas?'

'I don't have a doubt in the world about who or what you are. Annie, you're everything to me.'

She put her fork down on her plate and looked into the evening shadows on the yard.

'I don't think I can handle this,' she said.

'There nothing to handle. It's over. I just had to find out if he was wired into the government. The Treasury people told me he wasn't.'

But she wasn't hearing me.

She looked down at her plate, then back at me again. Her eyes were wet and her chin was dented with tiny dimples.

'Dave, I feel just like I did the night that man put his hands on me.'

'Your family is involved with the peace movement, and the FBI probably collected some gossip on you all. It doesn't mean anything. They have files on all kinds of people, most of it for no explainable reason. They followed Ernest

Hemingway around for twenty-five years, even when he was receiving electroshock treatments right before his death. Joe Namath's and John Wayne's names were on a White House enemies list.' I touched her on the arm and smiled at her. 'Come on, who was more American than the Duke?'

'I was seventeen. He was a Mennonite student from Nebraska, working in the home-repair program in Wichita for the summer.'

'You don't need to tell me this.'

'No, goddamn it, I'm not to have the lies of those people in our lives. I didn't tell him about the baby. He was too young to be a husband. He went back to school in Nebraska and never knew about it. When I was seven months pregnant we had a terrible electric storm at the farm. My parents had gone to town, and my grandfather was harrowing on the edge of an irrigation ditch. He was an old-order Mennonite and he harrowed with a team instead of a tractor. But he'd never quit work because of weather, unless it washed him right out of the field. I was watching him from the front porch, and I could see the wind blowing dust around him and lightning jumping all over the horizon. The sky was blue-gray, the way it gets in Kansas when you see tornadoes start spinning out of the earth, way off in the distance. Then a bolt of lightning hit a cottonwood tree next to the irrigation ditch, and I saw him and the team and the harrow topple over the side.

'I ran across the field in the rain. He was under the harrow, with his face pressed down in the mud. I couldn't get him out, and I thought he was going to suffocate. I cleaned the dirt out of his mouth and nose and put my shirt under his head. Then I got one of the mules untangled from the harness. The phone in the house was dead, and I had to ride four miles down the road to a neighbor's house to get help. I miscarried in their front yard. They put me in the back of a pickup with a roof on it and drove me to the hospital in Wichita. I almost bled to death on the way.'

'You're one hell of a girl, Annie.'

'Why did that man tell you those things?'

'He wanted to rattle me, get my mind on something else. He figured he had one play left, and he was going to take it.'

'I feel afraid for you.'

'You shouldn't. Four of them are dead, and I'm still walking around. When I was in Vietnam I used to try and think everything through. Then one day a friend told me, 'Forget the complexities. The only thing that counts is that you're still on top of the ground, sucking air.'

'Except you don't believe that.'

'A person has to act and think in the way that works for him. I can't control all this bullshit in my life. I didn't deal any of it. In fact, I tried to deal myself out. It didn't work out that way.'

I saw the sadness in her eyes, and I took her hands in mine.

'The only thing I'm sorry about is having brought problems into your life,' I said. 'It's the cop's malaise.'

'And problems I have with you are problems I want.'

'You don't understand, Annie. When I told you about Biloxi I made you an accessory after the fact.

So when I came over here this evening, I guess I did know what I have to do. I'd better go now. I'll call later.'

'Where are you going?'

'I've got to set things straight. Don't worry. Things always work out before the ninth race.'

'Stay.'

She stood up from the table and looked down at me. I got up and put my arms around her, felt her body come against me, felt it become small and close under my hands, felt her hands under my chin and her sandaled foot curve around my ankle. I kissed her hair and her eyes, and when she opened them again, all I could see was the electric blueness in them.

'Let's go inside,' she said. Her voice was a low, thick whisper in my ear, her fingers like the brush of a bird's wing on my thigh.

Later, in the darkness of her bedroom, the sunset an orange and purple glow beyond the half-closed blinds, she lay against my chest and rubbed her hand over my skin.

'One day you'll have a quiet heart,' she said.

'It's quiet now.'

'No, it isn't. You're already thinking about the rest of the night. But one day you'll feel all the heat go out of you.'

'Some people aren't made like that.'

'Why do you think that?' she asked quietly.

'Because of the years I invested in dismantling myself, I was forced to learn about some things that went on in my head. I don't like the world the way it is, and I miss the past. It's a foolish way to be.'

★

I left Annie's and drove over toward St. Mary's Dominican College, where Captain Guidry lived with his mother in a Victorian house, not far from the Mississippi levee. It was a yellow house, in need of paint, and the lawn hadn't been cut and the lower gallery was overgrown with trees and untrimmed shrubs. The windows were all dark, except for the light of a television screen in the living room. I unlatched the picket gate and walked up the cracked walkway to the front porch. The porch swing hung at an angle on rusted chains, and the door bell was the kind you twisted with a handle. I thought it was about time the captain seriously considered marrying the widow in the water department.

'Dave, what are you doing out here?' he said when he opened the door. He wore a rumpled sports shirt, slippers, and old slacks with paint stains on them. He held a cup with a tea bag in it.

'I'm sorry to bother you at home. I need to talk with you.'

'Sure, come in. My mother just went to bed. I was watching the ball game.'

The living room was dark, smelled of dust and Mentholatum, and was filled with nineteenth-century furniture. The furniture wasn't antique; it was simply old, like the clutter of clocks, vases, religious pictures, coverless books, tasseled pillows, and stacked magazines that took up every inch of available space in the room. I sat down in a deep, stuffed chair that was threadbare on the arms.

'You want tea or a Dr Pepper?' he said.

'No, thanks.'

'You want anything else?' He looked at me carefully.

'Nope.'

'Thataboy. Jimmie's still holding his own, isn't he?'

'He's the same.'

'Yeah, I checked on him at noon. He's going to make it, Dave. If they get through the first day, they usually make it all the way. It's like something down inside of them catches a second breath.'

'I'm in some serious trouble. I thought about just riding it out, then I thought about getting out of town.'

He reached over from where he sat on the couch and clicked off the ball game.

'Instead, I figured I better face it now before it gets worse, if that's possible,' I said.

'What is it?'

'I had to kill Philip Murphy last night in Biloxi.' I saw his jaw set and his eyes light angrily.

'I was going to bring him in,' I said. 'That's the truth, Captain. I let him go into the bathroom to take a leak, and he had a Walther taped inside the toilet tank. He called the play.'

'No, you called the play when you started acting on your own authority, when you refused to accept the terms of your suspension, when you went as a vigilante into another state. I asked you at the hospital to have a little patience, a little trust. I guess those were wasted words.'

'I respect you, Captain, but how much trust have people had in me?'

'Listen to what you're saying. Can you imagine making a statement like that in a courtroom?'

I felt my face flush, and I had to look away from his eyes.

'You still haven't told me everything, though, have you?' he said.

'No.'

'You left the scene and you didn't report it?'

'Yes.'

'What else?'

'I think Purcel killed Bobby Joe Starkweather.'

'What for?'

'I don't know.'

'Maybe he was just riding in St. Charles Parish one morning and decided he wanted to blow away a redneck,' the captain said.

'There was a witness. I have her name and where she works.'

'But you didn't bother telling this to anyone before?'

'She's a doper and a hooker, Captain. Her brains are as soft as yesterday's ice cream. I didn't know what would happen to her if they kept her as a material witness, either.'

'I'm having a hard time assimilating all this, Dave. I hate to tell you this, but this Purcel business sounds like it came out of a bottle. Maybe his personal problems are about to screw up his career with the department, but he's not an assassin, for God's sake.'

I felt tired, empty, my options all spent, and all of it for no purpose whatsoever. The captain was a good man. I didn't know what I had expected of him, actually. In going to his house with my strange stories, I had given him even fewer alternatives than I had myself.

'Give me the address,' he said. 'I'm going to call the Biloxi police department. Then we need to go down to the station, and I think you should call an attorney.'

He made the long-distance call, and I listened glumly while he talked with someone in their homicide division. I felt like a child whose errant behavior would now have to be taken over by a group of bemused authority figures. The captain finished and hung up the phone.

'They're sending a car out there and they'll call me back,' he said.

I sat in the silence. 'Did that black kid ever find anything in the mug books?'

'No, he was too scared, poor kid. We found out he's a little bit retarded too. You don't think Murphy pulled the trigger?'

'No.'

The captain blew air out of his nose. His fingers made a design on the arm of the couch as we sat in the gloom.

'Captain, did you hear anything about Didi Gee being indicted?'

'No, but you know how they are in the prosecutor's office. They dummy up on us sometimes, particularly when they're thinking about a roll of drums on the six-o'clock news. What did you hear?'

'He thinks he's going to he indicted.'

'He told you this? You've been talking with Didi Gee?'

'He asked me out to Mama Lido's. He gave me the line on Murphy.'

'Dave, I'm advising you at this point that you should be careful of what you tell me.'

'I believe he thinks he might actually go to Angola.'

'If the prosecutor's office is taking Didi Gee before the grand jury, it doesn't have anything to do with homicide. We had two cases I thought we could tie to his tail, and the prosecutor sat on his hands until one witness blew town and another time a clerk threw away a signed confession. You remember two years ago when somebody cut up a bookie named Joe Roth and stuffed him into the trash compactor in his own house? The next-door neighbor heard a Skilsaw whining in the middle of the night, and saw two guys leave the house at dawn, carrying a bloody paper sack. We found out later it contained the overalls they wore while they sawed up Roth's body. The neighbor picked out one of Didi Gee's hoods from a lineup, the guy had no alibi, his car had blood on the seat, he was a two-time loser and psychotic who would have sold Didi Gee's ass at a garage sale to stay out of the electric chair. But the prosecutor's office messed around for five months, and our witness sold his house at a loss and moved to Canada. So I can't take their current efforts too seriously. If they want to put the fat boy away, they should be talking to us, and they're not.

'I'm not sure what you're getting at, Dave, but it doesn't make any difference. It's our territory now, not yours, even though we're talking about your brother. What's the word they use when they're talking about characters in Shakespeare's plays?'

'Hubris?'

'Yeah, that's the word. Pride, a guy not knowing when he should sit one out. I think maybe that's the origin of our problem here.'

Captain Guidry turned the ball game on and pretended to watch it while we waited for the call. He was clearly uncomfortable. I suppose he was thinking he might actually have to arrest me. Finally, he got up, went into the kitchen, and brought us back two bottles of Dr Pepper.

'You remember a drink called Dr. Nut when we were kids?' he said.

'Sure.'

'Boy, those were good, weren't they? The closest thing to it is a Dr Pepper. I guess that's why Southerners drink Dr Pepper all the time.' He paused in the silence and brushed the tops of his fingers with his palms. 'Look, I know you think the bottom's dropped out of everything, but try to look at what you got. You've put the cork in the jug, you've still got good friends, and you have a hell of a fine record as a police officer behind you.'

'I appreciate it, Captain.'

The phone rang, and he answered it with obvious relief. He listened for almost a full minute, his eyes blinking occasionally, then he said, 'That's what he said – on Azalea Drive, the last pink stucco duplex. Next to a vacant lot.' He looked at me. 'That's right, isn't it, Dave? It's the last place on the street, and the apartment next door has newspapers on the lawn?'

I nodded.

'You got the right house,' he said into the phone. 'Did you find the landlord? . . . I see . . . No, sir, I don't understand it, either. I'd appreciate it, though, if you'd keep us informed, and we'll do the same . . . Yes, sir, thank you for your time and courtesy.'

He hung up the phone and touched the hair implants in his scalp.

'The place is empty,' he said.

'What?'

'There's no Philip Murphy, no body in the shower, no clothes in the closets, nothing in the cabinets or drawers. The next-door neighbor says a couple of guys were there this morning with a U-Haul trailer. The only thing that checks out is that the glass is gone from the shower doors, and it looks like somebody sawed a piece out of the bathroom doorjamb. Did it have some lead in it?'

'Yeah, I caught the edge of it with the first round.'

'I don't know what to tell you, Dave.'

'What about the landlord?'

'He lives in Mobile. They haven't talked with him yet.'

'What about blood?'

'The place is clean. You're off the hook, at least for now.'

'This means there's more of them out there. They're like army ants that trundle off their dead.'

'I have thirty-two years in the department. Only once before have I run into something like this, and to tell you the truth it unnerved me for a long time. About twenty-two or twenty-three years ago, a car with three soldiers in it got hit by a train on Tchoupitoulas. They were all killed, and I mean really ground up under the engine. What bothered me was that all three of them were wearing seat belts. What are the odds of three fatalities all wearing their seat belts? Also, guys that are that careful don't put themselves in front of trains. Anyway, it was winter and they were supposed to be on leave from Fort Dix, New Jersey, but they had suntans like they'd been lying on the beach for six months. I think they were dead before the train ever hit them. Somebody belted them in their car and put them on the track at three in the morning.

'But I'll never know for sure, because the army claimed their bodies, bagged them up, and that's the last I heard of it. We'd better talk to the Treasury people tomorrow morning.'

'They have a way of becoming comatose when they hear my voice on the phone.'

'I'll call them. You did the right thing, coming here tonight. Things look a little better than they did a while ago, don't they?'

'Yes, sir, they do.'

'There's something else I want to tell you. It looks like the prosector's office is going to drop the concealed-weapon charge against you.'

'Why?'

'Elections are coming around again. It's law-and-order time. They're going to make a lot of newsprint about gambling and narcotics, and they don't want people accusing them of wasting taxpayers' money while they try a cop on a chickenshit weapons charge.'

'Are you sure?'

'That's what I heard. Don't take it to the bank yet. But those guys over there are on their way up to higher things, and they don't care about our little problems in the department. Anyway, coast awhile, will you, Dave?'

But scared money never wins. You don't ease up on the batter in the ninth, you don't give up the rail on the far turn.

The next day it rained just before dawn, and

when the sun came up, the trees along Carondelet were green and dripping, and the air was so thick with moisture it was almost foglike, suffused with a pink light the color of cotton candy. I parked down the street from Clete's house in a working-class neighborhood that would eventually be all black. His lawn had been recently mowed, but it had been cut in uneven strips, with ragged tufts of grass sticking up between the mower's tracks, and the cracks in the sidewalk and driveway were thick with weeds. His garbage cans had been emptied yesterday, but they still lay out front, their battered sides glistening with dew. At seven-thirty he came out the front door, dressed in a white short-sleeved shirt, a striped tie, and seersucker pants, his coat over his arm. His belt was hitched under his navel, the way a retired football player might wear it, and his big shoulders made him look as if he had put on a boy's shirt by mistake.

I followed him across town in the traffic. Up ahead at a red light, as the heat and humidity of the day began to gather and intensify among the tall buildings and jammed automobiles, I saw him yawn widely, rub his face as though he were trying to put life back in dead tissue, and rest his head against the door. There was a man with a real dose of the yellow-dog blues, I thought. By midmorning he would be sweating heavily, emptying the water cooler, debating whether he should eat more aspirin, hiding with his misery in the darkness of a toilet stall; at noon he would emerge into the sun's glare and the roar of traffic, drive across Canal to a café where nobody knew him so he could drink beer with his meal until one o'clock and glue his day back together. He was serving hard time, but it was about to get worse.

He double-parked in front of the Greyhound bus depot and went inside, putting on his coat. Five minutes later he was back in his car, working his way into the traffic, looking around as though the whole world were coming at him in the rearview mirror.

I went back to my houseboat, called the hospital about Jimmie, pumped iron, ran four miles along the lakefront, cleaned and oiled my twelve-gauge, and cooked some redfish and dirty rice for lunch while I listened to a recording of Blind Lemon Jefferson:

> Dig my grave with a silver spade
> And see that my grave is kept clean
> Oh dear Lord, lower me down on a golden
> chain.

I wondered why it was that only black people seemed to treat death realistically in their art. White people wrote about it as an abstraction, used it as a poetic device, concerned themselves with it only when it was remote. Most of Shakespeare's and Frost's poems about death were written when both men were young. When Billie Holiday, Blind Lemon Jefferson, or Leadbelly sang about it, you heard the cock of the prison guard's rifle, saw the black silhouette suspended from a tree against a dying red sun, smelled the hot pine box being lowered into the same Mississippi soil a sharecropper had labored against all his life.

That afternoon I went up to the hospital and

spent two hours with Jimmie. He slept with the remoteness of someone who had moved off into another dimension. Occasionally his mouth twitched, as though a fly had settled on it, and I wondered what painful shard of memory was at work under the almost featureless, ashlike mask that had become his face. I hoped he was not remembering the gun flashes fired point blank at his head through the door of the toilet stall. Few people appreciate the level of terror that a person experiences at that moment. Soldiers learn not to talk about it. Civilian victims try to explain it to friends and therapists, and are often treated with the sympathy we extend to babbling psychotics. But the best description I ever heard of it was not from a soldier or victim. We had a serial killer in an isolation cell at the First District, and he gave an interview to a woman reporter from the *Times-Picayune*. I'll never forget his words:

'There's no rush in the world like it. They drown when you point it at them. They beg and piss their pants. They cry, they tell you to do it to somebody else, they try to hide behind their own hands. It's like watching somebody melt into pudding.'

But I had no way of knowing what battle Jimmie was fighting inside himself. Maybe nothing went on inside Jimmie. Tomorrow they were going into his skull with the brace and bit to pick out the fragments of lead and bone that were stuck in his brain. But maybe they wouldn't simply find brain cells that were prized and broken as though they had been teased with an icepick; it was possible that the injuries were larger, the doctor said, like the dead and pulpy edges of bruised fruit. If so, his mind could deteriorate to the point that his thoughts would be little more than sand pattern drifting back and forth under the currents of a dull sea.

At five o'clock I was parked a block down Basin from First District headquarters when Clete walked out the front door. I followed him again to the Greyhound bus depot and watched him double-park, go inside, then return a few minutes later to his automobile. Even though I was now sure what he was up to, I had trouble believing it. We were required by department policy to carry our weapons both on and off duty, but his wife's fears and objections about guns were evidently enough to make him put himself in a position that was incredibly vulnerable.

I watched his car head off into the traffic, then I drove to an open-air café on Decatur across from the French Market, sat at the raw bar and ate a bowl of shrimp gumbo and two dozen oysters on the half-shell, and read the afternoon newspaper. A young crowd was in the café, and they were playing Island music on the jukebox, drinking Jax on tap, and eating oysters as fast as the Negro barman could rake them out of the ice bins and shuck them open on a tray. After the traffic had thinned and the streets had cooled in the lengthening shadows, I drove back to Clete's house off Carondelet.

When he opened the door he had a can of beer in his hand, and he wore a pair of baggy swimming trunks and a T-shirt that said DON'T MESS WITH MY TOOT-TOOT on the front. His eyes were bleary, and I suspected that he had skipped supper and had already committed himself to a serious evening of mentally sawing himself apart.

'Hey, Dave, what's happening?' he said. 'Come on out on the back porch. I'm tying some flies. I think I'm going out to Colorado and do some trout fishing.'

'Where's Lois?'

'She took the girls to a show. I think they go to about ten shows a week. I don't care, though. She gets discount tickets from the bank, and it's better for them than watching that MTV stuff. They're her kids, anyway, right? Say, tell me something. Did I see you down on Canal this morning?'

'Maybe.'

'Going down to see Jimmie?'

'I saw him this afternoon.'

'Oh. How is he?'

'He goes into surgery again tomorrow. We'll know a lot more then.'

'I'm real sorry about Jimmie. He's a fine guy.'

'I appreciate it, Clete.'

'Excuse the mess out here. Just throw those magazines on the floor and sit down. You want a Coke or coffee or something?'

'No, thanks.'

He had built the sun porch himself three years ago. It looked like a cracker hammered onto the back of the house. Vases of unwatered brown ferns and wilted spider plants hung in the windows, and the throw rugs he used to cover the concrete pad looked like discarded colored towels. He had set up a card table in the center of the room, and on it was a fly-tying vise, spools of thread, different types of bird feathers, and a tangle of tiny hooks. An unfinished, ragged fly was clamped in the vise.

He sat down in a canvas chair and took another beer from an ice-filled cooler.

'I'm going to take two weeks' vacation time, and we're going to head out to Colorado,' he said, 'Lois is going to visit her Buddhist priest, maybe get him out of her system, then we're going to camp on the Gunnison River, fish, backpack, live in a tent, do all that health stuff. I can get off cigarettes, lose some weight, maybe cut down on the booze. It's a chance for us to get a fresh start. I'm really looking forward to it.'

'I've got your nine-millimeter.'

'What?'

'I followed you to the bus depot.'

The stiff skin around his mouth tried to wrinkle into a smile.

'What are we talking about?' he said.

'I followed you there this morning and again this afternoon. Then I got Bobo Getz to open your locker for me. You remember him. He used to buy room keys off the hookers at the Ramada.'

His face became wooden. He lowered his eyes and slid a cigarette in and out of the pack.

'What are you trying to do to me, Dave?' he asked.

'Nobody has done anything to you. You jumped into the pig flop by yourself.'

'So I'm ashamed of leaving my weapon in a bus locker. But this isn't a home. It's a goddamn lunatic asylum. Who the hell set you up as my judge?'

'Run that game on somebody else. Ballistics will match your weapon to the bullet that come out of Bobby Joe Starkweather. You should have lost it somewhere.'

'Yeah? Maybe I didn't expect my partner to boost it from me.' He took the cigarette out of the pack, lighted it with a Zippo, dropped the lighter loudly on the tabletop, and rubbed his hand over his face while he blew out the smoke. 'So you gonna put me in the wringer?'

'Why'd you do it?'

'Ten thousand bucks.'

I didn't say anything. I looked at his big hands, the way a cigarette looked so small in them, his scarred, poached face, and wondered what had happened to the good-humored and intelligent man I used to work with.

'Come on, he was garbage and you know it,' he said. 'The credit union wouldn't give me another loan, I'm still paying alimony to my first wife, I owe the finance company, and I was paying fifty a week to a shylock. I could have handled it, but I had some complications with a girl. She said she was a month late, and she stiffed me for a grand to get lost without having a talk with Lois. That's about all it would have taken to put her in hospital.'

'Who paid you, Clete?'

'Murphy.'

'Why did he want him killed? Why did he want a cop to do it?'

'What difference does it make?'

'You're going to have to explain it sometime.'

'He said the guy was an asshole, he was out of control or something.'

'Murphy didn't need to pay cops to hit somebody.'

His brow wrinkled. He wiped a piece of tobacco off the corner of his mouth.

'You said "didn't".'

'He's not a player anymore.'

It took a second for the recognition to work into his eyes.

'Man, you don't fuck around, do you?' he said.

'Come on, Clete, why a cop?'

He waited a moment, and I saw the heat come back in his face.

'He said he worked for a guy. I suppose that general, what's his name, the guy whose house you got busted at, he said the guy didn't believe in whacking his own people. It's probably bullshit. All of them are slime, anyway.'

'So you knew Murphy before?'

'No. He knew me. At least he knew I was paying a shylock.' He drank from his beer can, inhaled from his cigarette, studied his hands, then raised his eyes again.

'Where do we go from here, partner?' he asked.

'I don't know.'

'Is a piece of shit like Starkweather this important?'

'You not only killed a man for money, you could have brought him and Murphy in. You could have gotten me off the hook.'

'I don't read it that way. But I don't guess that's important now. Are you going to give them my piece?'

'I don't have it.'

'What?'

'I just guessed you were dropping it and picking it up at the bus locker.'

He shook his head and blew out his breath as though I'd kicked him in the stomach.

'Damn, if you aren't slick, Streak.' He began to flick the fly clamped in the vise with his fingernail. 'What do you think I ought to do now?'

'I don't care what you do,' I said. 'Get out of town. Go to Colorado. Take up Zen with Lois. I just know one thing for sure – don't ever call me "partner" again.'

12

Jimmy went into surgery at eight the next morning, and they didn't wheel him into the recovery room until almost noon. The doctor found me in the waiting room and sat down in his greens on the leather couch next to me. He was prematurely bald and talked with a west Texas accent. His fingers looked as though they could cover a basketball.

'I call this kind a dusting-and-cleaning situation,' he said. 'There was a messy spot or two, but most everything was on the surface. All things considered, it cleaned up beautifully. I'm still concerned about that eye, but at least I don't think we're talking about paralysis anymore. I hope that's good news for you this morning.'

'It is, Doctor.'

'Now, about the other stuff – general recovery, post-effects, psychological trauma, we can't really tell you. There's a lot about the brain we don't understand. I've had to cut 'em open and go in with an ice-cream scoop, and somehow the other parts of the brain compensate and the person can live a fairly normal life. Then I've seen a simple fracture cause a guy headaches that almost drove him to suicide. It's like the jack-in-the box. Sometimes you just don't know what's going to jump up at you. But we've got a great eye man here and fine therapists, and every day it's going to get better for your brother. You follow me? In other words, we've got it turned around, and that's what counts.'

We shook hands, then I stopped by the gift shop downstairs and had fresh flowers sent up to Jim's room. I saw a big plastic crawfish in the gift case, and I had the salesgirl tie it with a bow to the flower vase.

I went back to the files and the *Picayune*'s morgue. Once again, the photographs and news stories sent me back across the sea, back into the era that would always be mine, whether I had wanted it or not. As I stared at the pictures of grunts loading their wounded into a dustoff, the elephant grass flattening around them, their dust-filmed faces streaked with dried sweat, their heads twisted back at the gunfire they still heard behind them, I felt like a leper who could not stop picking at his own crusted lesions. And like that leper, I knew I was about to sink my finger into a dark recess of pain and grief that did not cauterize with time. I flipped the frames of microfilm up on the viewing screen until I saw again the series of photographs taken during and after the My Lai massacre. I had never been able to rid myself of one of those photographs since I had first seen it in *Newsweek* magazine fifteen years ago. The villagers had been herded together, a GI with an M-16 was facing them, and a woman was begging with clasped hands while her little boy, not more than five, held her skirt and looked out from behind her with uncomprehending terror on his face. His mouth was open, the skin of his face was stretched tight with fear, and his eyes were wide with the knowledge that his mother's words could not protect him from what was about to happen.

The next frame on the microfilm showed the ditch where they were executed. On the floor of the ditch, amid the tangle of dead adults, was the body of a little boy who wore the same short pants and T-shirt as the child in the first picture. This was the war that an American called a holy cause.

I knew that I would always be caught in that lens, too, locked inside a frame of film that people would never be able to deal with, because to deal with it would require an admission of responsibility that would numb an entire nation.

That is why the word *obsession* is a convenient one in the analytical vocabulary. We apply it to those who were trapped inside the camera, who can never extricate themselves from those darker periods in history that were written for them by somebody else. But I had a feeling that the general would understand what I meant, that he too had heard the click of the shutter in an unexpected moment, had realized with a quickening of the heart that some of us are meant to be only sojourners in the present.

Then a strange thing happened that afternoon. I drove back to my houseboat, ate a sandwich and drank a glass of iced tea, and suddenly felt very tired. I took a nap, with the fan blowing across me in the hot cabin, and awoke an hour later with the thick heat of the afternoon in my head. I pumped water into the kitchen sink, splashed my face and dried it with a paper towel, and stared abstractedly out the window into the gleaming sunlight. Then my eyes focused on a man who stood under a palm tree farther down the beach. His hair was absolutely white, his skin deeply tanned, his posture erect as he smoked a cigarette in a holder and looked out at the shimmering lake from behind pilot's sunglasses. I rubbed the moisture out of my eyes with my fingers and looked again. I suspected that possibly I was obsessed after all. I went out on my deck and saw him turn and look at me. Cigarette smoke drifted away from his mouth in the wind. I walked quickly across the gangplank onto the dock and headed down the beach toward him. He looked at me a moment longer, removed the cigarette from his holder and dropped it into the sand, then casually walked to a gunmetal gray Chrysler and drove away. The heat was like steam rising from a stove.

I put on my running shoes and shorts, did four miles along the beach, showered in my tin stall, and called Annie and told her I would pick her up for supper after I visited Jimmie at the hospital. But just as I was locking up, Captain Guidry parked his car under the palm trees by my dock and walked down the path through the sand dune toward me. He carried his coat over his shoulder, and he wore his badge on one side of his belt and his clip-on .38 holster on the other. He wore long-sleeved white shirts and a tie even in the summer, and there were huge loops of sweat under his arms.

'Give me a few minutes of your time,' he said.

I unlocked the door, fixed him a rum and Coke, made myself a glass of instant iced coffee, and sat down with him at my deck table under the canvas umbrella. The heat and humidity of the afternoon had started to lift and break apart in the evening breeze, and there were patches of dark blue floating in the green of the lake.

'I shouldn't drink this,' he said. 'I had a couple of belts right after work, and I probably don't need any more. But . . . so what? Cheers, Dave.'

'You're not a man we can accuse of many vices, Captain.'

'Yeah, but my life is pretty boring as a consequence. At least it is until I get hung up on a case. I want to get you back into the department. You're too valuable to be marking time out here on your boat. I'll tell you something straight out. You're probably the best investigative officer I ever had under me. You have honest-to-God talent and ability. There's nobody else I can depend on like I've depended on you.'

'That's kind of you, Captain.'

'Forget the kindness. I want people in custody for Jimmie's shooting. I'm ashamed of the number of homicides and attempted homicides we're not prosecuting. I'm convinced that almost every guy we don't nail keeps killing people until he finally falls. I've never bought this number that a murder is usually a one-time excursion. You remember that hit man from New Jersey we busted about five or six years ago? He's been a suspect in something like eighteen contract murders. That's hard to believe, isn't it? He'd still be out there if one of his kind hadn't stuck an icepick in his ear. Anyway, they're not going to walk on this one. I'm going to tie the ribbon on the package and carry it over to the prosecutor's office myself, but I might need a little help. Now don't you bullshit me, Dave. You knew something when you came out of Jimmie's room the day he was shot. I want to know what it is.'

'I didn't hold out on you. I just wasn't sure it meant very much. I'm still not sure it does.'

'What?'

'Jimmie put his fingers on my chest, like he was trying to trace the letters of somebody's name.'

'Okay.'

'I think he knew he couldn't spell out an entire name. But what about initials? Whose name sounds like initials?'

'No, you tell me.'

'Didi Gee. He used me. He had me out to lunch with him and his collection of assholes while Jimmie was being hit. I not only gave him an alibi, I allowed him to shoot off his mouth about his ethics and how people were forcing him to break his own rules.'

'Why would he want to hit Jimmie?'

'He's going up in front of the grand jury, and I'll bet you Jimmie's going to be subpoenaed, too. He knew Jimmie wouldn't perjure himself. He'd take his own fall, and Didi would end up falling with him.'

Captain Guidry drank from his rum and Coke and took his pipe and pouch out of his coat pocket.

'I'm going to tell you a few things, but I need to extract your word of honor about something first,' he said.

'I've stopped dealing in those terms, Captain. That's not meant to be cynical. Considering the kind of mileage I have on my odometer, I just have a hard time thinking about personal honor.'

'That's because you've convinced yourself you're one of the world's great sinners. Let me tell you something. Real honor means you're still intact and functioning after your soul's been shot out of a cannon.'

'What do you want?'

'A promise you won't try to take down Didi Gee.'

'I didn't plan to.'

'You didn't plan that situation over in Biloxi, but it happened anyway, didn't it?'

'As a police officer I've shot four people, and I won't tell you about my record in Vietnam, except that I'm sick of all of it. There's always somebody there to convince you we got to blow 'em away, just this one more time, and the world will be a safer place. If Didi Gee deals the play, that's another matter. But I'm off rock-'n'-roll, Captain.'

He fiddled with his pipe for a while, then stuck it inside the tobacco pouch and put the pouch on the table.

'I got a call from the Fort Lauderdale police department,' he said. 'They try to monitor their local talent, but one of them slipped off the leash and left town for a couple of days. They think he might have been over here.'

'Who is he?'

'A hit man that works for the mob in New Jersey and south Florida. They sent me a picture on the wire, and I showed it to the black kid with five others. He said that's our man.'

'Where's this guy now?'

'Eating lobster on the beach, but we're going to jerk him up short. We'll cut the warrant on the kid's make, they'll pick him up for us, and we'll extradite back to New Orleans. By that time maybe Jimmie can identify him, too. The important thing is we don't let this guy fly.'

'You'd better get a damn high bond, then.'

'It will be. Also, the word's going to be on the street that this guy is a traveling man, a very bad risk. There's one thing you got to remember, though, Dave. We'll need Jimmie for a solid case. I don't think the kid will hold up too well by himself.'

'What about Didi Gee?'

'We'll take it a step at a time. We won't have any trouble showing motive – the prosecutor was going to indict Jimmie and use him as a witness against Didi Gee. I think it comes down to how much time our contact man wants to spend chopping sugar cane in Angola. Fort Lauderdale says he's never had to do any hard time. The possibility of a thirty-year jolt in the Louisiana prison system might really increase his instinct for negotiation.'

'Don't send Purcel after him.'

'Purcel's *my* problem. Don't worry about him.'

'He got ten thousand for Starkweather. He'll take money again. It's never a one-time thing. If you don't believe me, run his nine-millimeter through ballistics. But I bet his house will be robbed by then. Maybe you can get a match off the slugs from the Segura shooting, if they're not too beat up.'

'I hope you have my job one day, Dave. Then you can be responsible for everything that's wrong in the First District. It's something to look forward to.'

'I'm just squaring with you.'

'Yeah, but give me some credit. I'm the one that warned you about protecting Purcel's butt in the first place. Right?'

I didn't answer. The wind was cool now, and it flapped the canvas umbrella over our heads. Twenty yards out, a half-dozen pelicans sailed low over the water, their shadows racing ahead of them on the green surface.

'Right or wrong?' he said, and grinned at me.

'You're right.'

Then his face became serious again.

'But no Didi Gee, no cowboy stuff, no bullshit of any kind,' he said. 'The fat boy's going away, you can count on it, but it's going to be by the numbers. Right?'

'Right,' I said.

But even as I spoke, I thought, *if we break promises to God, shouldn't we be allowed an occasional violation of our word to our friends and superiors?*

Monday morning I had to go through another interview with Internal Affairs, this time concerning my last encounter with Internal Affairs. The three of us sat in a closed, immaculate white room that was furnished with a wooden table and three chairs. My interviewers were takers of notes. The yellow legal pads they wrote on were covered with swirls of calligraphy from their black felt pens. I didn't know either of them.

'Why did you strike Lieutenant Baxter?'

'He provoked me.'

'How's that?'

'What do you care?'

'I beg your pardon?'

'I said why are you asking me these questions? You work with the man every day. You know him better than I do.'

'Should we just indicate that you do not choose to answer the question?'

'I punched Nate Baxter because he's a bad cop. He tries to bully and degrade people. In my case, he tried to ignore evidence in the torture and murder of a federal law officer. Those things aren't demonstrable, but they're true, and both of you guys know it.'

Both of them looked at me blankly across the table. I could hear the air-conditioning humming through a duct in the white silence.

On the way out I got a clerk to pull the computer sheet they had gotten on the hit man from the National Crime Information Center in Washington. It was brief, almost hazy, in its description, in the way that a facial image burned into rock with acid would be hazy and brutal at the same time.

> B. 1957, CAMDEN, NJ, GRADUATED H.S. 1975, ATTENDED MIAMI-DADE C.C. 2 YRS. VOC: DRY CLEANER, APT. MANAGER, SALESMAN. SUSPECTED INVOLVEMENT IN 6 HOMICIDES ORDERED BY ORGANIZED CRIME FIGURES. 1 CONTEMPT CITATION RESULTING IN 3 MONTHS' CONFINEMENT BROWARD COUNTY STOCKADE. CURRENT ADDRESS: CASA DEL MAR, GALT MILE, FT. LAUDERDALE, FL.

I tried to envision the man. The face remained an empty, dark oval, like the pitted center of a rotten piece of fruit, but I could see the simian hands. They were strong, ridged with knuckles, thick across the palm, but they were not made for work or for touching a woman's breast or even for tossing a ball back and forth with boys. Instead, they curved readily around certain tools that in themselves were only discardable means to an end: the .22 Magnum revolver, the .410 pistol, the barber's razor, the cork-tipped icepick, the Uzi. He loosed the souls from their bodies, the grief and terror from their eyes; he unstuck them from their mortal fastenings, sawed the sky loose from the earth's rim, eased them as a lover might into the wheeling of the stars. Sometimes at night he watched his deeds on the ten-o'clock news, ate ice cream out of a carton with a spoon, and felt a strange sexual arousal at the simplicity of it all, the purity, the strobelike glow where their bodies had been outlined with chalk, the remembered smell of death that was also like the smell of the sea, like copulation, like birth.

He had been busted at nine-thirty that morning and was now being held in the deadlock of the Fort Lauderdale jail, with no bond, while he awaited extradition to Louisiana. With good luck Jimmie would identify him, and with the right turn of the screw he would be willing to feed Didi Gee into an airplane propeller.

It should have been enough. But it wasn't.

I went back to the houseboat and found an old canvas money bag that I used to collect pennies in. The canvas had been cut out of a sail and sewn with a thick double stitch, and it closed and tied at the top with a leather drawstring. Then I sorted through my toolbox and found a half-dozen tire lugs, three ball bearings, and a huge iron nut that I used as a weight on my crab traps.

Rain clouds drifted by overhead, and my houseboat and the lake were suddenly covered with shadow, and the waves were capping on the slate-green surface. The air was cool and smelled of trees and salt and wet sand that was alive with shellfish. I could feel caution lights start to flash in my head, the way you do when you watch the amber light shimmer in a whiskey glass; you raise the glass to your lips and you're almost eyeball to eyeball with that protean and dancing balloon of yellow light, then its heated energy hits your stomach, surges through your chest, and rips open sealed places in your brain that you did not know existed. But the marriage is made, the hyena will have its way, the caution light is locked on red, you can't even have the pleasure of loathing yourself because the metamorphosis to which you've committed yourself is now the only self you have.

No, I wasn't out of control. It wasn't whiskey or an adrenaline surge like it that was loose in my system. I simply had to set some things right. And sometimes you don't set things right by being reasonable. *Reason* is a word I always associated with bureaucrats, paper shufflers, and people who formed committees that were never intended to solve anything. I don't mean to be hard. Maybe I'm just saying that what works for other people never worked very well for me, and that's probably because I shorted out a lot of my wiring a long time ago. I was never good at complexities, usually made a mess of them when I tried to cope with them, and for that reason I was always fond of a remark that Robert Frost made when he was talking about his lifetime commitment to his art. He said the fear of God asks the question, Is my sacrifice acceptable, is it worthy, in His sight? When it's all over and done with, does the good outweigh the bad, did I pitch the best game I could, even though it was a flawed one, right through the bottom of the ninth?

No, maybe I'm simply talking about honor. I could not define it in myself, but I recognized it when I saw it in others, and I was convinced that as a virtue it had little to do with being reasonable. And I knew absolutely that it was as dishonorable for a man to allow himself to be used as it was for him to use others. I also knew as a cop that the use of people, which is probably our worst sin, was considered the stuff of moralistic rhetoric by the legal fraternity.

So it wasn't an afternoon for caution lights, even though they reminded me of that amber-yellow heat that could almost soak through glass into my palm and crawl up my arm. It was a day of wind, of whitecaps turning into froth on the lake, of salt spray blowing through my windows, of palm leaves straightening against the gray sky, of swimmers chopping for the shore as thunder rolled overhead and I pointed my car toward the Eastern Expressway and the first raindrops clicked flatly against my windshield.

His office was in a huge liquor store he owned on Huey P. Long Avenue in Gretna, out of which he operated two beer distributorships, a catering and valet parking service, and a half-dozen delicatessens. The liquor store took up almost an entire block. It had wide, well-lighted aisles and buffed floors; music played from hidden speakers; spider plants and philodendron grew in the windows; glass collection jars for crippled children and stand-up posters advertising LSU, Tulane, and the Saints' fall football schedules stood on the front counter. Shoppers used arm baskets while they browsed through the aisles. The enclosed and refrigerated delicatessen counter was filled with shelled shrimp, squid, deviled eggs, lox, sliced cheeses, and meats from all over the world.

It was a place that probably compensated in some way for the deprivation he had known in childhood. There was an endless supply of food and drink; the interior was made entirely of glass, plastic, chrome, stainless steel, the stuff of technology, of *now*; and the people who bought his booze and gourmet trays belonged to the Timber Lane Country Club and treated him with the respect due a successful businessman. It wasn't that far to the waterfront neighborhood of Algiers where he grew up, but it must have seemed light-years away from the time when the sight of his convertible, with the bloodstained baseball bat propped up in the rear seat, made Italian merchants walk sweatily to the curb with the taped brown envelope already in their hands.

I felt a lick of fear in the back of my throat, like a pocket of needles in the voicebox, as I walked through the electronic sliding doors. The leather drawstring of the money bag was wrapped around my hand, and I could feel the collection of ball bearings, tire lugs, and the one big iron nut striking against my thigh as I walked. The shoppers in the aisles were the type you see in liquor stores only in the afternoons: by and large they're amateurs, they examine the labels on bottles because they don't know what they want, and they move about with the leisurely detachment of people who will not drink what they buy until hours or even days later. At the back of the store was an office area with a mahogany rail around it, much like the office area in a small bank. Didi Gee sat behind an executive's glass-topped desk, talking to a clerk in a gray apron and two middle-aged men who had the kind of heavy-shouldered, thick-chested breadth and slightly stooped stance that comes from a lifetime of walloping freights or lifting weights and drinking and eating whatever you want, with disregard for what you look like. Didi Gee saw me first and stopped talking, then all their heads were turned toward me and their faces were as flat and expressionless as people looking up the street at a bus about to arrive. I saw Didi Gee's lips move, then the two middle-aged men walked toward me with the clerk behind them. He was much younger than the other two, and his eyes would not focus on mine.

We stood in the center of the wide aisle, and I could feel the shoppers moving away from us, their eyes a bit askance, their brows slightly furrowed, as though a violent presence could come into their midst only if they looked directly at it. Both of the big men wore slacks and short-sleeved shirts and rested easily on the soles of their feet, the way boxers and oldtime career soldiers do.

'What do you want?' the larger of the two asked. He wore big rings on his thick fingers, and a gold watch with a black face that matched the black hair on his arms.

'So far you guys aren't in it,' I said.

'We're in everything. What do you want, Robicheaux?' the second man asked. He had a puckered scar in the center of his throat. He had been chewing gum, but now he had stopped.

'It's *Lieutenant* Robicheaux.'

'You want to buy some liquor? Go get him a fifth of Jack Daniel's,' the first man said to the clerk. 'It's on the house. Now what else you want before you leave?'

'It's not worth it for you,' I said.

'We'll walk you to your car. Charlie, put his bottle in a sack.'

Then the first man touched me slightly on the arm, just a brush with the callused inside of his palm. I swung the canvas bag from the side and caught him across the eye and the bridge of the nose, felt the lugs and ball bearings flatten against the bone, saw the pain and shock grab the rest of his face like a fist. He stumbled backward through a conically stacked display of green bottles, and the stack folded into a rain of wine and glass all over the aisle. I saw the second man's fist leap out at the side of my head; I bobbed, bent my knees, felt a ring rake across my scalp, and came around with the bag full circle and laid it right across his chin and mouth. His lips went crooked, his teeth were streaked red, and his eyes stared straight into mine with a fearful knowledge. I swung at him again, but he had his shoulders bent and his arms over his head now. A woman was screaming somewhere behind me, and I saw a man drop a red arm basket on the floor and walk quickly toward the electronic sliding doors. Others had formed into a crowd at the far end of the aisle.

Then the first man crunched through the glass and spilled wine and came at me holding a broken bottle of vermouth by the neck. The side of his face where I had hit him was red and swollen. His head was low, his shoulders rounded, his weight flat-footed, his eyes close-set and glaring. He poked at me with the bottle, as though it were a pike. I swung at his wrist, missed, heard the canvas clink on the bottle's tip, and he came forward again and lunged at my face. He must have been a knife fighter at one time, and even though he was heavy and breathed with the controlled rasp of the cigarette smoker, his reflexes were fast, his thighs and big buttocks were cocked like springs, and there was no fear in his eyes, but only a steady heated light that would accept any attrition to get to a murderous end.

But impatience was his undoing. He jabbed the bottle at my eyes again, and when he thought I was going to jerk backward, he raised it to slash at my head. But I didn't give ground, and I swung the heavy knot of metal from behind me, the canvas actually whipping in the air, and caught him solidly on the temple. His face went gray, his eyes rolled, the lids fluttered like bruised flower petals, and he crashed into the shelves and lay still.

Somebody was calling the police on the telephone. The second middle-aged man and the clerk in the apron retreated in front of me as I walked through the broken glass and the pools of wine, whiskey, and vermouth. Didi Gee rose from his desk like a leviathan surfacing from the depths. He had knocked over the ashtray when he stood up, and his perfumed cigarette was burning on the desk blotter. His face was still filled with disbelief, but there was something else at work in his eyes, too – a flicker, a twitch, the rippling edge of a fear he had hidden inside himself all his life.

'You're fucked,' he said.

Don't talk. Do it. Now, I thought.

'You hear me? Fucked. Your brother, your girl, you're all a package deal.'

'He thought you were his friend. You bastard,' I said.

I saw his eyes sweep the store, look impotently at his employees, who were having no part of it now, then his hand went inside the desk drawer and flattened on top of a blue automatic. I came straight overhead with the canvas bag, struck him across the forearm, and snapped the side panel out of the drawer. His fingers straightened and trembled with the shock, and he wrapped his hand around the swelling on top of his forearm, held it against his chest, and backed away from me. His lower buttocks and the backs of his thighs hit against the mahogany rail that surrounded the office area, bolts popped loose from their fastenings, and the rail suddenly snapped flat against the floor. Then he turned and ran with his head twisted back at me.

I followed him behind the delicatessen counter, onto the duckboards, into the midst of his countermen and butchers, whose faces at that moment dared show no partisan expression. Didi's breath was wheezing, his huge chest laboring, his black curly hair hanging in his face like snakes, his dark eyes hot and desperate. His breath sounded as though he was strangling on air bubbles in his throat. The fat across his heart quivered under his shirt. He tried to speak, to gain control of the situation a last time, to click over the tumblers that he had always used to make terrified suppliants of his enemies. Instead, he fell against the wooden butcher's block and held on to the sides for support. The block was streaked brown and covered with bits of chopped chicken. His stomach hung down like a huge, water-filled balloon. His face was sweating heavily, and his mouth worked again on the words that wouldn't come.

'You got a free pass, Didi,' I said, and dropped the canvas money sack on the butcher's block. 'Give your help a raise.'

I heard the sirens outside.

'Tell them cops to get an ambulance,' one of the clerks said. 'He's got blood coming out of his seat.'

They opened up Didi Gee that night. The surgeons said he had malignant polyps the size of duck's eggs inside his bowels. They cut and snipped, sewed and stapled until almost dawn. They closed his colon, implanted a drip tube in his side, and fed him through his veins. Later he would wear a plastic bag on an emaciated frame that would lose a hundred and fifty pounds in a month. He would listen to pyschologists talk to him in a vocabulary he couldn't fathom, learn to stand on a walker, sit in group-therapy sessions with people who talked about life when it was clearly evident they were dying, look dumbly at brochures describing vacations in the Islands, watch his children's discomfort at the smell that came from under his sheets.

He would sign over his power of attorney to others, draw his signatures across bits of paper that seemed now to have no more value than confetti, and try to think about the coming fall, about red leaves flying in the wind, about Christmas trees and brandy cakes and eggnog, and about the following spring that would surely come a-borning if only he could hold its shape clearly in his mind.

Somewhere down inside him, he knew that his fear of death by water had always been a foolish one. Death was a rodent that ate its way inch by inch through your entrails, chewed at your liver and stomach, severed tendon from organ, until finally, when you were alone in the dark, it sat gorged and sleek next to your head, its eyes resting, its wet muzzle like a kiss, a promise whispered in the air.

The next night I couldn't sleep. At first I thought it was the heat, then I decided that it was the insomnia that plagued me two or three nights a month and left me listless and disordered in mind the next morning. Then finally I knew that it was simply the price of ambition – the Fort Lauderdale hit man was in jail, Didi Gee was dealing with a punishment far worse than any court could impose on him, and I wanted to get Wineburger and the general. But I knew they had won the day, and accepting the fact was as easy as swallowing a razor blade.

Then about 3:00 AM I fell asleep and I dreamed. Shakespeare said that all power lies in the world of dreams, and I believe him. Somehow sleep allows us to see clearly those very things that are obscured by the light of day. I heard my father talking to me again, saw his huge muscles working under his flannel shirt as he pulled a ten-foot dead alligator up on a hook over the barn door. He pushed the point of the skinning knife into the thick yellow hide under the neck and then pulled it with both hands in a red line that ran from the mouth to the white tip under the tail.

I didn't see him, no, he said. *That's 'cause I was thinking like me, not like him. That 'gator don't get out on them log when he hungry. He hide under them dead leafs floating next to the levee and wait for them big fat coon come down to drink.*

I woke up at dawn, dripped a pot of chicory coffee, heated a small pan of milk, cooked a half-dozen pieces of toast in the skillet, and ate breakfast out on the deck while the pink light spread across the sky and the gulls began to wheel and squeech overhead. I had always thought I was a good cop, but I was still amazed at how I sometimes overlooked what should have been obvious. My father didn't read or write, but in many ways he had learned more from hunting and fishing in the marsh than I had from my years of college education and experience as a policeman. I wondered if he wouldn't have made a better cop than I, except that he didn't like the rules, authority, and people who took themselves seriously. But maybe that was his gift, I thought; he laughed at seriousness in people and consequently was never distracted by their subterfuge.

I left the houseboat at seven-thirty and was at the Jefferson Parish courthouse when it opened at eight o'clock. I found what I was looking for in a half hour. I was actually shaking when I went into the phone booth in the marble corridor and called

Fitzpatrick's supervisor at the Federal Building.

'I found Larry Wineburger's warehouse,' I said.

'Oh yeah?' he said.

'Yeah, that's right.'

He didn't respond.

'The one the Nicaraguan mentioned on the tape,' I said. 'I assume you've listened to the tape.'

'We did.'

'It's way down in Jefferson Parish, off Barataria Road. I was looking for it under "deeds" in the parish clerk's office. Then it hit me: Why would a slumlord like Wineburger want to buy warehouse property? He makes his real-estate money off welfare clients. A guy like Whiplash doesn't own anything that doesn't bring in a high, immediate return. So I checked leases in the Registrar of Deeds office. The law doesn't require anyone to record a lease, but a lawyer would do it automatically to protect himself.'

'Can you tell me why it is you have to share this omniscience with us?'

'What?'

'Who gave you this divine calling? Why is it incumbent upon you to direct our investigation?'

'You want the information or not?'

'We sealed that place yesterday afternoon and cut the warrant on Wineburger last night. This morning he's developed an enormous interest in the protected-witness program.'

I felt the skin of my face pinch tight in the half-light of the phone booth. The line was quiet a moment.

'What was inside?' I said.

'It's not really your business, Lieutenant.'

'It is. You know it is.'

'A lot of modified AR-15s, ammunition, medical supplies, and, believe it or not, a Beech King-Air B-200, outfitted with racks for electronic surveillance gear.'

'A big day for the cavalry,' I said.

'We're high achievers.'

'What about Abshire?'

'Plays second base for the Dodgers, right? Take it easy Robicheaux.'

'You'll never win their hearts and minds.'

'Before I hang up, let me add one thing. You didn't do half bad for a guy locked out in the cold. You were a good friend to Sam Fitzpatrick, too. We're not unappreciative of that. And finally, I hope this is the last conversation I ever have with you.'

So I didn't know what plans, if any, they had for the general, but I knew I had to see him. I didn't like him, certainly, but I felt a peculiar kind of kinship with him. I felt I had learned something about him in the morgue at the *Times-Picayune* that most other people would not understand. Like those Confederate soldiers buried under the lawn of Jefferson Davis's home, some people share historical real estate that will always be their private country. And I also knew that to be free of the tiger you sometimes had to look right into the beaded orange light of his eye.

After lunch, I visited Jimmie in the hospital. He was out of intensive care now, and the blinds were open in his room and the sunlight struck across the vases of roses, carnations, and dahlias on the windowsill and dresser. The nurses had him propped up on pillows, and although one of his eyes was taped and his face was still gray, he was able to smile at me.

'In a few more weeks we're going to be stringing some green trout,' I said.

He started to whisper something, and I had to sit on the edge of the bed and lean over him to hear his words.

'*Je t'aime, frère*,' he said.

I didn't answer him right away. I didn't need to. He knew I loved him as much as he loved me, in the way that only two men can love each other. I picked up his water and glass straw and helped him drink.

'It's always today, Jim, and it's just going to get better and better,' I said.

His mouth was like a bird's on the glass straw.

I left the hospital and drove my rental car back to the Hertz office downtown. I couldn't afford to keep it anymore. I figured if I was reinstated with the department, and hence with the credit union, I would buy a new automobile; and if I wasn't reinstated, it would probably be time to liquidate and look for new horizons, anyway. There were always options. I remembered the worst afternoon in my gambler's career. My wife and I had gone on a vacation to Miami, and by the end of the ninth race on our first day at Hialeah I had dropped six hundred dollars. I sat in the emptying grandstand, dozens of torn parimutuel tickets at my feet, a cold wind blowing paper across the track, and tried not to look at the disappointment and anger in my wife's face. Then I heard a small plane's straining roar overhead, and I looked up into the gray sky and saw a biplane towing a long canvas sign that read,

GET EVEN AT BISCAYNE DOG TRACK TONIGHT. Even the loser had a future.

I took the streetcar down St. Charles Avenue to the Garden District. It was wonderful riding down the esplanade with the window open under the trees, the iron wheels clicking on the tracks, the sunlight and shadow flicking across my arm. At each stop, black and working-class white people and college students waited in the shade of the oaks and palm trees, and black teenagers sold ice-cream bars and snow cones out of bicycle carts, and the sidewalk cafés in front of the hotels had already started to fill with the early supper crowd. For some reason every day in New Orleans seems like a holiday, even when you have to work, and there is no better way to enjoy it than rattling down the esplanade in the breezy streetcar that has been running on those same tracks since the turn of the century. I watched the pillared and scrolled antebellum homes roll by, the spreading oaks hung with Spanish moss, the small courtyards with their iron gates and whitewashed brick walls, the palm fronds and banana trees that shaded the old, root-cracked sidewalks. Then we crossed Jackson Avenue and I got off at my stop, drank a lime coke in Katz and Besthoff, and walked down the short, brickpaved street to the general's home on Prytania.

I paused at the front gate. Through the umbrella trees along the fence I saw him sitting at a white iron table in the side yard, peeling oranges and avocados into a bowl. He wore sandals and khaki shorts with no shirt, and his sun-browned skin and white hair were dappled with the light shining through the oak tree overhead. Under his arms were the wrinkled webs of tissue that old people have, but his physique was still robust, the movement of his hands strong and confident as he pared the fruit into the bowl. By his elbow were an ashtray with a cigarette holder in it and a corked bottle of wine. He unstoppered the bottle, poured into a small glass, and then his acetylene-blue eyes fastened on mine.

I unlatched the iron gate and walked across the lawn toward him. His face was empty, but his eyes watched me as they would a creature who had suddenly been released from a cage.

'Are there others with you?' he asked.

'Nope. I'm still operating on my own.'

'I see.' He looked up and down my body, watched my hands. He slipped the paring knife into an orange and peeled back the rind. 'Do you want revenge?'

'They'll come for you. It's just a matter of time.'

'Maybe. Maybe not.'

'There's no maybe about it, General. If the feds don't, my supervisor will. He's a better cop than I am. He does it by rules, and he doesn't mess things up.'

'I don't understand why you're here.'

'What were you doing out by my houseboat?'

'Sit down. Do you drink wine or do you want some fruit?'

'No, thank you.'

He put a cigarette in his holder, but he didn't light it. His eyes looked across the yard where some gray squirrels were running up an oak tree.

'I want to apologize,' he said.

'Oh?'

'For all the things that have happened to you. You shouldn't have been involved in it.'

'Cops automatically become involved when you break the law.'

'I've brought you serious grief, Lieutenant. Some of it was done without my knowledge, but ultimately I'm responsible. I offer you my apology now. I don't expect you to accept it.'

'I came here for a personal reason, too. I won't be the one who comes up your walk with a warrant. Somebody else will do that. But I think I'm the only one who knows why you got into this Elephant Walk project, or whatever you call it.'

'What makes you privy to my soul, Lieutenant?'

'You were a soldier's soldier. You're not a right-wing crazy. You have the reputation of an honorable man. I suspect that people like Wineburger, Julio Segura, and Philip Murphy make your skin crawl. But you went on the other side of the street with the lowlifes and the paranoids and started shipping arms down to Central America. A couple of innocent people are dead in this country, and God only knows what damage those guns have done in Guatemala and Nicaragua. So a man who probably doesn't respect politicians in the first place has become part of a political conspiracy. It doesn't fit, does it? I think it has to do with your son.'

'Maybe you're well-intentioned, but you're being intrusive.'

'I was over there, General. Your knowledge and mine won't go away. But you've got to look at it for what it is. You can't bury something awful inside yourself, then pretend it's not there while you fight another war that makes you break all your own rules.'

'What do you mean?'

'The massacre at My Lai. You're blaming it on your son. Or you're blaming it on the VC that made him set those mines.'

'No.'

'Yes. Tear it out of yourself and look at it in the light. They captured him around Pinkville and made him string mines through those rice paddies. Then Calley's people got blown up by those same mines before they went into My Lai.'

He set the orange and the paring knife down on the table. His hands were flat on the table's surface. His eyes blinked rapidly and I could see the pulse in his neck. His deeply tanned, smooth skin was spotted with the sunlight shifting through the oak leaves overhead.

'I've apologized to you. I'm deeply sorry for what's happened to you. But you haven't the right to do this.'

'It wasn't your son's fault. He was forced to set those mines, and you have to forgive him for it. Maybe you even have to forgive the people that made him do it.'

'Do you know what they did to him?' One blue eye trembled at the edge.

'Yes.'

'They put his head in a cage full of rats.'

'I know.'

'He didn't like the army. He was going to medical school. But he was never afraid of anything.'

'I bet he was a fine young man, General. A friend of mine over on Magazine knew him. He said your kid was first rate.'

'I don't want to talk any more about this, if you don't mind.'

'All right.'

'Your supervisor . . . you say he's a good man?' He picked up the orange and pulled a piece of rind off it absently.

'Yes.'

'Will he see that you're given back your position?'

'Probably.'

'I'm sure that he's a man who keeps his word. How long before they'll be out here?'

'Today, tomorrow. Who knows? It probably depends on who takes jurisdiction. Why not walk in on them?'

'I don't think so.'

'You must know by now they've got Wineburger. He'll turn you for the pennies on your eyes.'

He lit his cigarette. The smoke curled around his holder. His eyes looked into the shade of the trees.

'Well, I guess it's not your style,' I said, and got up from the table. 'I'll go now. Read Saint John of the Cross. It's a long night, General. Don't try to get through it with apologies. They're all right between gentlemen, but they don't have much value for the dead.'

I walked back to the streetcar stop on St. Charles. The esplanade was shady under the spreading oaks, and the wind blew pieces of newspaper through the intersection. The streetcar tracks were burnished the color of copper, and they trembled slightly from the rumbling weight of the car that was still far down the esplanade. The wind was dry, full of dust, the burnt-out end of a long, hot afternoon, and I could smell the acrid scorch in the air that the streetcars made when they popped across an electric circuit. Overhead, clouds that had the dull sheen of steam floated in from the Gulf, where the sun was already sinking into a purple thunderhead. An elderly black woman who waited at the stop with me carried a flowered umbrella hooked on her arm. She wore a pillbox hat clamped down on her small head.

'It gonna rain frogs by tonight,' she said. 'First it get hot and windy, then it smell like fish, then lightning gonna jump all over my little house.'

She smiled at me with her joke. I helped her on the streetcar, which was crowded with black people who worked as servants in the Garden District. She and I shared a wooden seat in the back of the car as it rumbled along the esplanade under the trees, past the scrolled iron balconies, the sidewalk cafés in front of the hotels, the green-blue lawns that were now streaked with shadow, the marble-columned porches where Confederate officers once tethered their horses and drank bourbon with their ladies. Out over the Gulf I heard a long peal of thunder, like a row of ancient cannon firing in a diminishing sequence. The black lady shook her head gravely and made a wet, humming sound in the back of her throat.

Epilogue

I was reinstated in the department with no disciplinary action other than a letter of reprimand for punching out Nate Baxter. In two days a half-dozen cops called up to congratulate me. I had heard from none of them while I was on suspension. I discovered that I was not ready to return to work, that my file drawer of gargoyles and grief would have to remain in abeyance in that old Basin Street building that had once housed slave auctions and cock-fights. I took two weeks of my vacation time, and Annie and I went to Key West, walked along the ficus-shaded streets by the bay where Ernest Hemingway and James Audubon had once lived, scuba-dived on Seven Mile Reef, where the water was so clear and green at thirty feet that you could count the grains of sand like fragments of diamond in your palm, fished for cobia, grouper, and wahoo, and ate trays of boiled shrimp and conch fritters down on the dock while the shrimp boats rose and knocked inside their mooring slips.

When it was time to return to work, I put in for my remaining week's vacation. Finally I had no days left. The summer had burnt itself out; the heat had lifted one day in a breeze off the Gulf, the sky turned a darker blue, the trees a deeper green. Stubborn boys still tried to hold on to baseball games in sand lots, but each morning was cooler now, the sunlight gold and warm at noon, and you could hear high-school marching bands thundering on afternoon practice fields. I walked into the First District at eight o'clock on the day I was to resume work, filled out a request for return of my retirement funds, and resigned.

It was time for somebody else to fight the wars. Captain Guidry argued with me and said that I had been vindicated. But vindication is of value only if you're interested in keeping score. I think by that time I had learned that the score takes care of itself. You just keep bearing down on the batter, then one day you look over your shoulder and you're pleasantly surprised at the numbers that are up on the board.

Clete blew Dodge like the town was burning down. He packed two suitcases, forged his wife's signature on a check against their joint account, and left his car double-parked in front of the airport with both front doors open. A month later I received a postcard from him that had been mailed in Honduras. The card showed a Mayan pyramid in Guatemala.

Dear Streak,

Greetings from Bongo-Bongo Land. I'd like to tell you I'm off the sauce and working for the Maryknolls. I'm not. Guess what skill is in big demand down here? A guy that can run through the manual of arms is an automatic captain. They're all kids. Somebody with a case of Clearasil could take the whole country.

See you in the next incarnation,

C.

P.S. If you run into Lois, tell her I'm sorry for ripping her off. I left my toothbrush in the bathroom. I want her to have it.

I used my retirement money to buy a boat-rental and bait business in New Iberia, and had my houseboat towed from New Orleans through Morgan City and up the Bayou Teche. Annie and I rode on the boat the last few miles into New Iberia, and we ate crawfish *étouffée* on the deck and watched our wake slip up into the cypress and oak trees along the bank, watched yesterday steal upon us – the black people in straw hats, cane-fishing for goggle-eye perch, the smoke drifting out through the trees from barbecue fires, the crowds of college-age kids at fish-fries and crab-boils in the city park, the red leaves that tumbled out of the sky and settled like a whisper on the bayou's surface. It was the Louisiana I had grown up in, a place that never seemed to change, where it was never a treason to go with the cycle of things and let the season have its way. The fall sky was such a hard blue you could have struck a match against it, the yellow light so soft it might have been aged inside oak.